C000022609

DON'T STOP
for Anything...

Tony Irwin

**Grosvenor House
Publishing Limited**

All rights reserved
Copyright © Tony Irwin, 2022

The right of Tony Irwin to be identified as the author of this
work has been asserted in accordance with Section 78
of the Copyright, Designs and Patents Act 1988

The book cover is copyright to Tony Irwin
Cover images – credit to Trentinness/Dreamstime.com
and Ultrakuik/isotckphoto.com

This book is published by
Grosvenor House Publishing Ltd
Link House
140 The Broadway, Tolworth, Surrey, KT6 7HT.
www.grosvenorhousepublishing.co.uk

This book is sold subject to the conditions that it shall not, by way of
trade or otherwise, be lent, resold, hired out or otherwise circulated
without the author's or publisher's prior consent in any form of binding or
cover other than that in which it is published and
without a similar condition including this condition being imposed
on the subsequent purchaser.

This book is a work of fiction. Any resemblance to
people or events, past or present, is purely coincidental.

A CIP record for this book
is available from the British Library

ISBN 978-1-80381-117-8
eBook ISBN 978-1-80381-118-5

I dedicate this book to my wife, Jean.
Without her help and patience,
you wouldn't be reading this.

Preface

Witnessing the destruction of beautiful Aleppo on television was the inspiration for writing this story. Previously having worked and socialised with the innocent people of Syria who were so brutally treated was hard to bear. The Western World stood by and watched as atrocities were inflicted indiscriminately as a tool to break their spirit. Western Governments pledged the guilty would not go unpunished in the hope that it would stop the barbarity of this insane war. No one has been punished; the crimes have been well documented. Nothing has changed.

Move forward ten years to Mariupol; the Western World is watching as the evil skills honed in Aleppo are used again. Western powers are once more claiming the guilty will be brought to justice for the War crimes committed there. Crimes are being documented. Nothing has changed.

Prologue

Syria was an imperfect jigsaw assembled over centuries. The 'Few' had all the wealth and power.

The 'Many' had little of either.

Ill-fitting pieces were forced together.

The 'Many' asked whether the pieces could be rearranged fairly to suit all.

The 'Few' refused.

The 'Many' remonstrated.

The 'Few' used all their power to force the 'Many' to capitulate.

They didn't succumb as they had nothing to lose.

The jigsaw fell apart under the stress of discord.

It couldn't be reassembled because the ill-fitting pieces were glued together by a blend of 'Tolerance', 'Fear', and 'Hatred'.

'Tolerance' dissolved, leaving 'Fear' and 'Hatred'.

This is Syria today.

This is a work of fiction. Unless otherwise indicated, all names, characters, businesses, events and incidents in this book are either the product of my imagination or used in a fictitious manner. Any resemblance to actual persons, living or dead or actual events is purely coincidental.

Each civilised person should admit he has two home countries,
the one he was born in and Syria.

French Archaeologist, Andre Parrot

Table of Contents

Chapter 1

Aleppo 19th July 2012

I am an ordinary man who has lived a relatively safe and secure life. At times, I thought my life had been difficult. Sometimes I feared I wouldn't quite measure up to its challenges. Witnessing the destruction of Aleppo, bodies discarded on the streets like garbage outside their destroyed homes. Terrified that, soon, the corpses could be my family. Terrified, I wouldn't be able to save them. That is fear. Getting my family to safety was the greatest challenge I would face. The memory of what I was forced to do would forever haunt me.

* * * * *

For about a year, the unrest throughout Syria, known as the Arab Spring, was escalating. It started in Tunisia when a protesting fruit seller, Tarek el-Tayeb Muhammad Bouazizi, committed suicide by setting himself on fire. Though a non-political gesture, it became the catalyst for the Tunisian revolution and became widely known as the 'Arab Spring'. His suicide was in response to the humiliation caused by an overzealous municipal officer confiscating his wares. Neighbouring

1

Arab nations joined the protest, bringing unrest throughout the Middle East. There were one hundred and seventy political copycat suicides throughout the Arab world. These protests enflamed a movement in Syria attempting to oust President Bashar al-Assad. Various domestic and foreign forces were opposing the Syrian government and each other in varying combinations. Simply, it was shambolic: the self-interests of governments worldwide added coals to the fire by taking sides.

I was half-listening to Amina and the children, disturbed by the distant dull thudding sound of bombs exploding and the rattle of machine guns that had become more persistent over the last week. The sound emanated from the deprived eastern side of the city. Assad's troops and allies were making a concerted attack on the rebels encamped in the ancient, neglected area of the city. The rebels integrated with the poorest people for protection, using them as a shield; many had joined the movement with the promise of a better life. The militants encouraged the poor to risk everything as they had little to lose, only their squalid homes and lives. The more successful Assad became, it only encouraged the more impoverished to join the movement. Militants, mercenaries and radical Islamist extremists flooded in from neighbouring Arab countries – and the rest of the world – to join them in their fight for justice. The rebels were being pushed back by the full might of Assad's army and his allies' firepower. They retreated into the citadel and souqs in the centre of the city.

Aleppo is one of the oldest, best-preserved cities in the world and one of the most beautiful. Perhaps because of this, the rebels assumed Assad would not destroy such a beautiful and extraordinary place with World Heritage status. How wrong could they be? Government forces were raising this part of Aleppo to the ground. Historic buildings and artefacts were destroyed at an alarming rate, along with the livelihoods and homes, regardless of affiliation. Aleppo was home to three million people of all religions, creeds, colours and stature; before the civil war, they mixed regardless. The eastern side of the city was where the most impoverished people lived. On the western side lived the wealthy. Like other significant cities, the standard of housing and the quality of life reflected where you lived. Regardless of their differences, rich and poor mixed peacefully and with respect for each other: status and faith caused little conflict.

Before the uprising, it was a joy for us to spend time in the Al-Madina Souq, the largest covered market globally, with thirteen kilometres of narrow passageways, cafés, shops and stalls. Everyone treated each other with respect and politeness. The Arab has a way of making you feel welcome. Unlike other nationalities, this friendliness and openness will only come after you have shown them the same respect. Over time, the relationship develops, and you can feel a part of their life and become their friends. I had worked with Arabs before in Saudi Arabia. It was probably easier for me to become accepted as, over time, I had learnt the Arab psyche by trial and error.

Our home was on the city's western side and considered a good neighbourhood by Western standards. I lived with my wife, Amina, and our children, Amara and Amal. We both worked at Aleppo University. Amina taught English language, and I taught Mechanical Engineering. We both had well-paid, enjoyable jobs. Our family life could not have been better.

I was sitting in my comfortable chair in the lounge of our townhouse as usual. My wife, Amina, and children were lounging on our low-seated traditional Arabic majlis, as close as possible to each other. Amina told the children a Syrian folk story in the same enthusiastic, animated way she would have been told as a child by her parents. I was only half-listening, trying to ignore the sounds of war, but couldn't. The children giggled as the story evolved. I could understand some Arabic, so I gathered it was about a man with an ulcerated leg. A doctor amputated the good leg by mistake, but fortunately, his bad leg got better. I noticed recently that the storytelling became more regular, and she often repeated the same one. I mused she was distracting the children from the noise emanating from the city as the sound of conflict coincided with the storytelling. Amina and the children loved to lounge on our majlis as they found them more inviting and relaxing. To me, it was like slumping on the floor, and they were impossible to rise from easily. Amina and the children would only sit on chairs at home when we had company or were dining with friends. Unlike me, they made sitting and rising from the floor appear effortless and graceful. I found it a difficult and embarrassing task.

Our closest friends in Aleppo were Ali Mansour, a retired captain in the Syrian army, and his wife, Margaret, an ex-Oxford University lecturer in Middle East history. There had never been people in our lives that we owed so much. The debt owed was all one-way, although they didn't see it like that. As Ali would say, "You are our friends." You need to be an Arab to understand the concept and duty of a true friend; I am still learning as a non-Arab myself. Margaret was the person who brought my wife and me together. She had a wicked sense of humour, a sort of gentle sarcasm. After a while, I could detect from her facial expressions when she was serious and when she was winding me up. However, she still managed to catch me out now and then and draw an imaginary number one in the air with her index finger and smile. Amina had difficulty understanding her witty remarks to begin with but soon became adept and would often join in. Then the two of them would draw the imaginary number ones, followed by calling out 'gotcha'.

Ali was a career army officer and intended to remain so until retirement. However, he found his army role challenging with the increasingly authoritarian actions of the government towards its own people. He joined the military to help keep the country safe from foreign powers, not oppress his fellow countrymen. So, at a certain point, he reluctantly decided to retire from the army and work for Conch Oil as their security adviser, purely for peace of mind. Ali could be very opinionated and argue, with arms crossed, until he won the argument. He then uncrossed his arms to indicate the discussion was over as far as he was concerned. Occasionally, sometime later, he might remark, "I think you may be right." Holding both his arms outstretched with palms flat, shrugging his shoulders and muttering, "You win," followed by, "Maybe," and another shrug.

We often discussed the Middle East's troubles, particularly in Syria. I learned from these discussions that the issue that divides the Sunni and Shia sects of the Muslim faith became a problem in the twentieth century when radicals captured idealism; this escalated into conflict. I knew very little about the history and still don't fully understand it because it's so complicated. Ali and Amina had lived in Syria all of their lives, and even they disagreed. Margaret had studied it at university, so she saw the problems from a different perspective. So their interpretations were often at loggerheads, making the debates quite colourful. Individually, they all believed to know the solution, but none could agree upon it.

One night they called round; the sound of the conflict was louder than usual. Amina took the children upstairs to bed. When she returned, we soon dived into questioning Ali about how bad our situation was. Ali advised us that we were safe for now because we lived on the city's western side. Government troops were massing in our area to protect us because we were considered wealthy and happy with our lot and were not considered a threat to the government.

"How long will we remain safe?" I asked Ali.

"Inshallah," he replied.

I interpreted the situation as very fluid from this remark, and he didn't really know. Ali's disclosure magnified my concern for our friends and acquaintances on the poor side of the city. Their lives, homes and businesses were being destroyed by their own government. Men, women and children were being killed for wanting a little bit more. We were angry and frustrated at not being able to halt the obliteration. Not being able to help in any way was challenging for all of us to come to terms with.

Later that evening, after Ali and Margaret had left, Amina was sitting crossed legged on the majlis as always, reading a book. Scattered around her were a dictionary, thesaurus and encyclopaedia; she was flicking from one to another, making notes.

My thoughts went back to my conversation with Ali. We would have to decide on our options very soon. This triggered my memory back over the years to the events that brought me to where I am now. The chance events that changed both our lives were the direct result of someone's stupid, callous actions; I found myself immensely grateful for that person's stupidity.

Before Syria was another life. Ex-pats often repeat this remark. Those memories from the other life drifted into my mind, as though they had happened to someone else, not me. It was like a dream.

Chapter 2

Life Before Aleppo, 1987

I was raised on a housing estate in a poor district of Coventry, in the West Midlands, England. I was expected to follow my father; my schooling and training pointed me in this direction. Like his father before him, he worked in a factory as a skilled tradesman, with no ambition to do anything else. Initially, I did follow in his footsteps but soon realised this life was not for me. In my early twenties, trapped within factory walls for ten hours a day, the thought of doing the same tedious, monotonous job for the rest of my life was beyond my comprehension. My wife, Jane, and I decided to move from the industrial Midlands with our family to work at a refinery on the west coast of Wales. Both sets of our parents agreed it was a better place to bring up children, though they would miss us dearly and probably their grandchildren more. With the promise of spending time with us on holidays and us making regular return trips to visit several times a year, they reluctantly came to terms with our decision.

At least I wouldn't be imprisoned inside a dreary, smelly, noisy building, but outside in the fresh air, or so I thought. The added attraction was being close to the sea and the beautiful beaches and countryside of Pembrokeshire. In reality, the working environment at a refinery is more toxic and hazardous than any factory I had ever worked in. However, we could take advantage of living within the beautiful national park of Pembrokeshire. It was the ideal place to raise a family: living in an area where we had previously enjoyed holidays was surreal. Helen, our oldest, and Paul would be able to take advantage of growing up away from the dirty, smelly Midlands. My wages as a mechanical fitter were just enough to maintain my wife and two children. The salary was sufficient as long as you were satisfied with just getting by, like everyone else.

Some of my workmates in a similar position decided to go to the Middle East to earn more money. When they came home on leave, they encouraged me to try it for myself, which I eventually did. At the time, I didn't realise, dream or imagine where this would eventually lead me.

Earning triple my salary in the UK and employed by an American company that rewarded those that put in the effort with promotion encouraged me to stay there for four years. I was promoted twice and moved from maintenance supervisor to chief planning engineer. This enabled me to send more money home. My wife seemed content looking after the children and the home; we bought a bigger house and luxuries that we couldn't afford before. Working abroad for extended periods away from my family was difficult for us all. I started to question whether it was really worth it. I decided that there's more to life than money. I missed seeing my wife and the children growing up. Eventually, we decided that there were enough savings for me to return to the UK.

Naively, I started my own business from nothing, using most of our savings. The economic climate was in recession. Running a plant maintenance company with no business experience and lacking the required contacts was doomed to fail. It was a case of who you knew and your reputation; I had neither. The business went under after two years of hard work trying to keep it afloat. Starting over afresh, and back in the same position as before, I felt a failure. I was lucky to find another job, but it paid an income far less than we had become accustomed to. We were only just getting by again, like most people.

I returned home from work one day at the usual time, after one of those days at work, where 'the shit had hit the fan'. It was not an unusual experience, as the machinery at the plant was coming towards the end of its life expectancy. So, I was pretty knackered and looking forward to a lovely relaxing evening home with my family. Putting the kids to bed, telling them one of their favourite stories, perhaps watching a bit of television and drinking a couple of glasses of a delicious red wine we had recently discovered. That was what I had planned in my head, so I was a bit disappointed to find my wife waiting in the hall, wearing a coat.

I was waiting for my children to come running to greet me as usual, or even shout 'hiya, Dad', if they were engrossed in something, but the house seemed unusually quiet. *Strange*, I thought.

"Hiya, love. You look like you're going somewhere."

She didn't reply. She just stood there with a poker face, not indicating what was about to come. I hung my coat up. She was still standing in the same spot.

"Still here?" I said.

She looked vexed and handed me a letter at arm's-length, saying, "Read it now!"

I opened the letter, and she watched my shocked reaction as I realised it was a divorce petition. "You can't be serious; this is a joke, yeah?"

"No joke. I've had enough."

"But you're claiming unreasonable behaviour; surely that's a joke?"

"That's what it says," she said, smirking.

Unable to think clearly, my first thoughts were whether she was leaving me at that moment. "Hang on now! Divorce has never been discussed; why can't we talk?"

"There's nothing to talk about; I've made up my mind."

"Bloody hell. Don't I get a say in it?"

"No, you don't; I am leaving you right now, this minute."

When I realised this was really happening, I became furious. I hadn't seen this coming. I had thought things were getting better between us recently. It occurred to me, though, that this wasn't a spur of the moment decision. It had been planned behind my back.

"Why was my behaviour unreasonable?" I shouted, losing my temper.

"See you in court," she replied, with a false smile she sometimes used. She knew how to wind me up and waited for my response with satisfaction written on her face.

"Where are the kids? What have you done, you stupid, selfish woman?" I yelled, moving close to her. You, bloody you, that's all you think of, poor you, you haven't done a day's work in your bloody life. It's been up to me to provide everything while you do as you please; that's unreasonable behaviour, you stupid, selfish bitch. You're always taking, never giving back." I paused before shouting again, "Where are the kids?"

"It's none of your business," she said to provoke me further.

I resisted her provocation; she had played these games before. So I bit my tongue and just glared at her.

"Don't try and find us! Bye, bye. See you in court!" were her leaving remarks as she sarcastically blew a kiss goodbye.

I slammed the door behind her and kicked it in frustration. The house was empty and felt eerie. This was how it would be now, I thought. I sat on a chair opposite the sofa where my children should be sitting, trying to get my head around what had just happened. In a few minutes, my life had just fallen apart. I looked forward to a lovely evening at home with my family. Now alone, in an empty house, was a stark reality.

I would usually plop on the sofa between them. Always Helen on the right and Paul on the left, as though they had their own invisible zones. Helen would move slowly towards me, then lean her head on my shoulder, sitting upright, very ladylike. Paul would push himself into me as though I was an invader but then settled as I put my arms around both of them. They would fall asleep when they were younger, and I would carry them to bed. Helen's head would gently nestle on my shoulder, but she seemed to be in control of her limbs. Paul was completely different; it was like trying to carry a rag doll, his arms and legs flopping everywhere. As they got older, annoyingly, I would nag them to get ready for bed. Staring at the empty sofa, I realised how much I would miss what I took for granted. I was sobbing aloud on my own with no one to hear.

Since my parents died, Jane was the only person I could confide in or get comfort or support from. I was now completely alone. The grief of losing my parents returned. They left without me saying goodbye. When my dad died, my kids said, "We will miss most the walks he used to take us on." I knew what they meant as we did the same when I was a child. Regardless of the weather, if he said we were going for a walk, we were going. His favourite saying was "There's no such thing as bad weather, just the wrong clothes." His favourite walks were through the woods and open countryside. He identified and named most plants, trees and animals.

The picture of Mum, spitting on her hankie, dabbing my kids' grazed knees the same way she did mine. When we cringed, she would say, "Better than anything from the chemist."

My parents died relatively young, in their sixties, only a little time between their deaths.

People say you can die of a broken heart. I am not sure if that is true or not. My father was the first; he died of a heart attack, which shocked me and everyone who knew him, as he always kept active. He was rushed to hospital, garden dirt on his hands, but was dead on arrival. Mum struggled to come to terms with his death and was never the same. She would say, "The better half of me is gone." I asked Mum to come and stay with us; she refused, explaining she was surrounded by good friends. I thought she realised that Jane wasn't keen on the idea, which she wasn't. Mum died a year later; a neighbour found her sitting at the kitchen table, cup of tea in front of her, cat on her lap. Apparently, she had an aneurysm; she hardly ever saw a doctor. It took me a long time to realise that my parents wouldn't see my children grow into adults, and I would miss that.

I poured a large Scotch, knowing this was precisely the wrong thing to do, then another, and another.

Then the phone rang; it was Derek from work. "Are you all right?" he asked.

"Why shouldn't I be all right?" I replied, confused as to why he should be asking.

"Come on, Allan, I don't need to spell it out, or do I?"

"Bloody hell. You know? Who bloody else knows?"

"My wife told me. Sorry, Allan. I was sworn to silence."

"Derek! Who bloody else knows?"

"Sorry, Allan. Everyone at work knows. You know what this place is like for rumours."

"How long have you known, Derek?"

"For some time, I didn't have the bottle to tell you."

"Derek, you are supposed to be a bloody mate. Some fucking mate you turned out to be!" I replied angrily, slamming the phone down before he could answer.

My head was not in a good place, so I poured another Scotch. This became my excuse to drink myself into oblivion most nights. Being the injured party gave me some justification. During these drinking bouts, I wondered if the affair she had admitted to having while I was working abroad had ended. Or was it still going on under my nose? The thought that my kids probably knew before I did caused me a lot of anxiety. I can't remember much about those nights other than standing drunk in front of a mirror, looking at myself and thinking what a pathetic sight I was. Not realising I was suffering from depression, my friends disappeared because of my behaviour. My mates at work avoided me because I was behaving like an arse. I felt like a leper. I now realise they would have supported me if only I had asked.

One evening, a month or so later, Derek unexpectedly popped round to see me. "Can I come in for a chat?" he said, standing at the front door. He wasn't a welcome visitor, but reluctantly I let him in any way. He looked embarrassed. "Sorry, mate. I haven't been in touch recently; I needed to pluck up the courage. I felt guilty not telling you what was going on."

"So you bloody well should. I bloody well would have told you, if it happened to you. We are supposed to be mates, for fuck's sake."

"Maybe you would have. I'm here now as a mate. Is that okay?"

"Some bloody mate," I shouted in a temper. The couple of drinks I had already consumed didn't help my mood.

"It is what it is; get a grip, man! You're better than this, and it's all for the best."

"How do you know what's best for me? Are you bloody psychic or something?"

"Allan, for God's sake, you did everything. You couldn't have done more. Trying and failing is nothing to be ashamed of, is it?"

"That's all right for you to say that; you haven't a clue what it's like, have you?"

"No, I haven't. I was lucky. I have a wife that cared, not one that didn't care a shit."

"I failed! Not her. She didn't, did she?"

"Allan, put the boot on the other foot; what would you have done if she struggled?"

"Helped, of course; anyone would."

"Open your eyes, man; she did nothing to help. She watched you fall apart and did nothing. You're well rid of her. You would have been dragged further down if she had stayed."

"I suppose so. I always thought everything was my responsibility."

"Allan, you should be celebrating. She's gone now, not your responsibility anymore; that should be a weight lifted off your shoulders."

"That's so easy for you to say. Soon the house will go, she's taken the kids, and everything I worked so bloody hard for will be gone."

"I know it's hard, but you're young enough to start again; you are well rid of her. It's time to think of yourself. You only come this way once; make the most of it. Do something!"

There was silence for a bit. Taking in what Derek had just said was consuming me. I could feel he was looking at me for some sort of reaction. I avoided eye contact as I didn't want him to see me struggling to cope.

"For Christ's sake, Allan, she didn't even want to take your name. Jane Hudson-hyphen-bloody-James – what the hell was that about?"

"She always said it was stupid having two Christian names – 'Jane James' – so I went along with it."

"Allan, every woman I know has taken their husband's name without question."

"It didn't matter to me; she said Jane James sounded weird."

"It's a shame her first name wasn't Jessie; that fitted her personality better!"

"Well, she was always quick on the draw with her sarcastic remarks," I quipped in response.

"She robbed you blind and shot you in the back," Derek said, smiling.

I didn't respond; what he had just said hit home. I was trying to be strong but failing.

Derek broke the silence. "Sometimes it has to get worse before it gets better."

"It can't get any worse," I said.

"There you are then; better times ahead!"

I felt like he had physically beaten me up; I was weak and useless, but I knew that everything Derek had said was true.

"Come on, mate, you can do this. Leave the booze alone and think over what I've told you."

When Derek left, I poured a Scotch and drank it, before thinking about what he had said. Yes, I was better than that. *Come on*, I said to myself, *there are many people in a far worse place; get a grip.* That was the last Scotch I drank because I felt I needed it. From then on, I did things I wanted to, for me. That was the kick up the backside I needed and stopped me from fretting over something that was out of my control. On reflection, I decided there was no point fretting as it made no difference.

So, I decided not to waste money on solicitors but let her have what she wanted. That weekend, I did what most women would do in my situation. I went on a spending spree. I bought clothes for myself, not clothes that someone else decided suited me. I moved the furniture about and changed where ornaments were placed and some I even put in the rubbish bin. I was starting afresh and in control of where I went, what I did and with whom. I felt free; a feeling that had been a distant memory. I started to see my children again and felt guilty that my own predicament had gotten in the way.

After the divorce, nothing much was left for me. The judge awarded my wife the house, maintenance allowance for her and the kids and virtually everything else. Despite the judgement, I felt joy and freedom. I could really do what I wanted with nobody reigning me in. My only responsibility was to my children, which I would not duck. In my late twenties, I was broke, with no home, living in digs, with no prospects. Somehow, I had to do a reset and take a life-changing direction. I didn't want to use the kids as a ping-pong ball. I saw them regularly and tried to be polite to their mother. Hopefully, as they grew older, they would understand. I had to earn enough to support them and myself. The economic climate in the UK was making that difficult. I started to check the daily papers for advertisements for skilled workers in the Middle East to get out of my predicament.

* * * * *

Amina brought me out of my daydreaming over the past. She passed me a nightcap of hot chocolate. "The thuds have stopped. Perhaps we will sleep peacefully tonight," she said.

"I hope so." I sipped my drink. Now back in reality, I looked across to Amina and thought how different my life was. "Thank you for being you."

"Thank you, too. What's brought this on?" she asked, looking surprised.

"I've just been thinking about my past life and realise how lucky I am."

"Me too," she said, smiling, holding out her hand. This was her signal that it was time for bed.

Chapter 3

Applying for a Job in Syria 1996

One of the disadvantages of a non-Muslim living in a modern Muslim city was being woken by the call to prayer at sunrise. The unavoidable noise of many muezzins calling to prayer from minarets fitted with loudspeakers, all chanting simultaneously was like an alarm call. Sunrise was between half-past five and six in the morning, so not often welcome. If that prayer call didn't wake me, another four during the day would. Once awake, I usually slipped drowsily downstairs. I made chai to bring back to bed, hoping not to wake Amina or the children who, for some reason, could sleep through the racket. When younger, if one of them realised I was up, they would come bounding noisily into the bedroom; peace and quiet would be lost. Amal liked to wrestle and tumble over me, making it impossible to sip my chai. Amara had always laid between us; she chattered about all sorts of things, not bothered if anyone was listening. Now older, they could sleep through anything, just like their mother. This morning, I sat in bed sipping my chai; sometimes, I would sit on our bedroom balcony, which had views over the rooftops to the centre of Aleppo. Later, Amina would join me; admiring the sunrise over the city was a beautiful way to start the day. Since the conflict began, we couldn't do that anymore; it was difficult to witness the progress of the city's destruction.

That morning, I had been woken by the din. Amina was still asleep, her chai going cold as usual. Still partly in a dream, caused by the previous day's contemplation, I started to recall my route to my new life in Syria. It all began when I spotted an advert in *The Daily Telegraph* for planning engineers in the Middle East. I contacted the recruitment company. The package was good, so I attended an interview in London at the Royal Gloucester Hotel. The interview was a success, and I was offered the job there and then. The work schedule was one month's work, followed by a month's vacation. The salary was £50,000 per year, all expenses paid, tax-free, subject to a complete medical examination. I was requested to stay at the hotel one extra night for a medical examination the following day. Having been through these medicals before, I realised how impersonal they were and wasn't looking forward to being treated like a piece of meat.

Two weeks after completing the medical, I received an information pack that included a set of instructions. Cash in Syrian pounds and pound sterling to cover all my expenses over the next month. The recruitment company explained that I was required urgently, which was fine: I needed the money immediately. The instructions were to meet up with a chap called John Collins at Charles de Gaulle Airport, Paris.

I met my contact, John, in the departure lounge bar as instructed. I was greeted with 'hiya, aite, geez', which I presumed meant 'hello, are you okay?'. He was a flash Essex boy, with obviously highlighted blond hair and teeth whiter than white. Wearing a flowery, designer, fitted shirt, white leather belt, blue chinos, and fancy shoes. We had a few drinks at the bar, and later we were joined by two others that John had agreed to escort on their first trip to Syria. The first to introduce himself was Matt from Edinburgh. Matt was a tall, red-haired Scot with a goatee beard, who spoke perfect English quietly, in a measured way. Matt dressed in a smart tweed jacket, shirt, tie and slacks and looked like an engineer to me. He greeted us with 'gled tae meet ye' with a subtle Scottish accent, I think to indicate he was a proud Scot. He reminded me of Fyfe Robinson, the TV presenter, in appearance and his articulate use of the English language. Fyfe could make the most mundane article enjoyable by getting the audience interested in his unique use of the English language mixed with his warm Scottish accent and phrases. Why do some Scots have such a better command of English than the English? I had previously worked with Glaswegians, who were impossible to understand. Although Glasgow and Edinburgh are not that far apart. That always puzzled me.

Then Doug introduced himself. It was apparent he was a Geordie when he greeted us by uttering, "Are ya alreet?" My previous thought about the English language forced me to smile. He looked a little older than us three. Doug, just the opposite of Matt, appeared to have been sleeping in his clothes. He was stout and short; his face was partly shaven. Attention to detail wasn't his forté as he had missed as much as he had shaved. His uncontrollable matted black hair, which was covered in grease and still had a mind of its own, flopped over the grey hairs poking out of his ears. When Doug spoke, his

Geordie accent was so broad that it was challenging to understand. By the time I had, the topic of conversation had already moved on. I wondered if the others understood or if they were just nodding in agreement as well. I had just taken a swig of beer when I realised Doug reminded me of Robert Newton's portrayal of Long John Silver. The resemblance was uncanny, except for the wooden leg and Captain Flint uttering 'pieces of eight'. I almost choked and had to turn away, wiping beer from my chin, trying to control a laughing fit.

"What's up? You okay?" Matt asked

"I will tell you later," I replied.

Doug was making up for a lost time, swiftly consuming drinks at the bar. He wasn't shy about paying his way either. We all tried to slow him down to no avail. We explained that the rounds should be shared between us all, and we would tell him when it was his turn. The contrast between my fellow travellers couldn't be further apart. I found myself drawn to the company of Matt as we seemed to have most in common. I started to feel less apprehensive about how quickly my life was moving in a different direction. Being with others doing exactly the same thing and seeing their excitement encouraged me. I was glad that Matt was employed in the same role as me, not that we had a lot in common personality-wise. I was glad it was him, not the other two, I would be working closely with. I got the impression Matt was thinking precisely the same thing as we seemed to agree with nods during the conversations.

John held Matt's and my attention whilst explaining what we were about to experience. Matt and I asked pertinent questions, and the three of us started to learn a little about each other. John described himself as an electrical engineer, although we were to discover later that was an exaggeration. Matt was engaged in the same role as a maintenance planner. Later, after one of his many trips to the bar, Doug told us he was a welding trainer. John advised us to buy as much alcohol as possible, suggesting vodka was the best option. He claimed that, from his previous experience, the Syrian customs were too lazy to check. Shortly after boarding was announced, we made our way to the boarding gate. Doug was walking beside me but having difficulty keeping in a straight line. I wondered whether he had a wooden leg. When he wasn't bumping into me, he was bumping into furniture or other passengers. We managed to control him between the rest of us and negotiated through the gate and onto the plane.

When boarding planes, I often scrutinise the passengers in the boarding queue, noting how big they are, how tidy, drunk etc., and select the one I would least want to sit next to. I didn't have to look very far; he stood next to me. Luckily, I had booked the connecting flight from Heathrow to Damascus and been allocated a seat, so I was also 'Doug free' for a few hours. I fell asleep straight away, probably due to the drinks consumed earlier, and seemed to land at Damascus airport in no time.

Chapter 4

First Impressions of Syria

On arrival at Damascus airport, John guided us to the visa office. John collected our passports from us and joined the queue at the desk. One customs officer was attending to the queue. From where I was standing, I could see into the visa office. A car front bench seat was on the floor. Two customs officers were sprawled across it, smoking cigarettes and completely ignoring the queue. After a long time, John started handing out the visas, but mine wasn't there. John explained the whereabouts of passport control and our transfer bus to me, if I managed to sort out my visa and left with the others.

I pushed myself to the front of the ever-increasing queue and asked the customs officer to check for my visa again. He went to a pile of papers placed on a table in clear view and flicked through the stack. He returned to me, shrugging his shoulders. I asked could he look again, but he showed no interest and continued to serve others in the queue. In frustration and fear of becoming stranded at the airport, I leapt over the counter and picked up the visa pile. Unbelievably, mine was fourth from the top. I was back on the other side of the counter in minutes, on my way to passport control without being noticed by the officers. As directed by John, I joined the Conch Oil bus outside the airport, which was now almost full. The impatient workers already onboard jeered as I climbed on. John told me we were to meet them later in the evening at their hotel because it had a bar serving alcohol.

We arrived at our hotel in Damascus. A charming young Syrian booked us in, speaking in perfect English. She exchanged pleasantries as she was trained to but with a controlled deadpan expression. After showering and changing, we arranged to meet in the hotel restaurant for a light meal before going sightseeing. Leaving the hotel, I asked the clerk what the best things to see in the short time we had were. With the same deadpan expression on her face, she gave us tourist tips and warned us not to eat outside the hotel because the food would be too strong for us. We didn't know what she meant, but we were about to find out. She had recommended visiting an old part of Damascus called Bab Touma, which was nearby. We walked through the very narrow streets. The buildings on both sides had different coloured striped canopies, almost touching each other, creating a covered walkway, like a scene from *Ali Baba and the Forty Thieves*. It also reminded me of the souqs at Hofuf in Saudi Arabia, not far from the oil field where I worked previously. Similar types of merchandise were grouped close together.

We found ourselves in an area selling meat. The stench of rotting flesh was unbelievable. Outside of the butchers were filthy 40-gallon oil drums full of waste meat. The butchers threw unwanted bits of animals with indifferent success into drums. Some bits were spilling onto the pavement, disturbing the mass of black flies covering the rotting meat. In between the canopies, we could see the buildings were four-storey-high. Hanging on these walls were baskets of eggs, painted different colours, also live and dead poultry dangling close together. The smell was unbearable; gasping for fresh air, we quickly moved on. Then there were premises selling bread and cakes displayed on counters outside, again covered with swarms of black flies. I realised what the clerk meant when she had warned us the food would be too strong for us. Looking down a side street, I saw what appeared to be a slaughterhouse, outside of which animals' carcasses were thrown into the back of an open truck.

We couldn't get out of the narrow streets and confined space fast enough. We found ourselves in a modern, wider street. We decided perhaps the food would indeed be too strong for us.

"I'm clamming," Doug uttered, which translated into 'I'm hungry' I think.

As we walked back to our hotel, we forced him not to buy any displayed foods. Our hotel was at a busy junction; the noise of the car horns was deafening. Workers going home, people going out, it's the same as the world over, all in a hurry. It seemed all the drivers had their hands on their horns simultaneously; it was complete chaos. The vehicles were driving far too fast and too close in an undisciplined and bad-mannered fashion. It reminded me of Dhahran or Istanbul, where taking a taxi ride was both frightening and exhilarating.

Every street corner had a large advertising board with a photo of Hafez al-Asaad, the incumbent president. Every shop window had an enhanced image of the president, a statue, photograph or painting. You couldn't look in any direction without seeing him in various uniforms and poses. I could understand the logic as all religious countries display their deities in abundance. It's a way of controlling the people, elevating the poser into a god-like status. Although, as I concluded that, no, you can't brainwash all the population, Hitler popped into my head; what do I know?

We made our way to the Beit Al Wali Hotel on foot to meet the rest of the Conch Oil workers as arranged; it was only a short walk away. Their hotel was far grander than ours, probably classed as five-star, whereas our hotel was perhaps two. In the foyer was a quintet of European musicians performing classical chamber music. This all-female quintet seemed a bit odd to me and out of place. We walked past the ensemble into a sizeable luxurious bar. Chaps from the bus occupied the noisy, crowded bar front. The noise was similar to any bar anywhere where alcohol consumption was a little in excess. There was much talking over each other; I couldn't hear a single word, just a drum of chattering and laughing. Having lived in Arab countries before, I was surprised by the variety of alcohol on display and freely and openly consumed. The bar became even more crowded when a British Airways flight crew joined us. It was getting harder to hear anyone speaking; all I could do was nod in agreement as everyone was talking excitedly. When the flight crew left, John mentioned they had their own club in Damascus. We realised then that Doug was missing. John, Matt, and I had avoided Doug, as we needed a break from him. John had noticed he was buying a lot of drinks at the bar again. I shared with the others that Doug reminded me of Long John Silver.

"Aye, canny resemblance, but 'Long Gone' probably a better description," Matt quipped.

We had an early start in the morning, so we decided to walk back to our hotel without Doug.

The three of us were up early for breakfast, but there was still no sign of Doug. We checked out and were about to leave when Doug appeared, looking worse for wear, even more than usual. He handed over his room keys at the checkout as we sat in the foyer, waiting for our bus to arrive. We could hear a bit of a commotion, so we reluctantly went to see what was going on. Doug demanded his passport whilst the clerk demanded payment for the night's stay. Doug turned to us and asked for help with the bill. The bus was due any minute, so we paid his bill between us out of embarrassment and agreed to sort it out later. We then sat in the foyer, waiting for our bus to take us on the rest of the journey.

"What a canny neet. I'm paggered," Doug said.

"It's a wonder you can remember anything," Matt said.

"Why can't you pay your bloody bill?" John asked angrily.

"That gadgie's a propa doylem, man," Doug replied, looking at John.

"Repeat in English!" I asked; I couldn't understand anything Doug had said.

"Doylem – idiot," Doug replied again in Geordie speak.

"Idiot? Me? I've done the trip loads of fucking times; it's never been an issue. You're a right stupid twat," John said, raising his voice, glaring at Doug.

"Divn't shoot ya gob off, man," Doug muttered, shrugging his shoulders.

Doug had managed to get our backs up in such a short time, and it wasn't just that we couldn't understand what he was talking about. His appearance, manner, inability to walk straight, lack of common sense, and the whole Doug package was a bloody nightmare. To put it politely, there was something not quite right about Doug.

We got on the bus, ready for our journey, and luckily there were spare seats, so we all managed to avoid sitting next to Doug; we each had a whole bench seat. We left the affluent area of Damascus and soon found ourselves on the outskirts of the city. I was amazed by how quickly the view changed from a well-maintained suburb to a heart-wrenching slum. As far as the eye could see were homes constructed of materials which others had discarded: pieces of wood, rusty metal and corrugated iron sheets. I noticed some homes were made of newer materials, indicating the size of the slum was increasing, confirming the problem was escalating. The word 'home' conjures up a warm and inviting place to me, somewhere to come home to and be safe. I couldn't imagine coming home to what was before me, but thousands had to. Not surprisingly, there were no photos of the president here. The homes were garden shed-like in size, packed close together on the side of a hill. I wondered how people could live like that, and more importantly, how a government could condone it. I wondered whether 'condone' was the correct word; perhaps it was a necessity, and the government was compelled to accept the situation. Sometime soon, these people would want a better life; it would only take a spark to start a fire. That spark could be someone with a vision of a better life for these poor people. A spark like Che

Guevara, to rise out of this hellhole and start a bloody revolution. The consequences made me cringe. The hotel we had just left, with all its glitz, and the homes of the poor in front of me, were a million miles apart.

Then the banter started; it reminded me of returning to Saudi after being on leave and watching my children's faces, begging me not to go. Blokes attempting to hide their emotions by making crass remarks as though they didn't care, in an attempt to dull the anguish they really felt. Someone from the back of the bus shouted, "What was the first thing you did when you got home?"

"Knocked on the front door and ran around the back," John shouted back in his unmistakably cockney accent.

A ripple of laughter followed.

"Not to be rude, the second thing I do is put my suitcase down," a Dutch voice shouted out.

More laughter followed.

"They won't cut the grass, you know," someone shouted.

I realised I was laughing like everyone else on the bus, but I didn't understand the joke.

"I always tell my missus I'm coming home a day later; I haven't caught her out yet," another voice from the back of the bus shouted.

There was a short silence while everyone thought about the last remark.

"I couldn't do that and risk spoiling my holiday," Matt spoke quietly.

Matt could have been talking about me. My thoughts turned to my own situation; Jane hadn't apologised but inferred the divorce was my fault. *Maybe it was?* I pondered. Unlike most of the chaps on the bus, I didn't have that worry anymore. The banter would probably be the same on my next trip. All ex-pats returned to work with trepidation and never got used to the loneliness.

Matt's remarks reminded me of what a risky business it was to spend so much time away from your family. In the four years I spent in Saudi, I witnessed many of my fellow workmates' heartbreak after receiving news from home. There was even a suicide following a phone call from a wife. The poor chap, distraught, drove off a plateau in the middle of the night, and his body wasn't found for days. Mostly it was mates returning to work after being on leave with bad news. We thought we men were making all the sacrifices, stuck in the desert with nothing to occupy us but work. When the broken-hearted returned, they turned to their mates for solace. But wives and partners were also feeling the strain; they were just as lonely as we were. I found it hard to fathom why the break-ups happened; and why in such a cruel way. Witnessing a mate uncontrollably crying is challenging to cope with. I definitely didn't have the correct tools in my toolbox for that, but I tried my best. One of my mates returned home to find his dreams shattered. The riding stables they had bought together through his sacrifice of working away weren't his anymore. He had given his wife power of attorney because it made sense while he was away. She had met someone else, sold the business and moved away. He described the joy of approaching the stables, proud of their achievements. His happiness turned into utter despair when he realised what had happened. I knew of at least four similar circumstances and how fragile such long-distance relationships were. Later, I discovered that my marriage was no different.

We left the slum area, which went on for miles, on our way to Deir ez-Zur. I understood from John that the journey would take about eight hours. From the window, for mile after mile, all there was to see was desert scrubland covered in waste and rubbish. Floating in the air were thousands of plastic shopping bags, but there were no shops. The scrubland must have been convenient for uncontrolled waste disposal; it was a filthy and uninviting place. This is one of my early memories of Syria that I will never forget. We passed through the odd village of concrete block-built homes that didn't appear finished. I wondered who had constructed them so poorly, with no pride, and why they weren't completed. The buildings seemed deserted, but the evidence of washed clothes drying outside confirmed that they were inhabited.

Gazing through the window and listening to the various conversations around me, I gleaned that most of them worked for Conch Oil and not as contractors like us newbies. This was probably why their hotel was five-star and ours only two. I started to see from the window what appeared to be the odd carved stone or piece of carved pillar littering the roadside. Then, to my amazement, amongst the scrubland appeared a magnificent Roman city protruding above the horizon. Curious, I asked John the name of these ruins. He told me it was Palmyra. I had never heard the name before and wondered why. The ruins went on for mile after mile and were magnificent. The bus stopped at Zenobia Cham Palace Hotel at the centre of the city ruins. We were greeted by smartly dressed staff, wearing grey and maroon uniforms, who led us into an opulent foyer and then through into a lounge. The attentive staff served us a delicious Arabian-style meze. We were the only visitors at the hotel; perhaps that is why we were treated so well. I couldn't understand why it wasn't flooded with tourists. Previously, I had visited Ephesus in Turkey, Parthenon in Greece and similar historic places swarmed with tourists. Palmyra, in my opinion, was far superior in size and far more impressive; there was far more to see.

After lunch, we headed off towards Deir ez-Zur. The scenery was just the same, with scrubland and the occasional settlement. We were driven through Deir ez-Zur, the principal city on the Al Farat river, also known as the Euphrates.

I learned that most Conch Oil refineries were almost identical in design and construction on the eight-hour journey. We were dropping off workers as we went. The refineries were very similar, sitting amongst barren scrubland. Surrounded by two sets of high wire mesh perimeter fences, about five meters apart, topped with razor wire, reminding me of pictures of concentration camps. They all had long fenced vehicle entrances, with two sets of manned security barriers to be negotiated. The guards didn't appear to be that interested, other than raising and lowering the barrier. I mused that fitting automatic gates would save some money without any loss of security. Then John shouted that Al Omar was our stop. It had been a long and tedious journey. The early start meant that it was still light, but the sun was quite low in the sky. It would be dark within minutes.

Chapter 5

Al Omar (work)

John introduced Matt, Doug and myself to Henk, the plant superintendent, on arrival at Al Omar. He passed us to a Brit supervisor named Paul, who showed us around the residential and office complex while relaying a bit of interesting information as we went. Paul explained that the plant was almost brand new, recently commissioned and handed over by Conch Oil to the Al Farat Oil Company. He explained that most of the staff we had met were involved in the building of the plant. Paul told us we were the only three contractors on site. The other staff were mainly Dutch and employed by Conch Oil as contractors to the Al Farat Oil Company. We were contracted through a recruitment company because it was easier to hire and fire. Paul escorted us to our residential block. Our rooms were large and sparse, with just a bed, wardrobe, kitchen table, chair, shower and toilet. Although not very inviting, they were palaces compared to the slums of Damascus and the settlements we had just passed through. At least we had the luxury of clean running water, showers, clean beds and our own space.

We agreed to unpack, shower, rest and meet later in the canteen. The canteen was self-service with quite a good selection of food. We helped ourselves and sat down, ready to eat, and Paul joined us. Paul looked at our plates. "It's up to you, but we avoid any meat or fish products that don't come from a tin and avoid fresh salad," Paul advised.

"What does that leave?" Matt asked.

"Fruit, eggs, boiled vegetables, tinned sardines, etc.," Paul responded.

"I could do with losing a bit of weight," I said.

"The food comes from Damascus in an unrefrigerated van, except for the eggs and bread, which are local," Paul explained.

"I saw the disgusting way meat was handled in Damascus," I commented.

We all nodded in agreement, confirming Paul's suggestion was a good idea.

"No matter how picky you are, you will develop a tummy bug; it's just the ways things are," Paul warned.

The following morning at 6am, Henk led the communication meeting. I recognised some of the faces from yesterday's journey. The Dutch were easily recognisable as most of them displayed incredible facial hair. To me, each was trying to outdo the other with flamboyant waxed moustaches and beards. They reminded me of old sepia photographs from the Victorian era when it was the fashion for men to have great walrus moustaches, sideburns and overgrown beards. They reminded me of characters often depicted on seaside postcards: odd and humorous. I found it challenging to keep a straight face and wondered if Dutch women were attracted to this look or did they laugh behind their backs, as I was trying hard not to.

My thoughts were then drawn to the four well-dressed Syrian men at the meeting who, in contrast, looked completely normal. They said nothing, made no eye contact with anyone, but just watched what was going on. After the meeting, Henk took Matt and me to our office. He explained that our role was to set up a maintenance programme for this plant and the identical sister plants. He mentioned that we needed to be very careful of the Syrians at the morning meeting. He intimated that they may be undercover spies or religious police monitoring us, checking that we behaved appropriately. I noticed that they had a military look about them; they never slouched and looked extremely fit, clean-shaven and were in their early thirties. I had come across religious police in Saudi Arabia. There was no comparison between those and the ones here. In Saudi Arabia, they were usually older and dressed in traditional thawbs and sandals, not in freshly laundered Western-style trousers, short-sleeved shirts and polished shoes.

Matt discussed where we should start on this mammoth task. I had previously done something similar and suggested that identifying the essential plant items would be an easy start, using their plant accountancy numbers. We searched through the office, which had cupboards and filing cabinets full of various documents and found very little that could be of use. Matt opened a large, heavy, sealed cardboard box stored in the corner of the office.

"Bloody hell, take a look at this!" Matt exclaimed, passing me a lever arch file. On the front, in bold letters, was written 'Conch Oil Planned Maintenance Schedule Al Omar'. Inside the cardboard box were about twenty lever arch files titled the same. We were a bit bewildered, to say the least, and started to examine the files in detail. The files were detailed and complex, with maintenance schedules for all plants. They also provided a manual job card index system – not computerised, but a good start. We were more than puzzled and spent the rest of the day familiarising ourselves with the information discovered. We discussed how it might be possible that Paul wasn't aware of the maintenance plan's existence. We had found it almost immediately, so it didn't make any sense.

That evening John, Matt and I met in my room for a few drinks. Matt and I felt we had earned it. We hadn't mentioned the arrangement to Doug, as we wanted a relaxing evening. It wasn't long after our first drink of vodka when we heard somebody knocking on the door. Doug was accompanied by two Syrian canteen staff and asked if they could come in for a drink.

"We don't have any drink, piss off," I retorted firmly. "You don't have any drink either, do you?" I challenged.

Doug first looked confused. I thought he then realised his mistake of encouraging Muslims to drink alcohol. "Nee, nee, divvin," he said and then left.

"What the hell! How do they know what he's saying, because I don't?" Matt asked.

"It's a mystery to me. Do you know, John?" I asked.

"Meshugenah," John said.

"What?" Matt asked, looking incredulously at John.

"Meshugenah is cockney slang for crazy," John replied.

"For fuck's sake; it's bad enough with one talking in riddles," I added.

"Sorry," John said, smirking.

"What you just said, John – 'crazy' – sums Doug up in one word," I said.

They both nodded their heads.

"Aye, a bampot, a reet eejit."

I couldn't help joining in the banter. "He's a bedlamite, alright. Can we now speak in English?"

"Nobody could have been born like it; he wouldn't have survived this long. A recent bang on the head, maybe?" John commented.

"I bet he's taken them to his room for a drink, stupid arse," Matt replied.

"I don't think he's that stupid. He came here to drink our booze, not his; think about it!" John said.

"Maybe he has a brain cell after all," replied Matt.

"Maybe, but just the one," I replied.

After the communication meeting the following morning, we asked Henk to come to our office to show him what we had found.

"Well, I never knew about this," Henk said, looking amazed.

"The files here are for this plant only; that means there must be similar files for all the plants, doesn't it?" I asked.

"Well, it certainly looks that way. I will check with the other plants and let you know," Henk replied.

"It seems weird that nobody discovered these files; I can't believe we are the first to discover them," Matt said.

"It seems strange to me as well," I agreed.

"I can't see the point of both of you working on the same plant. If they have similar files, I will let you both know tomorrow," Henk added after a bit of deliberation.

After Henk had left the office, we had a chat and concluded something was wrong; indeed, someone must know that the files had been here for a long time. The following morning, Henk told me to continue working with Matt for the next week to ensure we were singing from the same hymn sheet. We continued to work twelve hours a day. The only break we got was Doug popping into the office, which was not a welcome respite. Doug was struggling with his job and entirely out of his depth. Doug's role was not as a welding trainer as hired, but as a pipeline engineer. He was tasked with designing pipelines correctly, with appropriate valves and equipment. This was totally out of his knowledge range, so he would appear in our office asking for help from time to time. Matt had far more patience than me and also had more pipeline work experience. He was a skilled draughtsman and helped Doug as much as he could.

Doug told us that he had been in touch with the contract company during these visits, to explain that the expenses were insufficient. Matt and I didn't have a cash flow issue, but we agreed to support him in requesting more cash, as we realised that if we didn't, we would have to finance Doug ourselves. Later that day, we had a phone call from the contract company informing us that they would get more money to us. It wouldn't be included as expenses, but come out of our salaries.

In the evening, John asked if we wanted to join him for a few beers (surprisingly) outside of the camp. This would be a change as the twelve-hour days were a tedious drag. John drove Matt, Doug and me in his crew cab to a petrol station, of all places, on the main highway. We sat on a bench outside the petrol station drinking a few

Belgian beers. I thought a petrol station was a strange place to consume alcohol in an Arab country. Unfortunately, the beer was a magnet for persistent irritating flies. We sat there with our thumbs firmly pressed on the necks of our bottles, our hands covered in flies.

Doug passing his medical was a puzzle, so I purposely discussed how stringent and thorough mine had been. My medical had been held at a company called Medical Express in London. The building was modern, upmarket and impressive. I was shown into a large waiting area and told to sit and wait. The receptionist called my name and pointed to a changing room door; she told me to strip naked, put on a paper gown tied at the back, and knock on the door when I was ready. The rooms had linked doors, which went from one room to another. Entry was by knocking and waiting for the command to enter. The first room was audiology, next ophthalmology, heart, lungs, etc. In the final room was an attractive young woman sitting behind a desk. She requested me to take off the gown and lie on the examination table naked.

"Shouldn't I wait for the doctor?" I said.

"I am the doctor," she replied.

Embarrassed, I lay naked on the table while the young lady examined every inch of my body, every muscle, every limb, stretched and rotated, and every orifice inspected. I've had medicals previously, but nothing as thorough or embarrassing as this. Whether because she was young and female or possibly because she was new to the job. For whatever reason, though embarrassed, I was impressed with the way she managed the examination as though I was an inanimate object.

"You are acceptable for your age," the doctor said as I left the room, "but have an elevated BMI."

"Thank you very much; that's good, isn't it?" I replied jokingly.

"No, it's not. You are a bit overweight, but the scaffolding is good," she replied.

My flippant remark went entirely over her head.

I looked at Doug to see if there was any sign his experience was similar. He had a weird look on his face; I took it as lust and asked him, "Was yours anything like this?"

"Haddaway, man, my medical was by a locum doctor in Toon. It only took a couple of minutes."

As usual, it took me a few seconds to work out that Doug had just confirmed that, no, and it was in Newcastle.

"Not a proper medical then?" Matt asked.

"Whey aye, man," Doug replied.

"Do you mean, yes, it was not a proper medical?" I asked, trying to decipher Doug's meaning.

"Are yee daft? I had a mini-stroke the year before but luckily not picked up," he replied.

"Did you have a technical interview?" I asked Matt.

I already knew the answer as we had discussed it during the day, but I was trying to move the conversation towards finding out about Doug's interview without appearing too obvious.

"Aye, a full technical interview. What was yours like, Doug?" Matt said.

"A right nebby bugga phoned me; I told him nowt." I translated this as 'a nosey bugger phoned me, so I told him nothing'.

Doug had somehow slipped through the system, either by chance or, more likely, because the contract company was desperate. After a few more beers, Doug explained he had been out of work since his stroke, desperate for money and with hardly enough to go to the pub every night.

Doug's disclosure helped explain his irrational behaviour. He was having physio treatment to regain his balance and his confidence. This admission put him in a different light to us. Maybe he couldn't help being an irritating arse. He was here, wholly out of his depth, because of the shortcuts of a recruitment company. Unfortunately, the fault was not his; we were stuck with him. The reward was lucrative for supplying contractors, and the posts were urgent, so they filled them regardless. An unspoken mutual understanding developed; we would do our best to look after him, as difficult as that may be.

Matt and I continued to work out a framework for the maintenance plan during our twelve-hour days. We were the only workers in the office complex. After the morning communication meetings, everyone seemed to disappear into thin air and didn't reappear until the end of the day. Matt, Doug and I ate what we could at lunchtime, but tinned tuna was losing its attraction. Fortunately, breakfast was a little easier to negotiate. It was mainly cereals, toast, eggs, jam, honey and plenty of coffee and tea.

On the seventh day, Paul told me to pack my bags at breakfast as I was to be taken to Al Taim, a sister plant to Al Omar, by a German called Karl. Karl appeared to be a product of Hitler's experiment; tall, athletic, blonde, and with a superior air about him. We left Al Omar in a crew cab designed to seat up to five or six people with two rows of seating. The back was kitted out with a comprehensive set of toolboxes. We travelled in a direction I hadn't travelled before. I was sitting in the front, my suitcase placed on the back seat. The scenery was lush instead of the desert scrubland. We were skirting along the banks of the Al Farat river. On either side of the river were cultivated fields of various crops and colours. We could see women and children working in the fields, who waved back at us as we waved at them.

"What a hard life for the women, children and men, toiling in the sun all day with no shade," I commented.

"It is what it is," Karl replied, shrugging.

His remark showed little compassion, but when we passed children on the track, he stopped the truck to give them sweets. The children clamoured for the boiled sweets he handed out. The children made guttural sounds and pointed their hands towards their mouths to gain attention as they scrambled to the front of the mêlée. I felt slightly ill at ease to see the begging children's faces cracked and weather-beaten. Their bare feet and ankles were like leather, their heels swaged out by continual pounding on hard surfaces. They were dressed in what were once white thawbs, which were now stained grey, ragged and dirty by continual use. I imagined their full attire and one-size-fits-all, occasionally laundered in the Al Farat and worn for many years. Was Karl handing out the sweets in an act of kindness, or was he reinforcing his ego? It crossed my mind that he thought himself superior as he never smiled.

"The difference between them and us is the accident of birth," I commented, but he didn't respond.

We drove through the city of Deir ez-Zur and stopped to admire the ornate metal suspension bridge over the Al Farat river. Karl explained the French had built the bridge, and it was the main attraction in the area. The locals were very proud of it and established picnic areas with permanent barbecues on the riverbanks. Families were walking the pathways at the side of the river as they would be on a Sunday afternoon in the UK. Well, almost; there was no holding of hands or show of affection.

As we drove past a school engaged in a sports day, the children were dressed in Western-style clothes. They wore blue blazers, grey trousers or tartan skirts for the girls, socks and shoes on their feet, and, as only excited happy children can, they were making so much noise. It prompted me to muse on how different they were to the sullen, unhappy, working children in the fields, only a short distance away. Though it was lovely to see well-cared-for schoolchildren enjoying themselves, I couldn't get the picture of the poor children in the fields on the riverbanks out of my mind.

We left the city's suburbs on our way to Al Taim, stopping only for refreshments from a small shop, where we both topped up the supply of boiled sweets. Outside the shop, children were begging again. They received boiled sweets in return. We were soon driving along a highway where there was a Bedouin camp on the left-hand side. As the road passed the centre of the campsite, Karl slowed the crew cab and came to a stop. Women wearing brightly coloured clothes came running out of the camp towards us. They surrounded our vehicle with their right hands outstretched, making the same guttural sounds the children had earlier. Their right hands were thrusting to their mouths, eyes wide and pleading. Some of the women were looking at me and shouting, "Jig-jig alsayaarat." later, Karl told me this meant 'sex in the car'. Karl appeared to be enjoying the women's attention, whilst I felt very uneasy. After a few minutes, he drove the crew cab away, leaving the hungry, disappointed women in our wake.

We arrived at Al Taim. Karl introduced me to another Dutch superintendent called Hans. He donned an awesomely crafted waxed moustache that curled up his cheeks to a needlepoint. I found it challenging to take someone seriously who displayed facial hair that must take a considerable time preening in front of a mirror to perfect. The waxed moustache was something to behold. I couldn't decide if it was a joke or just strange vanity. I managed to control my amusement at how ridiculous he appeared by not openly laughing. Once again, Syrian observers attended the morning communication meetings, similar to those in Al Omar. Hans took me to the planning office to discuss what Matt and I had discovered and what we had agreed with Henk.

"I am surprised you've found the maintenance files," Hans said.

"It doesn't make sense to me; surely someone knew about them?" I asked.

"Honestly, I didn't have a clue about them until Henk asked me to have a look," Hans replied.

"There's something fishy going on here. Surely they were handed over on completion of the plant?"

"Nothing to do with me. Bente was in charge of the handover."

"Who the fuck is Bente?" I replied.

"He is in overall charge of the plants, the big boss."

"Surely he must know about the files then?"

"I wouldn't know. We only meet on changeover for a few minutes, and he likes to keep things to himself."

"When is the changeover then?"

"In about a week. The way it works is the superintendent's changeover occurs halfway through your stint, so you get the joy of working with the two of us. The joke is, working with both is supposed to be for continuity."

"Okay, I will ask him then."

"Be careful, Allan; he doesn't suffer fools gladly."

"I am nobody's fool."

"Sorry, just a figure of speech, but be careful. He has a hell of a temper."

Hans decided that our action plan was the correct one and we should continue. He left me to carry on with it. I realised at the communication meeting that the main difference between the two plants was the staff at Al Taim were mainly British, not Dutch. Here, some of the team were also Syrian nationals on training programmes. I continued to develop the maintenance card programme for the rest of the week.

The maintenance supervisor, Mike, was a West Country boy with a broad accent. Mike was unhappy that he would no longer be in complete control of the maintenance. So our collaboration was tricky. His responses to me mainly were 'dreckly', which was his term for 'directly'. I took this to mean he might show some interest in what I was doing at some point in the future. For the time being, he was going to do as he wished, and he showed this through his reluctance to help me. After the communication meeting, I noticed that the office complex was again empty of staff, except for a few plant operators and trainees. I assumed that rest of the maintenance crew were out on the plant working.

The twelve-hour day was long and tedious, interrupted only by the odd conversation with Matt over the phone. After a couple of days, the Syrian trainees started to take an interest in what I was doing. They seemed to be left to themselves, unsupervised, for long periods. I explained the new system to them; it helped pass the time away and keep me on track. Describing the work plan to them helped me ensure that it was easy to understand how the programme would work. A couple of the trainees were exceptionally bright and understood the need for a programme but questioned why it wasn't already in place as it was so crucial. I tried to make excuses, but I realised that they knew the real reason from their facial expressions. On the fourth day, after the communication meeting, Mike came into my office.

"You haven't been stuck in this office every day since you got here, have you?"

"Where else would I be?" I replied sarcastically.

"Well, today, come with me. I will show you the sites."

That was a relief as the sun rose at six and set at six in the evening. The monotony of working every day for a month inside an office with no outside windows, barely getting a glimpse of sunlight, was oppressive. Being almost entirely on my own, any occasional visitor was welcome; sometimes, I would go for days without talking to another person. So, I was relieved that I could escape the office's four walls to see something different. I was expecting to see more of the plant, but at least I would be in the sun and fresh air.

Chapter 6

The Scam

We drove out of the refinery and headed for the Al Farat river. I soon realised that Mike didn't mean the sites, but sights; the views of green fields and women and children working. Again, the boiled sweets were handed out by Mike to demanding children as we went.

"Where did everyone disappear to after the communication meeting in the morning?" I asked.

"Some men go back to their rooms to rest, read, or work out."

"Don't they have work to do?" I asked, shocked.

"Well, the plant is new and fully automatic. The crew takes it in turns as there is hardly anything to do."

"What if something goes wrong?" I asked, troubled by his response.

"We're not completely stupid; there's always a couple of us about, and we have the trainees trained pretty well. They do all the leg work, as long as someone's there to supervise."

"What about the management? Don't they mind all the skiving?"

"The management is probably worse. Like Paul at Al Omar, he has a relationship with a woman in Deir ez-Zur; I don't think he is the only one."

"Do you mean he spends nights away with his girlfriend?"

"Not only nights, days too."

Curious, I asked, "Isn't he married back home?"

"Yeah, not much chance of being caught out if you're into that sort of thing."

"Aren't you concerned someone will find out what's going on?"

"Everyone knows, and as long as someone doesn't 'rock the boat', I can't see any problem."

"Why are there no Syrian trainees at Al Omar? Who does the leg work there?"

"The Dutch work it out between them. They will be getting trainees soon. They are just a little behind us, that's all."

I interpreted Mike's comment, 'rock the boat', to imply why he was reluctant to help with the planning programme. It would mean that they would have to start doing some work. I deduced that he was taking me out for the day to soften me up to his way of thinking. I mentioned the Bedouin camp incident with Karl.

"There was a rumour that a few of the staff, including Karl, were visiting the camp, but I wouldn't risk it," Mike said, shrugging his shoulders.

"Changing the subject, how long have you been here, Mike?"

"I started as a contractor like yourself but got transferred to Conch's books after commissioning. It's well worth it; the money is a lot better."

"Can I ask how much more dosh?"

"About double what you're on."

"Crikey, you mean a hundred grand a year?"

"Thereabouts. We could put a word in for you, if you're interested?"

He explained that some of the employees worked on rigs in the North Sea during their months off and formed offshore consultancies to avoid tax.

"So, what do you do?"

"I am building a house; hopefully, it will be worth a fortune when finished."

It crossed my mind that Mike was trying to influence me not to be too conscientious as I might spoil his days like this.

"Mike, who are the Syrian guys at the communication meetings?"

"Spies, maybe religious, not sure which; they never interfere with anything."

"So you are not sure?"

"They are probably checking that we're not trying to convert nationals or knocking the Muslim faith."

"Don't you think there could be another reason they are possibly reporting back to head office?"

Mike shrugged his shoulders and uttered, "Regardless, keep your distance, and they won't bother you."

We were driving along the main road when Mike turned down a small track towards the banks of the Al Farat river. At the end of the track was a small bar with a veranda overlooking the river. Mike parked his cab under the shade of a tree and then guided me onto the veranda. We sat on a majlis admiring the view of the flowing river and the lush green vegetation. In the distance, we could see workers in the fields, stooped over, harvesting crops out in the fierce sun without any protection.

Two ice-cold beers appeared on the table; this was obviously a regular occurrence.

"As-salaam Alaykum, Mr Mike," a young man uttered.

"Alaykum salaam," we replied.

Mike introduced me to the young man as Mr Allan. We sat there for a few hours talking, putting the world to rights, between the occasional beer and bowls of nuts and crisps.

We left, calling out 'masa lama' as we went on our way back to Al Taim.

We drove through empty villages. The only signs of life were outside bakers; everywhere else appeared deserted. When the bakers opened their shutters, crowds clamoured outside for their bread for the day.

I enjoyed the day out, but it was a one-off for me, although I realised it was a regular occurrence for many ex-pat workers. Did they realise it couldn't go on forever?

The following day, after the daily morning meeting routine, Hans told me he would pop in to see me later that morning. He came into my office to tell me that he started his leave the following day. His replacement, Bente, would be taking over. Bente was the most senior of all the superintendents and a stickler, so I was to make sure I kept on the right side of him. Again, he advised me why superintendents were not on the same rota and warned me not to annoy Bente, as he had a 'short fuse'.

After the morning meeting on the following day, Bente entered my office. Unlike the rest of the Dutch, he was clean-shaven, tall with an athletic build, and stern.

He glanced around the office as though he was expecting to see something different.

"What the fuck have you been doing?" was his opening remark delivered with a booming voice.

"Working hard, and there is no need to swear or shout. I am not deaf," I responded, not used to being addressed in this manner and stuck for words.

"Show me what you have been working so hard on," he yelled, looking around the office again.

So I showed him the planning manuals and how I was developing the programme. He became angrier.

"You haven't been wasting your time on this, have you?" he shouted.

"It doesn't look like a waste of time to me," I replied, raising my voice slightly.

"Well, it fucking is!"

"Hang on, I have done quite a lot."

"Show me!"

I showed him the card index system I had produced from the manuals.

"Who gave you permission to work on this rubbish?" he boomed, even more agitated.

"Rubbish! Someone has gone to a lot of trouble putting this lot together; it's not rubbish."

"Are you serious? Who told you to do this crap?"

"Henk and Hans; why?" I replied, bemused.

"Because I never told them to; it's a complete waste of time."

"Why? It's a good system, and you have to start somewhere."

"They should have known better! Another pair of bloody idiots!"

"Perhaps it would have been a good idea to tell them what you wanted, don't you think?"

"Of course, I knew the files were here. I ignored them because anyone with half a brain cell would realise that we haven't the manpower," Bente said in a slightly calmer voice. He paused. "Who do you think is supposed to be doing all this work? This system would take double our workforce," he then shouted.

"What about them doing twice the amount of work?" I retaliated, looking him in the eye. "Isn't that a simple solution? It shouldn't be hard from what I've seen."

"Who is going to make sure they would?" he said, shouting again.

"Hang on a minute," I said, "the maintenance programme was designed on your current manpower level; enforcing it would do that."

His face grew red as he realised he had lost the argument. Despite his bluster, it occurred to me that he was entirely out of his depth.

"That's precisely the reason for a proper planning schedule, utilising the manpower correctly, isn't it?" I reinforced.

"They're bloody useless; that's the problem," Bente replied.

"That's not my problem, is it? It's my job to install a maintenance programme, isn't it?"

"You are here to do what you are fucking well told," he screamed.

"I am doing what was agreed and what I was employed to do. I thought the idea of employing me was to provide a proper maintenance programme?"

"Your office looks like any other office. Does it look like a planning office to you?"

"What should a planning office look like then? Give me a clue," I queried sarcastically.

He grew angrier. "Bloody wall charts," he spat, looking around the room, and pointing his hands at the bare walls; his face was now bright red.

"What bloody wall charts? There isn't any," I retorted.

"Well, make some!" he blasted.

"Why, how and with what?"

"You should have made them two weeks ago. Are you thick or something?"

"I am not thick, nor am I a bloody mind reader either."

"I suppose that Hans and Henk were too busy trying to shag the local population to be interested?"

"Perhaps I should have joined them, rather than wasting my time here. At least somebody might have got some satisfaction!" I retorted.

Bente calmed down. The conversation between us became more constructive. He told me that the Syrian minister for energy would be visiting the site in a week. Apparently, there were concerns about how much it costs to run our oil refineries compared to those maintained by Syrian nationals. They were not modern or automatic like ours; they relied on far greater manpower. Though not as reliable, the running cost was lower due to lower wage costs, although our workforce was considerably smaller.

Bente outlined what he wanted from me: colourful wall charts with planned work identified and indicating it was all maintained and up to date. He told me the planning office was the largest in the complex. He wanted it to look the most impressive. It was my job to achieve this by covering the wall space with charts – as many as possible.

It dawned on me that Bente had been caught out by the unplanned visit of the minister. He had probably only heard about it on his return from leave. As the chief superintendent, he realised guiltily that the buck should stop with him. The responsibility was squarely on his shoulders as it was his decision to keep the existence of a maintenance programme secret. His bluster and blaming others was a way of convincing himself that he was doing the right thing. The downside was that it was left to me to fabricate a web of deceit the best I could, which was a place I'd been before! On several occasions in my work experience, incompetent people had risen to the top on the backs of others.

"What do you need?" Bente asked me quietly.

"I have never done anything like this before. Off the top of my head, I'll need a drawing board, drawing equipment, good quality card, paper, stickers, a small printer, etc."

"Okay, do your best," he replied.

"It's a massive task. I would have to interpret what was in the manuals and design the charts accordingly."

"You are missing the point entirely. I don't want to waste your time doing that," Bente continued calmly.

"Are you telling me what you want is bogus wall charts instead of setting up a proper plan?"

"You have the plant equipment list. Invent the rest as you go on. After all, you are a maintenance planner. It's not for real. Just make it look good. No one will pay any attention to it. Make the office look like we're maintaining the plant efficiently."

"Is that all? What will I do in my spare time?" I replied sarcastically. "And once I've finished it, where does that leave me?"

"Don't worry, you will be all right; I will see to that. This is the only plant the minister is inspecting, so a lot is resting on you, so you'd better not let me down!"

"Inshallah," I retorted sarcastically.

Later that day, everything I asked for was delivered to my office. I started to design and fabricate the bogus workflow charts and inspection schedules. I worked for the next six days for twelve hours a day, and I was handing so much paper my fingertips grew sore. Bente popped in every day to check my progress, sometimes suggesting colours and design, but nothing on content. I was skipping the communication meetings and was utterly shut off from the outside world. Mentally, I had come to terms with what I was doing. I reasoned that I had two choices: do as I was told and work on the stupid wall charts. Or carry on installing a maintenance system that wouldn't be used. So I decided that doing what I was told was the best choice; it would mean less angst with Bente. I had resigned myself that I would not return after my leave. I remembered my dad's words; 'if it doesn't feel right, don't do it'. On the sixth day, Bente visited my office, looked around the walls and was pleased. I had almost completely covered the walls with my nonsensical charts. He was delighted; I only had his opinion on how it would appear to anyone else. I was practically brain-dead and didn't care anyway by this time.

"This now looks like a planning office," he said as he left.

"Whatever you say," I responded.

The following day at the communication meeting, Bente told everyone of the minister's visit. He expected everyone to appear busy, work efficiently, and remain at the plant. The Syrian observers looked especially smart and seemed to be paying more attention to what was said. I realised that none of them had ever spoken, so I was unsure if they knew what was happening.

Later that morning, Bente introduced me to the minister in my office. In his late fifties, he was dressed in an expensive suit and looked like a typical Western politician. He spoke good English, was pleasant and well-mannered, and had an aura of confidence. The difference between the two men in my office could not be further apart. One was animatedly talking nonsense while the other listened intently without expression. I wondered if he fully understood what he was being shown. If so, why wasn't he asking any questions? Bente explained that the planning charts on the wall ensured that the plant was well maintained and up to date. Going from chart to chart, he pointed out the advantages of keeping work under tight control. The minister didn't say a word; he just looked at each one without indicating whether he understood the content.

"Good maintenance is a cost-saving exercise ensuring the plant will work with the minimum number of shutdowns due to unscheduled breakdowns Bente said enthusiastically."

The minister studied each chart, one at a time, as he walked around the room, occasionally glancing at me as he went. I found it odd. The minister said nothing to Bente or me.

"God be with you," he said in perfect English.

"Maa al Salama," I replied out of courtesy as he left my office.

In the afternoon, Bente returned to my office with a beaming smile. "Don't plan anything tonight. We have a barbecue in the desert to celebrate."

"So you managed to pull the wool over the minister's eyes then?"

"Hook, line and sinker," he replied confidently with a beaming smile.

"He's not as bright as he looks, then."

"The minister was pleased and agreed there was a need to educate the Syrians on running their plants as efficiently as we do ours."

Hope not, I thought, but kept shtum.

That night we drove out into the desert in a convoy of about twenty vehicles. When we arrived at the chosen location, it was dusk. We parked high on a plateau, overlooking a plain that went on as far as the eye could see. There was no sign that the area had ever been inhabited. Grey scattered rocks and sand stretched as far as the eye could see. It reminded me of photographs of the moon's surface: completely desolate. A crew cab joined us from Al Omar containing Matt, Doug and a Syrian driver, Ibrahim.

I asked Matt, "Is it just you three then?"

"Well, it should have been just the driver and me, but I felt sorry for Doug. He isn't doing anything, so I brought him along."

"Did you clear it with the super?"

"He sort of suggested it; it was his idea I came and saw what you were doing. I seem to be the only one that can keep him under control."

"The super did know it was a drinks party?"

"Not sure, we better keep an eye on Doug, or you can, for a change."

"You're joking. I am going to get blethered tonight; I've earnt it."

"Ah, well, he can't do much damage out here, can he?"

The drivers unloaded crates of beer from the backs of their trucks so we could help ourselves. Doug was immediately there to help with the unloading.

I couldn't resist saying, "See, he is good at something."

Matt replied, with a grin, "Yeah, he thinks he is unloading his quota."

The rest of us set up a sizeable homemade barbecue constructed from 40-gallon oil drums. We piled up wooden crates to create a bonfire. Night fell quickly. A few beers helped relax us all as we sat around the fire. Within an hour, the goat meat, freshly slaughtered by the Syrian trainees, was roasted on the barbeque and laid on a table with fresh bread for us to help ourselves to. It was like a banquet; fresh bread and a freshly roasted goat were delicious compared to the bland canteen diet we were used to.

The scene became the most magical thing I had ever seen. The desert sky, jet black, was studded with millions of stars, glittering like diamonds, which can only be seen in total darkness. It was like looking into a world far beyond. The bonfire was roaring and illuminating where we sat. Thousands of bright red sparks floated over the plateau, drifting upwards into the sky, joining the stars.

We were all in awe, sipping our cans of beer, stuffing our faces with goat and bread, and mesmerised by the scene before us: it was absolute magic.

Looking at the starry sky, Matt broke the silence, saying, "Something this beautiful couldn't have been an accident; it had to be created."

"It was supposed to have been created by a 'big bang' billions of years ago. It's beyond me. It's still growing. This planet is such a minuscule part of the universe; it does my head in trying to work it out," I replied.

Matt passed me another beer, saying, "Drink, and just look."

I will never forget this memory; this one stands out as the most magically beautiful of them all. Whenever I hear the words 'it's magic', the scene from that night always springs to mind.

This was the first time I had been able to have a face-to-face conversation with Matt for a while. He was staying the night at Al Taim on Bente's instructions, and I was to show him what I had achieved. We had already agreed our time could have been better spent; he also thought we were in a risky business. Sooner or later, the deceit would be discovered. Doug's company hadn't renewed his contract; it was apparent to everyone he wasn't suitable. John's contract wouldn't be renewed either. Apparently, he managed to shut down Al Omar, accidentally short-circuiting the control panel by connecting an AVOmeter across the wrong contact terminals. John had apparently trained as a wireman, not an electrician. His role had been tracing the pigging sensors and cables on the pipeline for accidental damage by goats, camels and Bedouins; this was within his capabilities. However, his superintendent ordered him to do a task entirely out of his expertise. As Matt explained simply: John was a 'bloody chancer'. I asked whether the superintendent was a chancer and whether he would be going home too.

"Apparently not; they make the rules, not abide by them," Matt replied.

The following day we were all tired after the boozy night. I showed the unimpressed Matt my wallchart-covered office. Matt shook his head. "What fucking idiot would fall for this? Excuse my language!"

"Only the big boss. It makes you wonder how he got to the top of the pile."

"Amazing! I cannae believe anyone would fall for this garbage."

"Garbage? I thought it was pretty well done myself." I said, trying to keep a straight face and failing.

"Aye, you might be right. Artistically, it's excellent. Content, though, is poor. It might look good in a modern art gallery."

"If you've seen enough of my artwork, perhaps we could do a bit of sightseeing? What do you think?"

"Aye, that would be great. I have been absolutely bored to tears on my own. Stuck in that bloody office, from dawn to dusk, is enough to make anyone bonkers."

We had a word with Ibrahim and told him to drive us somewhere interesting. Ibrahim, in his forties, spoke reasonably good English and agreed to take us out for a spin. So off we went on what felt like an adventure. Doug rode shotgun, with Matt and me in the back of the crew cab. We felt excited; we were escaping the humdrum of the office. Matt and I discussed whether we would come back for another contract. I relayed my conversation with Mike regarding getting transferred to Conch Oil. Matt thought he'd return and push to join Conch Oil himself.

* * * * *

Amina put her book down and returned me to the present. "You look deep in thought."

"I'm anticipating things might change for the worse: it's brought memories flooding back."

"Hope they are good ones."

"I was just thinking about how we met and what a piece of luck that was."

"Tell me again, please, while I make chai." Her eyes were laughing.

"This will take a very long time, especially if you butt in all the time, as you usually do."

"Just correcting your memory sometimes, as it isn't that good."

"I love to hear your side of the story as well, especially the bit about me rescuing you," I said jokingly.

Once again, I told 'Our Story'. She was never tired of hearing it, and I was never tired of telling it.

Chapter 7

Our Story

"Once upon a time, many years ago, a princess was held prisoner by an evil gang of thieves until…"

"Get on with it! Don't be silly, or it will take forever."

"Okay, but it will take some time, as always."

"We have plenty of that."

So I began the long story of how we met.

It all started the fateful day Ibrahim, our driver, took Matt, Doug and me out on a sightseeing trip. We were all chatting, not paying much attention to the surroundings.

A Bedouin camp came into view about thirty metres from the left-hand side of the road. Ibrahim slowed down the crew cab, wound down his window and poked his head out. I could see he was smiling and shouting at a hoard of approximately thirty women, who were running from the campsite towards our truck. The bright, colourful clothes were different from any I had seen before. As we came level with the centre of the campsite, Doug grabbed the steering wheel, overpowering Ibrahim. He jammed his foot on the accelerator, pushing Ibrahim's foot out of the way and steering the crew cab off the highway onto a track that led to the centre of the campsite. Ibrahim managed to bring the crew cab to a halt in the centre of the campsite by braking fiercely, and pushing Doug away from the steering wheel. He swore in Arabic.

The excited women immediately surrounded our vehicle. They indicated how hungry they were by jabbering and pointing to their mouths in the usual way. Ibrahim got out to talk to them. Matt and I were screaming at Doug.

"What the fuck have you done?"

Doug shrugged. "Just having a bit of fun," he said, pulling a stupid face.

Ibrahim got back into the cab, looked at Doug angrily, and cursed in Arabic at him. He then turned to Matt and me. "As long as the women get some money, it will be okay. I have arranged chai for a few Syrian pounds. Hopefully, that should be enough to satisfy them."

Matt and I were reluctant to stay; we just wanted to get out of there.

"Can't you just drive through the women, pushing them out of the way?" I asked.

"And risk running them over? I believe chai is the best solution," Ibrahim replied.

"Just a quick cuppa, okay?" Matt agreed.

We got out of the truck, and we were invited to enter one of the tents. The inside of the tent appeared bigger than the outside. We were told to sit in an area covered in carpets, cushions and goat skins. We sat cross-legged, in a circle, with a Bedouin woman between twenty and thirty years of age on either side of each of us.

"They looked older than they were," Amina butted in. "It's a hard life being a Bedouin woman."

"A young girl served us chai in small glasses. A heated conversation started between Ibrahim and the women. Their raised voices and body language indicated they weren't happy. I could see from where I sat there was an area with mosquito nets rising from the floor to the tent roof. Through the nets, I could see two separate bedroom areas covered in cushions, skins and carpets.

"The women are willing for jig-jig for twenty Syrian pounds," Ibrahim said. "It's not a lot of money." He shrugged his shoulders, indicating it was up to us.

Matt and I declined and, with difficulty, managed to convince Doug to also, although he was visibly disappointed. The women seemed angry, and the conversation continued with Ibrahim.

"They will dance for ten Syrian pounds," he eventually explained.

I just wanted to get out of there. A woman on my left was whispering 'jig-jig' in my ear. On the other side, a young girl, who looked about twelve years old, pointed at her tiny breasts, saying, "Me, Madam." We decided that paying for a dance might be a good idea. One of the women left the tent and returned with an old, bearded man. He dwarfed the women and carried an ornately decorated antique rifle in one hand and a homemade instrument in the other hand. The instrument was made from a gallon oil can, a stick with gut attached to it to make strings, and a wooden bow. The women took off their outer garments to reveal colourful pantaloons and short, tight, sleeveless blouses exposing their bellies. The man started to play his instrument whilst a woman provocatively stood in front of each of us. They began to dance erotically, rotating their hips close to our faces.

Arabian music always sounded like a strangled cat to me, but after my ears became used to it, it sounded okay, and bearing in mind the instrument used, it was amazing. The more excited the women grew, the closer their groins came to our faces. Until their groins rubbed into our faces, the women seemed to be going into a trance. I was concerned that the longer this went on, the worse the situation would become. I got the attention of the woman dancing in front of me by saying, "Jig-jig bukra." I waved my hands to intimate 'not now'. She seemed pleased and stepped back. I indicated to Ibrahim, by making a cut gesture across my throat, that I was ready to leave. Reluctantly, Ibrahim spoke to the women explaining that we would come back 'bukra', meaning tomorrow.

Eventually, we managed to get outside the tent but the women were clamouring for money. My father raised me to only carry enough cash to spend on any single day. I paid my dancer, as agreed, for the chai and her dance. I then gave her all the money in my wallet, ensuring she could see that that was all I had. I whispered 'bukra' as an additional precaution. Matt and Ibrahim were paying their dancers without any issue. We had forgotten to ensure that Doug fully understood when he started a heated argument with his dancer. Doug's wallet was in his hand, packed with the additional expense money given to him by the contract company. Doug was counting out money from a large wad to pay his dancer in full view of everyone. His dancer had her hands firmly grasped on his wallet. The rest of the women surrounded Doug, shouting and hitting him, trying to grab his wallet. Then, from nowhere, appeared about twenty Bedouin men. From their body language and aggressive appearance,

I feared the worst. The men pushed past the women, and Doug's wallet was forcibly removed from his hand by one of the men. The contents then passed between them, and there was a lot of exciting jabbering and nodding. The men turned to Matt and me, indicating they wanted our wallets and mobile phones. We had no option but to give them up. The men started to jabber excitedly at Ibrahim. Ibrahim indicated that he wasn't happy by shaking his head from side to side. We could see the fear in his face.

"They want your bank PINs," Ibrahim said.

"Do we have any choice?" Matt asked Ibrahim.

"No, not really," he replied.

"We're fucked aren't we?" I added.

"They will hold us until they have withdrawn the money from our bank accounts," Ibrahim explained.

We were all petrified, except for Doug, who didn't seem to realise the seriousness of the situation and was still shouting that he wanted his wallet back. A Bedouin approached him, drew his curved Arabian knife out and placed it across Doug's throat. Doug fell silent. Now it was easier to think without Doug jabbering on in his Geordie speak. Losing money was not as bad as having our throats cut, so, reluctantly, we gave them up.

The four of us were split up and taken in different directions. My arms were tightly gripped by a Bedouin on each side. One was carrying another antique rifle and had a large curved Arabian knife tucked into an ammunition belt. They roughly threw me inside a tent, similar to the previous one. The Bedouin remained outside my tent guarding the entrance. He used his hands to indicate my throat would be cut if I tried to escape. Alone in the tent,

I feared that once the Bedouins had our money, we may be of no further use to them. We might be set free, or something else might happen, which sent a shudder of fear through me.

After an hour or so, the night began to fall, and a woman appeared inside my tent. I could tell she was quite young from the layers of her clothes and the way she walked. She seemed to glide rather than walk. She carried a tray that held a lump of meat, rice and a milk dish she put in front of me.

"I served you goat meat, not the best bits either, like, eye, tongue or even brain; I wasn't allowed them. The Bedouin men keep those bits for themselves," Amina interrupted.

"Obviously, they were not out to impress me."

"A good job, too; you would have starved," Amina replied.

"Can I continue with the story?"

"Sorry."

You lit an oil lamp, illuminating the tent, then sat down in one graceful movement, with legs crossed, watching me eat. I couldn't help noticing your eyes, the only exposed part of your face.

"That was because I was wearing a shayla pulled across my face," Amina butted in again.

"Okay, now let me carry on, please, or we will be here all night."

"Your eyes were large and bright with dark brown irises. The light from the lamp was dancing in them. You watched me until I had eaten and drank everything in front of me. I awoke the following morning inside the bedroom. Through the mosquito net, I could see you preparing chai on a primitive oil stove. I couldn't remember anything after the meal the night before and wondered how I got to bed. As I stood up, I felt a little giddy and unstable, a bit like a hangover from a good night out."

"I guided you into the bedroom and you fell fast asleep like a baby," Amina butted in.

"Then, in the morning, you served me chai, bread, and honey. I couldn't help notice how beautiful you were. I could see the outline of your features through the shayla you were wearing."

Amina squeezed my hand. "Get on with our story!"

"After breakfast, you gave me a twig and water and showed me how to clean my teeth with it."

Amina butted in again, like a know-all quiz contestant with an index finger and thumb on either side of her chin. "It's a Salvadora persica twig, better than a modern toothbrush."

I clapped my hands in praise. "Clever girl," I said. "Your research into Bedouins is paying dividends. Can I continue? After breakfast, you disappeared, and I was left inside the tent on my own, anticipating something would happen. The guard escorted me outside to the toilet, a primitive hole in the ground shielded from the campsite by a frame and canvas sheet. Inside the toilet was an old oil drum filled with water and a jug for washing."

"The jug is called a 'lota' and is only used for toileting."

"I knew from my time in Saudi Arabia that washing after toileting is done with the left hand only, and the right hand is for eating."

"I noticed that you only ever used your right hand when I served you food."

"I was trying to please you. In Saudi Arabia, the right hands of thieves are chopped off as punishment. So they have to toilet with the same hand they eat with, which was considered very dirty."

"Not as dirty as using paper."

"Please let me finish! I couldn't wait for you to return to the tent; there was something about you that comforted me. You returned later that morning with two massive bowls, one of rice and one empty, and sat by the doorway of the tent and placed them in front of you. You were flicking the rice, grain by grain, from the full to the empty bowl and flicked unwanted chaff and sand onto the ground. My trainees in Saudi Arabia took it in turns doing the same thing every day. I sat down next to you and helped to clean the rice. Your eyes indicated that you were a little confused, but you were smiling."

"That's because grown men do not do such things. It's considered beneath them; it's a woman's work."

"I will remember that!" I said, grinning.

"Later that day, I was collected by an armed guard. I was terrified this might not be a good outcome but was pleasantly surprised when I met with the others. Ibrahim had managed to convince the Bedouins that we should be updated on what was happening. He told us the Bedouins would not withdraw all our money from the ATMs in one go. Instead, they would make a series of smaller withdrawals over a couple of days to avoid causing alarm. Despondently, we all returned to our tents. I was hoping that my evening meal would appear the same way as on the previous night, and it did. As dusk fell, your beautiful silhouette appeared in my tent, carrying a tray as before. You sat opposite but didn't eat or drink anything although I offered. I knew little Syrian language, so all the communication with you was through your eyes and hands."

"I was trying to convey to you that I was unhappy with your situation by keeping my head bowed."

"I woke the following morning, as before, not knowing how I went to bed or slept so well, and I had a similar hangover."

"That would be the effect of the potion."

"No doubt you will tell me what it contained, clever clogs?"

"It's a mixture of blue water lily, burnt hemp seeds, and seeds of the viper's bugloss."

"Every time I tell this story, you add to it."

"It's called education, darling. You should try it. It's an ancient combination of plants used by Bedouins to restrain people."

"Fine, whatever! Can you give it a rest? The following morning, you served me chai, bread and honey for breakfast, and we sat opposite each other. I pointed to myself and said, 'Allan'. You indicated to yourself and whispered very quietly, 'Me, Amina'. What you whispered next surprised me.

"In the English language, you said, 'Not Bedouin.'

'You speak English?' I asked, puzzled.

'A little,' you whispered.

'Not Bedouin, what then?'

'Syrian,' you responded proudly, hand on heart.

"You then stood up and walked out of the tent. I was alone again except for the guard outside. I approached the guard, positioned my nose as close to my armpit as possible, and pulled a face. The guard understood and led me to a small, tented enclosure. Inside there was an oil drum mounted on a crude wooden frame. A hosepipe was attached to the bottom of the drum; the end was crudely doubled and tied. The guard indicated that I should remove all my clothes and give them to him. Reluctantly I did. There was a lump of what I took to be soap. You have since told me it was saltwort. I felt very vulnerable standing there naked, but it wasn't long before the guard returned with a clean thawb. I felt a lot better and fresher returning to the tent. You returned later with my clothes, washed and dry. Your smile was amused, and your eyes were laughing."

"I haven't told you this before; white cotton freshly washed becomes transparent in bright sunlight."

"I was standing in front of the tent in full view, basking in the sun when you returned."

"I know; I remember it well for an obvious reason."

"You were smiling because you were impressed?"

"Darling, your use of the English language is awful; don't you mean disappointed?"

"That's an extremely unkind thing to say."

"I was extremely disappointed."

"What! I thought I looked a little like a Greek god in full splendour?"

"In some little way you did, the emphasis on little!" Amina drew a number one in the air.

"For that remark, just you wait; I am going to make you extremely disappointed tonight."

"Promises, promises! I can't wait."

"Is it true, or is it a wind-up?"

"Would I deliberately wind you up?"

"Yes, you would, and often do. Bloody Margaret's influence again! Now let me continue, please, without

7 3

you showing off how clever you are. Ibrahim had arranged with the Bedouins for us to meet again that afternoon. Ibrahim explained that their robbing of our bank accounts was going to plan. In his opinion, things would come to a head soon, maybe the next day. They would then have all our money. Ibrahim also shared that he had explained to the Bedouin leader that we would also be worth something to Conch Oil. They would pay a handsome ransom for our safe return. Ibrahim thought this would buy us a little more time and might allow us an opportunity to escape.

That evening, you glided into my tent. Your eyes looked more beautiful than usual; later, you told me it was khol, which certainly did the trick. That night, you served my meal and signalled me not to drink the milk by pointing at it and shaking your head. You tilted your head and rested it on your hands with your eyes shut, mimicking falling sleeping. I nodded that I understood and drank only the water. I asked where you were from using gestures and pointing but learnt nothing. Then I noticed that a tear had mixed with the Khol and left a black streak down your cheek. I moved my hand towards your face to wipe away the tear. You looked at me, and your eyes showed no objection. I removed your veil. For the first time, I saw your whole face. I felt lost in the beauty before me, and my eyes too swelled with tears. We were alone in the tent, staring into each other's eyes. Nothing else seemed to matter. The sadness in your eyes was overwhelming. Then, in an instant, you stood up, turned away, and left the tent. After you went, loneliness consumed me again."

"The reason for my unhappiness was that I knew there was a plan for you. Everyone was getting ready to move to another location, and it could only mean one thing."

"Which was what?"

"Bedouins are good at covering their tracks. No trace of you would be found."

"After you left me, I had this feeling that something was about to change. I sensed by your manner that you were saying goodbye. I was already terrified, but what I felt then moved up a notch. I guessed something would happen soon.

The tent had a skirt that could be rolled up during the day to allow cool air to circulate and shut for warmth at night. I pushed my head and shoulders under the skirt, so I could gaze at the night sky. I had done the same thing as a young child, camping out with my pals. On a cloudless night, we would lie on our back, gazing at the stars in awe, asking ourselves about the meaning of life. What is it all about? Why are we here? And for what reason? I didn't understand as a child, and I was even more confused as an adult. Only in the desert with absolutely no light pollution can the night sky look so magnificent.

I was shocked out of these thoughts by something firm pressing hard over my nose and mouth. I tried to move but couldn't. Something heavy was on top of me, pushing me to the ground. I was struck with fear. Every part of my body was held in a vice-like grip. I felt weak and helpless. I couldn't breathe. The more I struggled, the harder I was held by something so much stronger than me. My heart was racing; I was panicking. This is it, I thought. This is how it all ends: my fight for survival was leaving me. I was losing consciousness. My imagination was racing. What was holding me? Then I saw an alien face close to mine: a large shiny black head with no eyes with unrecognisable objects attached, pointing towards me. The front section of its body looked like a black turtle shell. The alien was straddling me, controlling all my limbs, pressing me harder to the ground. Then the alien whispered in perfect English, 'Don't be afraid. I am here to help you. Do as I say! When you hear a bang, run towards the road'.

The alien silently slipped away, and I lay as quiet as possible, trembling in shock and trying to control my breathing. What had just happened made no sense at all. I heard a thump from the front of the tent, then nothing. I crept out of the back of the tent and waited. After about a minute, I heard a muffled bang. The sky lit up with flares. I listened to all sorts of frantic screaming and shouting and ran as fast as my wobbly legs would carry me over the rough ground to the road. As I was running and stumbling, I heard three more muffled bangs, then silence.

When I reached the roadside, I could see three more identical aliens; they waved for me to join them. As I approached them, I realised they were soldiers. Further down the road, I could see other figures and people joining them. I walked towards the group and could make out Ibrahim, Matt, and Doug with more soldiers. They were in full battledress for night fighting. They were dressed from head to foot in black padded bulletproof uniforms, night vision binoculars, black visors with cameras attached to their black helmets. Strapped to their battledress were guns, bayonets and grenades. The padded uniforms made them appear massive.

The Bedouins must have been shitting themselves when the sky lit up, and they saw this bunch running towards them. The sight of them probably made them drop the antique weapons they had used to threaten us. We waited, grouped in a bunch. None of us spoke: the four of us were in shock. The soldiers appeared to be at ease and in control of the situation. A couple of trucks appeared, we were ordered to board and wait for the rest of the soldiers to join us. When they did, walking in front of them, I could see a group of Bedouins. I counted two men and four women. You were amongst them; unlike the other women, who were walking with heads held high, yours was bowed, as though ashamed."

"Yes, I did feel shame, but I was also glad that you were all rescued," Amina said.

"The Bedouins were handcuffed behind their backs and were roughly forced onto the back of another truck."

"I didn't realise that this was the start of another life for me."

"For me, too, thanks to Doug. Shall we make this the last time I retell our story? It's gone midnight now, and it's time for bed."

"Okay, but don't forget your promise."

Chapter 8

Meeting Ali

We were taken back to Al Taim in the truck. I thought that Matt, Doug, and Ibrahim appeared to still be very confused and wobbly on their feet, probably caused by the potion. We were taken to our rooms and told to remain there until the morning. I couldn't sleep, maybe due to adrenalin but also because I was concerned for Amina. The following morning, soldiers escorted Matt, Doug, Ibrahim and me to a building. We were kept some distance apart. Other than in the rescue truck, we hadn't had time to talk to each other. We were put in separate rooms. There was a table and two chairs in the room, and I was ordered to sit and wait.

The door opened; a Syrian observer I recognised from the communication meeting walked in, sat opposite me and introduced himself in perfect English as Captain Ali Mansour. That shook me a bit, as I had assumed that the observers didn't speak English and didn't understand what was going on at the meetings because their expressions never changed.

The captain explained that this was a debriefing and that he expected me to be perfectly honest with him, in which case, everything would be fine. "I am the soldier who whispered to you to get out after the bang," he told me.

"You're a soldier then?" I asked, curious, somewhat confused and stupid as he was in army uniform.

"Yes, a captain in the Syrian commandos."

"What is the point of you being at the morning meetings?" I asked.

His eyes locked onto mine. "I think you will find I am interrogating you, not the other way round. I ask the questions; you answer. Simple as that," he said with an air of superiority. "Relate everything that had happened! Everything is being recorded, so be very truthful."

I was careful, after his rebuttal, to give a detailed account. He went back over it and asked a few questions.

"Thank you for your account. You can go now. Your interview is over."

My curiosity got the better of me. "Why are you at the refineries?" I asked.

He smiled. "You are a nosey bugger, aren't you?" he said with a slight London accent. "To protect them, of course."

"To protect them from who? Surely not us?"

"Maybe you, or people like you, but it wasn't supposed to be Bedouins."

"What! People like me?"

"Not necessarily, but there are various factions that are trying to damage our country."

"But you disappear every morning?"

"Just because you can't see us, that doesn't mean we can't see you. We can't protect idiots who do stupid things, though."

"I haven't said 'thank you. Can I shake your hand?"

"That is not required; we were just doing our job."

"But you probably saved our lives."

"Do you shake your workmate's hands when they do the job they're paid to do?"

"Can I pat you on the back, then?" I said with a grin. I was desperately trying to thank him.

"I appreciate your comments, thank you," he said with a smile.

"Can you tell me, how did you know where we were?"

"Basic intelligence, something that appears to be missing from your bunch. When you didn't return after the first night, it was obvious something was wrong. We searched the highways and found nothing. When someone is missing, we check the activities around known suspects and banks. We spotted unusual Bedouin activity around the bank's ATMs in Deir ez-Zur. We discovered cash withdrawals from your bank accounts. It was then easy to follow them. As soon as we identified their location, we launched a drone to observe the camp to identify if you were safe and your exact location."

"Very professional. I'm impressed, and thanks for being so 'intelligent', so to speak."

"We watched you doing your ablutions, so we knew where you were."

"Oh, shit!"

"Precisely, not a pretty sight. I've got it on tape. Would you like a copy?" he said, grinning.

"Changing the subject slightly," I said, "the Bedouin woman tending to me seemed different from the others."

"Why would you think that?"

"Her exact words to me were said proudly in English – 'not Bedouin, me Syrian'."

"Why did she seem different?"

"Well, it was her demeanour mainly, as she was very passive and gentle, and difficult to get eye contact with, as though she was ashamed."

"Did you find out anything else about her?"

"Only that her name was Amina."

Captain Ali thanked me for my honest account and would reinterview me again once all the hostages had given their version of the event. The soldiers escorted me back to my guarded room; they had left refreshments inside. Later that afternoon, soldiers escorted me to meet the captain to continue the debrief.

"I am happy with your story, and all four have given the same account. I will not be taking action against Matt, Ibrahim, or yourself. The blame for the event is clearly on Doug's shoulders."

"I don't think he is quite right in the head; it's a mystery to me how he got here."

"He will never be allowed to return to Syria, and his contract is terminated. He will be denied an entry visa in future."

"What will happen to the Bedouins?" I asked.

"There will be a trial; the court will punish the guilty."

"How do you decide who to put on trial? There were so many involved."

"Good question. The two men we saw at the ATMs and the four women looking after the prisoners will be tried."

"But that's not fair, is it? The women were obeying the men, and what about the four men guarding us? Aren't they all just as guilty?"

"Possibly, but we can't arrest them all; I know it's not fair, but it's not up to me. I follow orders. It's the normal practice."

"But, why twice as many women as men? That makes no sense to me."

"It's because a man is considered to be worth twice as much as a woman."

"Bloody hell! It's like the dark ages."

"It's not up to me! Let it go!"

"Okay. What is the likely penalty?"

"Possibly life imprisonment; the court will probably assume that they would have killed you."

"That seems very severe to me," I replied.

"Well, kidnapping is a severe offence in Syria. Though, where girls are concerned, previous governments have tended to ignore the requests for ransoms. Returning hostages, especially girls, to families tend to instigate further crimes."

"What crimes?"

"The fathers of returned girls traditionally kill their daughters as they are considered defiled, and therefore of little worth."

"The Syrian woman feeding me differed from the others."

"In what way was she different?"

"The other women were aggressive and demanding. She was gentle, demanded nothing, and stopped me from taking the sleeping potion."

"Allan, this is the second time you have mentioned her."

"I know, it's just that I don't think she was the same as the others."

"Maybe not; we will see. I will be interviewing all the prisoners tomorrow. The taped evidence will be given to the courts, and they will punish those guilty. We only provide the evidence. That's where our duty ends. Officially, the interview is over; you can leave now. Or, Allan, would you like chai?"

"That would be nice."

"Okey dokey; interview over. We can talk about anything you like now, but not Bedouins, regardless of how pretty they are, okay?"

"How should I address you?"

"In uniform, Captain, which I hope this will be the last time, socially, Ali." He removed his tunic top and hung it on the back of the door with a flourish, turned and smiled.

"So, Ali, what made you decide to become a soldier?"

Ali poured the chai. "I returned home to Syria after studying in Oxford and enrolled in the Syrian Army. After my training, I was transferred to the 15th Special Forces Division and slowly rose to the rank of captain."

"There must have been a big difference between your life in Oxford and your life in Syria?"

"Massive. Really hard to readjust. I soon realised that I was not a good Muslim."

"What was the hardest thing to adjust to?"

"So many things. I no longer pray five times a day, I enjoy the occasional glass of wine – that's putting it mildly. My time in England altered my perception of non-Muslim people."

"In what way? I hope for the good, not bad?"

"Yes, you are right. When I first went to Oxford, I didn't trust anybody. My religious upbringing had led me to distrust everyone who was not Muslim. I soon found out, though, that most people are good."

"It was similar for me; Arabs initially looked pretty aggressive and threatening to me. But I soon discovered they are mostly gentle people, though it does take time to win their trust."

"Touché. I agree with you, Allan. It was the same for me. Gaining trust is the hardest thing."

"My father once told me when I was young that your first impression of someone is usually correct. You may change your opinion later, but at some point in the future, you will realise that your first impression was the correct one."

Ali thought for a while and then smiled. "I think he was correct. I have had precisely the same experience myself. Would you like to come to my apartment for a drink this evening?"

"Yes," I said, pleasantly surprised. "I would like to very much."

Visiting Ali in his room was to become a regular occurrence. When I first entered his room, I was taken aback by the contrast between my bare, uncomfortable bolthole and his luxury abode. There were comfortable chairs and furniture and no floor cushions. Looking around, I could see a drinks bar, proper glasses, tables, cupboards, carpets, bookcases, pictures on the walls and shelves.

"Wow, I didn't expect anything like this, Ali. It looks like somebody lives here," I said in amazement.

"Somebody does. You have to make the best of it. Sit down! Scotch, okay?"

"That would be great," I said as he walked towards the fridge. "No ice for me, please."

"A man after my own heart," Ali said as he turned to his drinks cabinet and poured two large whiskies.

We talked about general things while sipping our drinks. I noticed a few framed pictures faced down. I thought this strange, but felt it would be rude to mention. On the many subsequent visits, the picture frames were always turned down. That made me think that we had some way to go before he trusted me entirely as a friend. Why else would he hide them from me? Though curious, I didn't broach the subject.

Chapter 9

Back at Work

The following day, after the morning communication meeting, Bente came to my office.

"I am impressed. It looks more and more like a planning office every day!"

"I am glad you like it," I said, though it was a load of crap. I kept my opinion to myself as there was no point, and it was too early for a shouting match.

"I have just popped in to say that there is no issue with your contract regarding the Bedouin incident, so you can carry on with the good work."

"Bente, I am not happy with all this nonsense; I would sooner work on what I was employed to do. Sooner or later, it will have to be done; this is the ideal time before the plants start demanding attention themselves due to lack of maintenance."

He raised his voice slightly and said, "You worry too much, it will be fine, you have a job with a good salary. Make the most of it."

"Bente, I don't want to get involved in the financial side of things, I don't want to know what's going on, but surely you must realise that the budgets are there to be used."

With a redder face, Bente replied, "The budgets are nothing to do with you."

"I know that, but can I suggest that you look at setting up a proper Planned Maintenance Programme, using the maintenance manuals we already have?"

Bente, extremely irritated, shouted, "I have already told you we haven't the manpower to do that."

"You should have, according to the maintenance manuals. It designates a team of planning engineers, not just one, so it must be a part of the revenue budget."

Bente returned to his old ways by shouting, "You do as you are told to; that's the end of it."

"Bente, one of the first things you said to me was 'the planning office is the largest'; why do you think that should be?"

Irritated, he replied, "Because it is."

"So you haven't deduced that the designers understood a team of planners is required?"

He shouted, "What the fuck do they know?"

Realising that he was returning to bluster again, I said quietly, "If you listen to what I say, it should make your life easier. I can set up a maintenance programme with the information I have at hand. It could be done far faster if we had a few computers designated to it."

Bente, now at boiling point, shouted, "How are we going to buy and install them? You don't think things through; you've got your head in the clouds."

"Use your capital budget; it should be almost untouched. There is a saying, 'use it or lose it', you must be about to lose yours or have it cut."

Bente left my office, uttering again, "Just do as you are fucking well told to do." After a pause, under his breath, I heard, "Or I will find someone else that will do."

I resigned myself to the fact that it was a pointless task, trying to convince Bente. I had a choice between accepting what was going on and taking my dirty wages, if my conscience would allow it. Or not returning after my leave and finding another way of supporting my family. So I stopped going to the daily communication meetings as I couldn't see the point as it was a charade. I resigned to myself that I wouldn't return; at least I tried to do the right thing.

I only had a couple of days before this month's trip would be over. I was still working in my office on the maintenance programme; it was something to do to fill the time. I had stopped entering nonsense on the silly planning charts after the energy minister had left. When the communication meeting ended, after everyone skived off, Bente walked into my office. He seemed in a good mood, which, at the time, I thought unusual. The first time I had seen him smile. Trouble ahead, I deduced.

He said, "How are you? How are things going?"

I couldn't resist and answered, "Shit, and shit."

"Sorry to hear that." He waited for my response; I continued working without looking at him. "I have had an idea; why don't we get you some help."

I thought he was joking, so I said, "Is this a wind-up?"

"No, not all; I was thinking of installing some computers to help you."

"To do what, play *Tetris* all day, or maybe *Super Mario*?"

"No, no need for sarcasm, we could install a maintenance programme on them, what do you think?"

I replied sarcastically, "That's an excellent idea of yours."

He didn't flinch at my remark and asked, "Have you any idea what sort of computer you require?"

"Not my department, I'm afraid, you will need an information technology firm specialising in installing maintenance programmes; there are loads about."

He looked surprised and said, "Allan, I thought it was something that you could do?"

"I can use them, that's all, but I would need training on their system. I have used several different programmes before; they're all different, some you can buy off the shelf, but it will require IT for a while to iron out the gremlins." I could see the enthusiasm draining away from Bente's face. So I said, "While on leave, it's something I could look at."

Bente looked startled and said, "You would do that?" He paused, then remarked, "Any expenses, I will pick up the tab." As he left the office, he said, "See you soon, bye."

I now had a reason to return after my leave; it also gave me something to do, between seeing my kids and catching up with the few friends I had, as a month was a long time.

That evening, Ali told me what he had found out during the interview with the Syrian woman. He wasn't surprised by what she told him, as the story was all too common. Ali explained that Bedouins are uneducated nomads who move around the Middle East with impunity, crossing borders. They were a law unto themselves. Various tribes, all with different customs, doctrines, and rules, had been handed down since time began. Superstitions, fallacies, folk stories and contradictions were used to bolster their behaviour. The Syrian population didn't respect the Bedouins; most feared them. Some of the Muslim population considered their behaviour to be against their faith. One particular criminal activity of Bedouins which was feared most was the kidnapping of children, primarily girls. Unfortunately, if the rescued girls were returned to their families, that could be worse for them.

Ali told me that Amina was one of these children. From what he learned from the interrogation, she had been kidnapped in Damascus when eleven years old. She had been studying English at school and at home with her father. Her parents had been wealthy, and their family name was Yassin. Her father, Yoran, was a doctor, and her mother was called Souzan. Ali would be checking the accuracy of her story to see if she was telling the truth.

"Please be careful, as from what you have said, all may not go well for her."

Ali continued to tell me more about Amina. During the interrogation of the other prisoners, he had gathered that they didn't trust her. She had proven to be argumentative, strong-willed, and stubborn, unlike the compliant Bedouin women. She had been promised to the leader of another Bedouin tribe. It was traditional for the groom's female relatives to physically examine the betrothed bride to ensure her value and virginity. Amina had been reluctant, which caused some delay. Eventually, it was forced upon her, and it became known that she was beautiful and intact. Her leader then demanded greater financial rewards from the groom's family. This again delayed the marriage. Although Amina's behaviour had been challenging, the marriage arrangement was still in place.

I asked Ali, "Why didn't she escape?"

"I asked her the very same question; I wasn't surprised at the answer. When she was kidnapped, they took her to the Bedouin leader. Remember, she was a frightened child. The leader told her she must choose another name. She decided on Habiba because it was a friend's name she liked. He then told her if she tried to escape, if they caught her, they would cut off her head and put it outside her parents' door. If they didn't catch her, they would cut off her parents' heads and put them on spikes outside her home."

"She told me her name was Amina, not Habiba!"

"That was because she knew that you would not harm her."

Within a few days, Ali managed to locate Amina's parents. They still lived in the Malki district of Damascus, amongst the rich and privileged. Ali had sent a colleague to interview them to confirm what Amina had told him. And monitor their reaction to the news of their daughter being found alive and well. From his colleague's feedback, Ali was happy to share that they were thrilled and couldn't wait to see their child again. They had assumed they would never see her again and implored him to make arrangements to see her. He had to explain in detail the correct course to follow.

Chapter 10

Leave in the UK, 1996

The evening before my return to the UK on leave, Ali invited me to his room. Over a couple of drinks, we discussed the trial, amongst other things. The court had fixed a trial date for all those accused of the kidnapping. Ali promised to keep me informed while I was away. He doubted if the trial would start before my return because Matt, Ibrahim and I might be required as witnesses.

Early the following morning, I caught the bus with Matt, John and Doug for our return journey to Damascus. We would stay the night there before catching our flights to Paris. The bus pulled into Palmyra Hotel Zenobia Cham Palace car park on the trip back. We disembarked and were met by the staff, all lined up to greet us.

We were introduced grandly to Khaled al-Asaad, the respected archaeologist and head of antiquities in Palmyra, by a staff member. He explained how lucky we were that he had time to meet us and never missed an opportunity to explain the importance of Palmyra. He proudly announced that Palmyra was now a UNESCO World Heritage Site. During lunch, Khaled explained how he had held this position for over forty years, emphasising his life's dedication to Palmyra. He was friendly, pleasant and informative; it was plain to see how much he enjoyed passing on his knowledge. We were privileged to meet him. The day left an indelible mark in my memory.

Later, we drove to the Al-Zaetona Hotel in Damascus. I showered, changed, and met the others for dinner and later that evening, we made our way to the Beit Al Wali Hotel for a drink. The bar was as busy and noisy as ever; many ex-pat workers were journeying home on leave. Matt and I kept pretty much in each other's company all evening. It wasn't until later, when leaving the hotel, that we noticed Doug was missing again. The three of us decided to make our way back to our hotel. As we walked, we discussed Doug's issues and agreed it was difficult to sympathise with him, regardless of his health. His mindless, bombastic attitude outweighed any compassion we might have felt for him. John summed him up perfectly as a 'bloody nutter'.

We breakfasted the following morning and made our way to the lobby to check out before catching the bus to the airport. There was still no sign of Doug as we sat in the lounge; we caught each other's eyes without explaining our concerns.

"Where's Doug? It's like bloody Groundhog Day," Matt said, breaking the silence.

"Well, he will be on his own this time," I said.

As soon as I had spoken, the sound of Doug arguing with the clerk came from the checkout desk. It certainly was like Groundhog Day again, after all. As before, he wanted his passport, but the clerk was demanding he first pays his bill. Doug was refusing to pay his bill, jabbering on in Geordie speak. I couldn't understand what he was saying and the clerk probably thought he was talking gibberish. Then two men, who were waiting to check out, joined him at the desk. The clerk kept looking in our direction; it looked like she was hoping we would help her. One of the men waved us over, but we waved to show we didn't want to get involved. They beckoned us again, but we sat tight.

Finally, one of them came over furiously shouting. "What sort of mates are you? We don't even know him but we've chipped in to pay his bill!"

"More fool you," Matt chipped in. "Perhaps you can make sure he gets on the bus as well."

"And on the plane," I added.

"I hope you have enough dosh to buy him a few drinks in the departure lounge, too," John added.

The three of us left the hotel without Doug. I felt relief and presumed the other two did as well.

"So, we're Doug-free at last," Matt said.

"This should make the journey home far less stressful," I added.

"It's like going out for the night and leaving the children with a babysitter, hoping they can cope," John commented.

We all had different connecting flights from Paris, which meant we had differing amounts of time on our hands. We decided to have a few drinks at the bar while waiting for our boarding calls. Matt and I arranged to keep in touch while we were on leave. We were both wishing John all the best and thanking him for his help, when Doug appeared and sat down with us as though nothing had happened. I wondered if his newfound mates had sussed him out and realised why we ditched him. In a way, it was impossible not to admire Doug; he must have had skin thicker than a rhinoceros. I bought the four of us a beer, said my final goodbyes to John and Doug, and shook their hands. As I shook Doug's hand, I looked directly into his eyes to see if anyone was at home; the curtains were drawn and there was no sign of life. *Goodbye, Long John Silver*, I thought.

I will never forget Doug and will probably have a few nightmares over him. Perhaps his mini-stroke affected his behaviour and personality, in which case, who was the real Doug? God knows! I thought of his family waiting for him to return. Were they looking forward to it or dreading it? Maybe someone loves him. If it hadn't been for his stupidity and messing around with Ibrahim's driving that day, my life would have been entirely different, so, oddly, he did manage to do some good.

While I was on leave, Ali contacted me to confirm that the trial came under the Ministry of Justice's jurisdiction. All defendants were allowed legal representation. Under this system, all were presumed innocent and were allowed to present evidence and witnesses on their behalf. It would be a public trial in front of three judges. The trial should be over quickly as the evidence, including video, photo and audiotapes, were indisputable. Ali described the case as open and shut, as there was no defence and no mitigating circumstances. We had built up a good rapport and regularly kept in touch by phone. After Ali had established Amina's account of her circumstances was true, unknown to her, he was doing his best to help her. With Ali's help, her parents had procured the services of a respected lawyer for her defence. Her parents told Ali they had searched for years, placing adverts and posters throughout Damascus. In the end, they became reconciled that she was lost forever. Being the only child had made it worse for them. Finding their daughter was a dream come true, and no matter what had happened to her, they were still her loving parents. Ali was very impressed by them and told me he really liked them.

While home, I spent an enjoyable time with my children, who seemed to miss me as much as I missed them. When I hugged them, they hugged back just as hard; I felt their love, and I hoped they felt mine. Taking them out to parks and beaches was pleasurable but tiring; they had so much energy. I had forgotten what good fun they were to be with. They took me out rather than the other way around. I realised how much I missed them.

I contacted a few IT firms to establish which were the best equipped to install a comprehensive Planned Preventive Maintenance system to the scale required. I shortlisted two companies that seemed to fit our criteria and had done similar installations before. I contacted Bente with the information and also provided the companies with Bente's contact details. That was as far as I was prepared to go as I was still wary of Bente's real intentions. I spent the rest of the time visiting friends and generally whiling away my time. My return to Syria was always on my mind. I decided to give it another month and, if nothing changed, there was no alternative but to resign. What I had been doing there made no sense at all, but there was a glimmer of hope things might change.

Still, I had promised to appear at the Bedouin trial as a witness. My conscience and concern for Amina convinced me it was the correct thing to do.

I made a special effort to call in and see Derek and his wife, Liz and thanked him for the kick up the backside he had given me after my divorce. If he hadn't, I would have probably been halfway down the slippery slope into oblivion by then. They told me that they still saw Jane occasionally, with her new bloke; she seemed happy enough. I found it hard to believe how swiftly she had moved on. I didn't tell them the truth about how uncertain I was about my job in Syria; instead, I told them everything was great.

When I worked in Saudi Arabia, I most looked forward to coming home to be with my family, and my leave was never long enough. Returning to work was always a lonely and challenging experience, no matter how many mates I had out there. Friends weren't the same as having the family you love around you. What drove me to continue was the benefit of providing a better life in the future for them all. But returning from Syria was nothing like coming home from Saudi Arabia. On my own – locked up in a Travelodge most nights – was not pleasant but allowed me to focus on what I was missing. I realised that it was the company of Ali. Over such a short time, we had built up a friendship between us that I had taken for granted as it seemed so natural. Perhaps we both understood each other so quickly because we had spent time in each other's world and understood each other's cultures. But it seemed more than that; I liked Ali and enjoyed his company. We were different in so many ways, but that might be why we appreciated each other.

It gave me time to recall previous friendships with Arabs whilst working in Saudi Arabia. Three particular trainees were under my supervision all the time I had been there: Saud, Fahd and Mo. My three stooges, as I used to call them. They became very close to me, and we gained respect for each other. Saud, in particular, seemed to be more affectionate than the other two and was by far the brightest, and the leader of the stooges. When I returned from leave, the emotion they showed me was embarrassing; they had no hang-ups like me and openly said that they had missed me and embraced me. It may have been my upbringing, but I have never told another man that I missed him. A close family member or a girlfriend maybe, but not a male friend; something held me back, as it does now. I missed Ali, but I would never have told him to his face; I hoped my actions showed my feelings.

On my leave, I pondered a great deal over what I had learned from my trainees in Saudi Arabia over the years. Males and females didn't mix with each other. The men had to save a dowry to buy a wife, which could take years – on average, thirty. So they would spend most of their younger years in male company. Could that be why they showed each other open affection? They often held hands in public, which I found strange. It felt even stranger when they wanted to hold my hand as friends. They would rebuke me, hurt, when I pushed their hands away, saying, "You are my friend! Why did you do that?" I felt guilty but couldn't contemplate the idea.

Recalling an event in Saudi Arabia made me laugh aloud to myself one day. The head office had arranged an open day so that dignitaries, friends and relations could observe how much all the trainees had learnt in our area. In the workshop, I had set up various examples for my trainees to test their knowledge. I was sure of their ability, so I didn't rehearse anything, wanting it to look and sound natural. One of my tests was a pump shaft placed between centres with a dial indicator set up to check the bearing journals for trueness and micrometres for measurements. Saud was given the task of checking the shaft. He appeared confident as he went about his job, and I was proud that he was doing it correctly. A group gathered around Saud as he confidently went about his task. They looked impressed with how organised he was, writing down measurements and rechecking his results.

Saud's face lit up like a beacon, and he uttered, to the group surrounding him, "It's fucked."

Aghast, I said, "Saud, don't you mean it's beyond economical repair?"

Saud waved his index finger in the air, shook his head as though my suggestion was a trick, and repeated, "No, it's fucked."

I cringed as not only had he used the exact words I would have, but he said it using my Midlands accent. Saud is now probably passing on this knowledge to his own trainees, using the same expletive with my accent!

Chapter 11

Return to Work

I returned to Syria to work at Al Taim and remained convinced that what I was doing was a complete waste of time, pointless and soul-destroying. The first morning back, the communication meeting, led by Hans, was futile as usual.

Ali was there with his team, all with the same deadpan expressions, not saying a word or indicating they understood what was being said. I managed to get eye contact with him and a smile in return.

Later that morning, Hans came into my office. "Sorry about the misunderstanding," Hans said.

"What misunderstanding is that then?"

"You know, deciding that using the maintenance plan was the best option."

"Don't apologise to me as you were right."

"I think so too, but Bente doesn't, and his way is the only way."

"He blamed you for what I was doing; you do know that, don't you?"

"Yes, he doesn't listen; he is just a bully."

"Not only that, he is as thick as shit and dangerous, and he also gets away with it, shouting and blaming everyone else for his own failings."

Hans was looking browbeaten and said, "What can we do? He is the boss."

"Hans, as he told you about installing computers?"

"What computers? What for?"

"For fuck's sake, he hasn't told you anything?"

Hans despondently shook his head, indicating no.

"If someone doesn't bring him down, we will all be brought down sooner or later." I added, "I'm not happy doing this shit. I nearly didn't come back."

"Then why did you?"

"Well, I thought Bente had seen sense; not sure now. I have other reasons, Hans, but they're private."

"Okay. While you were away, your replacement didn't do much."

I realised that Bente hadn't discussed the new system with my replacement and wondered why. Disappointed, I said, "That doesn't surprise me. I won't be doing the same thing!"

"That's up to you, but be careful, don't rock the boat."

"I can't just spend hour upon hour doing nothing Hans. I was hoping that Bente had done the right thing; if he hasn't told anyone, I am not sure. He returns in two weeks, so I am carrying on doing the right thing."

"Okay, Allan, whatever, but keep Mike and me out of it."

Hans replied as he left, "I'll leave you to it then."

All that day, my mind was elsewhere, thinking of the trial. Later, before leaving the office, I spoke to Matt, who had also returned from leave; it was my first chance to talk to him. Matt agreed with me that we should carry on doing the same thing. Matt hadn't been sidetracked into fabricating the silly wall charts, so he was far ahead of me. I told Matt about my conversations with Bente and how pissed off I was. We both had ideas and were eager to set up a proper functioning system. He suggested that I pop into his office, maybe spend a day together brainstorming our ideas. I suggested maybe waiting until Bente was back, or it could be a complete waste of time. In his typical way, Matt replied, "Aye, maybe you're right, but your company would be nice."

I changed the subject to what had happened at the Bedouin camp and what we would say at the trial. His experience was similar to mine, except for his relationship with his Bedouin carer.

"I drunk my milk like a good boy," he said jokingly, "and jig-jig wasn't mentioned, and I was glad it wasn't."

"Well, there was no point, as they had all our money. I don't think they fancied us anyway."

"Aye, I know. The poor woman looking after Doug has just come to mind."

"I think they put a man with him. He was too much of a handful."

Matt didn't know of my relationship with Ali or the trial procedure. So I mentioned nothing about either.

"What will you say at the trial?" he asked in his perfect English.

"The truth, as it happened. That's all I can do."

The following morning, Ali phoned me and said, "The trial will be next week, and all six have been charged with kidnapping."

"What about me? Will I have to give evidence?"

"Yes, you will be called to give evidence, along with Matt and Ibrahim."

"All I can say is what happened to me. Have you found out any more about Amina?"

"Well, her parents have confirmed her identity using old photos and birth certificates, so she is who she says she is."

"That's great news; I bet she's delighted with the news."

"She doesn't know yet."

"Why not? Surely she needs to know?"

"Not according to the excellent lawyer I recommended to them to act on her behalf. He insists she shouldn't know they have been found, and he knows best."

"Surely, she must be distraught, knowing she will be punished the same as the others. Seeing her parents would help, don't you think?"

"I trust their lawyer; he knows best, and her parents also trust in him, so don't fret over it. The guilty will be punished, the trial will be fair, so why are you concerned about her? Ah! Or am I missing something? She hasn't taken your eye, has she?"

"I don't know why, but I feel responsible for her predicament. I know it doesn't make any sense, but I do, okay."

"Well, she is beautiful; I could see why she could turn your head."

"That's got nothing to do with it."

"If you say so," Ali said, indicating he didn't believe me with a beaming know-all smile.

"Ali, why don't you pop round to my room tonight for a drink? Sorry, it's only vodka."

"What? To your bare and inhospitable place? No, thank you! There are other reasons too. I can't be seen socialising with the enemy, and I am in your room every day anyway."

"You check my room every day? What for?"

"I check everyone's room; it's security, that's all."

"Hang on a minute! If I visit your room. What's the difference?"

"Well, yours is down a long corridor. Mine is accessed from an outside door. There's not much chance of anyone seeing you coming and going at mine. Even if you were caught, it would look completely different, as I could be ordering you there."

"Okay! Next time, I will bring a bottle."

"Only if it's a good single malt, which I know you haven't got. See you tonight."

After my evening with Ali, I called Matt to discuss being called as witnesses. He said he wasn't worried and would tell the truth, no more, no less and it was up to the courts. It seemed that I was alone with my concerns about giving evidence that would affect the lives of others and, in particular, Amina.

Chapter 12

The Trial

Ali collected Matt, Ibrahim and myself on the day we promised to give evidence in court; we didn't say much to each other on the journey. I suspected the other two were wary of Ali. When it was my turn to give evidence, a court officer guided me into a small dock opposite the accused. The courtroom was quiet and orderly.

I could see four women and two men in the dock. All except Amina were standing tall with defiant looks on their faces. Amina's head was bowed, which I interpreted as demonstrating her shame. When her defence counsel asked me to relate what had happened, an interpreter translated everything, word by word, into Arabic. I explained what had happened and how we were treated by our captors in as much detail as possible. When I began giving evidence, I could see Amina's head droop even further. As the questioning continued, she eventually raised her head and looked at me. Her eyes were full of tears as she realised the evidence I was giving was in her favour. A cry came from the small side gallery. Amina's eyes darted to where it came from. Amina let out a moan when she spotted her mother and father; she stretched out her arms as though attempting to touch them. They, too, were stretching out their arms in her direction, shouting, "Amina, Amina, eb-na-tee."

"Baba, Mama," Amina cried back, tears running down her face. Everyone in the court was watching the interaction between them, including the judges.

It occurred to me that this was precisely what the lawyer had anticipated and that it could help the court's ruling. The lawyer had strengthened his defence argument; he would later explain that Amina, too, was a victim. Whatever her crime, it was done under duress, and her circumstances were similar to ours; she, too, was a prisoner. The spectators in court watching the proceedings started talking between themselves. The previously quiet courtroom became noisy and unruly as the crowd began to shout angrily, 'harij ealayk' ('shame on you') at the prisoners in the dock. What I had just witnessed was so spontaneous and natural. In no way could it be perceived as a stunt. I looked across at her lawyer, who returned the knowing smile of a confident victor. He shrugged his shoulders upwards. His plan had been an easy success and he had never been in doubt of it. I felt like putting my thumb up in congratulations but restrained myself to a smile.

The lead judge hammered his gavel and demanded silence in court. The court fell silent; simultaneously, all the shouting stopped, and there was quiet again. The three judges nodded to each other. The defence counsel for Amina continued questioning me to verify that she had helped me. The defence counsel for the Bedouins declined to ask me any questions. I suppose they expected that my evidence would only incriminate them. The prosecuting counsel then cross-examined me, inferring my testament was false. He insinuated that I had formed a relationship of an intimate nature with the defendant, which I denied firmly.

Amina was now standing tall, looking at her parents, shaking her head from side to side at every wrong suggestion, and nodding her head when she agreed with me. Her parents were nodding their heads back to her, showing that they believed what I was saying to be true. Everyone in court, including the judges, watched Amina and her parents' reactions to the questions. They were not watching the prosecutor or me. It reminded me of a crowd at a tennis match, where, in unison, eyes follow the tennis ball backwards and forwards. The court was only watching Amina and her parents. Their heads moved as one. I swore that our relationship was not sexual, that she had disobeyed instructions to give me a sleep-inducing potion. I answered that I hadn't known she had been kidnapped as a child by the Bedouins but could tell she was different from the other women. At the end of my evidence, I hoped it was 'game, set and match.'

After completing my evidence and being dismissed by the court, I met with Ali. He told me Amina's defence counsel had cross-examined him and asked if the drone footage was evidence of an intimate relationship. He replied that it was just the opposite, confirming that Amina left my tent at dusk, and I spent the night alone, except for the guard, of course. Also, during the time we spent together, the tent was always kept open. There was no footage of us having any physical contact. Together with Matt and Ibrahim, I was allowed to return to work after giving evidence. Matt and Ibrahim returned to Al Omar, and I returned to Al Taim to continue with the so-called maintenance plan.

The trial continued for a couple of days. Ali told me during our evening get-togethers what happened in court. He teased that the drone footage of me doing my ablutions drew oohs and aahs in court. Before admitting that showing those parts was not deemed necessary or suitable for public viewing. The courts provided the Bedouin's defence lawyer, who had little interest in proving their innocence. All the undeniable evidence was stacked against them, and there were no extenuating circumstances. They had little chance of being acquitted.

"If Amina was found guilty, what would be her punishment be?" I asked Ali.

"Life imprisonment," he responded confidently without pause. "But I think it won't come to that. The prosecution evidence is weak, and the defence proof is strong."

"What worries me, Ali, is the reliability of the judges. They make the final decision, don't they?"

"I wouldn't worry too much about them, as there are three judges. Now, if it was down to just one judge, that would be another thing! Don't worry, Allan."

"But, Ali, I have seen examples on TV in the UK where courts in the Middle East keep innocent people locked up for years on jumped-up charges."

"Allan, you forget one thing. She is Syrian, not foreign, and her parents are respected, wealthy people. Now, can we put this to bed, please?"

After the verdict, Ali phoned to tell me that Amina had been cleared of all charges. The Bedouins received sentences of life imprisonment. Amina would be required to provide further information about her kidnapping, which is a severe offence and carries the death penalty. She refused to do this because she couldn't be responsible for another person's death regardless of what they had done to her. Most of all, she wanted the whole experience to be over, be back home with her family, and forget about the wasted years of her life. She wanted to return to normality. She had quoted a proverb to Ali, but he claimed it didn't translate well.

I met Ali in his room later and asked him about the proverb.

"Well, it goes something like this. 'He who sees the calamity in other people finds his own calamity light.' You see? It doesn't translate, does it?"

"I think Amina's trying to say, 'don't judge people until you have walked in their shoes.' Is it something like that?"

"Yes, Allan, similar. I'll give you that one."

I was trying to imagine how fantastic it must be for Amina to be home with her parents. It would be different being loved and cherished rather than being a possession to be traded. I was reluctant to meet her again because it might bring back bad memories, but I so much wanted to. Eventually, I caved in and asked Ali if it would be possible to arrange a meeting with her one last time, just to thank her for helping me. Ali said he would ask her parents. He thought they had a similar outlook to his own, as modern Muslims, so they would likely agree. After he had spoken to them, they also said they would like to thank me for what I had said in the courtroom. My monthly vacation was due, so it made sense to meet them in Damascus when taking my leave, so Ali arranged the date and time on my behalf.

Chapter 13

Meeting the Family

I was halfway through my working month, and Bente was back in charge. I asked him if he had followed up on the information I had given him and why didn't anyone else know. I wasn't confident the response that everything was in hand was accurate and I shouldn't worry. So I approached him concerning the possibility of a transfer to Conch Oil. He could see no objection, but it would mean a trip to the head office in Damascus at the end of my stint. This would enable me to spend a few extra days in Syria, which was convenient, as Ali had arranged a meeting with Yoran, Amina's father, and her family.

The interview went well at Conch Oil, and I signed a contract for a year. As everything had gone so smoothly, I unexpectedly had extra free time in Damascus. So Ali contacted Amina's parents, who were happy to meet me earlier than arranged. I was to meet them at their home.

Their detached house had a front garden set amongst similar dwellings far away from the busy road. My taxi dropped me outside. I apprehensively walked down the path to the front door, noticing the pretty front garden and a pergola covered with a mature grapevine shading a car from the sun. I took a deep breath and rang the doorbell. Yoran opened the door, smiled and greeted me with a traditional welcome – Alaykum Salaam – and a handshake. I replied, "Salaam Alaykum." Yoran led me into a large, rather bare lounge. Located slightly off centre to the room were two large wing-backed chairs with a round coffee table in between. Bookshelves covered almost all of the wall space. He asked me to sit.

"Isn't it traditional to have tea and cake in the afternoon in England?" he said in perfect English.

From where I sat, I could see a mixture of Arabic and mainly classic English novels. Daylight came through a large window overlooking the garden, illuminating a low, cushioned seating area in the room's far corner. "Yes," I replied, being polite, although it wasn't a custom I practised personally.

My reply seemed to please Yoran, who disappeared through a door in the far corner of the room. He returned with an English flowered teapot, delicate china cups and a sponge cake on a cake stand. *Very posh*, I thought. Yoran made a point of using the word 'tea', not 'chai'. I realised he was trying to impress me. He enquired about what I was doing in Syria, where I lived in the UK, my marital status, and about my family. He then changed the subject entirely and enquired about the Wimbledon tennis tournament.

"Do you follow the tennis at Wimbledon?"

"When I get the chance, but it's mainly played during working hours."

I thought at the time that he may have changed the subject because he felt that he was prying too much. So I returned his nicety by asking him about his work at the hospital. He was a doctor and worked at a hospital in

Damascus. The conversation eventually turned to how much Amina had been missed and how much time there was to make up, especially as far as schooling was concerned.

"Do you know the first thing she did after she settled down?"

"Being a young woman, I would have thought shopping for clothes?"

"Well, yes, there was a bit of that, but the thing that impressed me most was she collected books from here," he said, pointing to his shelving. "She carried them to her room. After reading them, she made comments in a notebook, documenting each one and writing about their content."

"Yoran, you have so many books. Have you read them all?" I asked out of politeness and curiosity.

"Most of them; some, though, are well-meant gifts I haven't read and probably never will."

"Have you a preference to what you read, or do you read anything?"

"Ah, that's a good question, Allan. I would say, mainly non-fiction. I have a thirst for knowledge, science and people, so I also enjoy biographies. I always have, but I also read the classics, though, and books by good authors like Dickens, Hemmingway, Shakespeare, and many others."

"How do you get the time?" I asked politely.

"Well, I make the time, and it's my way of relaxing. You will notice there is no television in the house, as I don't like the propaganda or hidden messages or the other rubbish they broadcast."

"How do you keep in touch with what's happening in the outside world then?"

"Ah, I have a radio and listen to the BBC's overseas broadcast mainly as that's probably the least political."

I turned the conversation back to Amina. "She showed me compassion; maybe that was because she was in a similar position to me."

"Maybe, but never underestimate her, she was strong-willed as a child, with a mind of her own, and little has changed," Yoran replied proudly.

"Is that why she tried to help me then? She was doing what she thought was right by me, don't you think?"

"Ah, I don't think she would have reasoned it like that. She was doing what she thought was right for her own conscience. For you, it was the right thing, but for her, it could have led to problems."

"I think I understand now; she would have done the same for anyone, and I shouldn't take it personally. Is that what you are conveying?"

"Yes, Allan, exactly that. She has the strength of character and resolves to find her way in the world, I am sure of that."

"You are very proud of your daughter, aren't you?"

"Yes, immensely proud and why not?"

I looked around the room while absorbing all that had been said between us.

"I will bring in another two cups, if that would be all right with you?"

"Yes, of course," I said.

He quickly returned with extra china and smiled at me. Following behind were Souzan, his wife, and Amina. The two women gracefully floated into the room. I thought they were the two most beautiful women I had ever seen. Yoran was observing my reaction as they came into view.

Yoran and Souzan exchanged glances, smiling. Amina's demeanour exuded confidence; gone were the many layers of clothing she had worn before. She wore a simple blue dress, which reached the floor and nothing on her feet. Her hair was loosely tied at the back. Her face and eyes bore no trace of make-up. She was stunningly naturally beautiful. I gazed at Souzan and could see where Amina's beauty came from; Amina was a younger version of her mother. The only difference was the slight greying of Souzan's hair.

Souzan and Amina sat gracefully and effortlessly. Although in conversation with Yoran, I was only half-listening. My eyes kept crossing the room to where the women sat. If Amina looked in my direction, I didn't see it. Every time I glanced across to her, she was looking at her mother.

"Would you like to join us at an informal garden party tomorrow afternoon?" Yoran asked. "I have also invited a few friends."

I accepted the invitation, unsure what to expect as we had little in common.

"Masa lama," I said as I was leaving the house. "Bukra." I smiled at Amina and Souzan and waved goodbye. Amina looked at me for the first time that day, and as our eyes met, something happened to me. I hoped that Amina felt the same way, but I couldn't know. Yoran kissed me on both cheeks and shook my hand as I left, accepting me as a friend.

The following day, I arrived at the house and was welcomed with the usual polite greetings. I was shown through the house into a large, walled garden. It seemed more like an orchard than a garden, with many mature fruit trees: I recognised figs, oranges, lemons and date palm. Compared to the dull grey, hot and dusty, uninviting street outside, it was like walking into a clearing in a rainforest. The vegetation appeared to be either lush green or brightly coloured. The noise of the traffic outside was replaced by a crescendo of sound from insects, frogs and birds singing, chirping, screeching and whistling simultaneously. After a short time, my hearing became accustomed to the sounds. It only became noticeable again when they stopped all at once for no apparent reason. For no reason I could understand, the crescendo restarted as if a superior being was conducting them in unison. The garden had been cleverly designed, appearing untouched by man but thoughtfully manicured by nature alone. There was a shaded area in the garden, created by magnificent flame and frangipani trees. Underneath was a large, low cushioned seating area.

Yoran asked me to make myself comfortable there, but I dreaded negotiating it. I waited until his back turned and tried to sit gracefully but failed. As I completed the tricky manoeuvre, I heard female voices. I turned to where the sound came from. Souzan and Amina were approaching with trays of iced drinks and Arabian pastries; basbousa, kunafeh, qatayef, and, of course, baklava, all exceptionally sweet and laced with honey. I struggled to stand without using my arms in one movement, but again I failed. They were both smiling openly, acknowledging my attempt at being graceful. As I greeted them, I was told to sit, and they both purposely looked away to save my embarrassment. Souzan and Amina placed the refreshments on a low table, indicating I should help myself, and then returned to where they came from. As soon as I was seated, I could hear voices coming from the door that led into the garden. I quickly got to my feet before anyone else could observe my struggle. To my amazement, Ali arrived with a woman, and Yoran was greeting them. I approached and greeted Ali with a firm handshake and a kiss on either cheek.

"Sorry for the surprise," Ali said.

"I didn't know you would be here," I replied.

"It was arranged previously," Ali said with a grin, flashing his white teeth.

"Aren't you going to introduce me?" I asked.

"Ah, this is my wife, Margaret."

"Well!" I responded, somewhat surprised. "Pleased to meet you."

"Likewise," she replied.

"Ali, you didn't tell me you were married." I turned to Margaret. "I have heard nothing about you, best-kept secrets and all that."

She held out her hand for me to kiss and then looked at me with a demure smile. She spoke with a slight London accent. "Well, hello. I, on the other hand, have heard much about you."

Later I learnt that she had been teasing me.

"Ali has told me nothing about you at all," I repeated.

She smiled. "Ali is a very private man, so he keeps the best things to himself."

She had a coy look on her face that I would come to know as the expression she used during a wind-up. I was only in Margaret's company for a few minutes before I realised that she was fun to be with, attractive, elegant, humorous and intelligent.

"Please be seated and make yourselves comfortable," Yoran invited. He guided us into the shaded seating area.

My previous attempts hadn't perfected the art of sitting and standing gracefully. I took my seat with some difficulty, but nobody said anything. Everyone was smiling. I was very interested in getting to know Margaret and I asked her many questions.

"This is a surprise to me. I wasn't expecting Ali to be here, but you are a real shock."

"I know; men always say I am shocking," she retaliated with a kittenish smile.

Margaret and Ali recounted to the party how they had met at university and were drawn to each other.

"Ali was shy, to begin with. It was me who had to approach him."

"I wasn't shy at all; bloody frightened, more like," he said quickly, looking embarrassed. He flashed a smile at Margaret.

"I suppose he had never met a proper woman before," she rallied.

"True; I have never met anyone quite like her before, Inshallah."

I wasn't sure how the other guests interpreted the banter, but it showed they were good fun to be with. I glanced across to Amina, who looked puzzled. I wasn't sure if this was because she didn't understand their witty rapport, the language, or Margaret.

We sat there talking, drinking and eating; the pastries, I learnt, were made from the products of their garden. My Arabic was poor, so the conversation was primarily English, with the odd Arabic phrase. Yoran's English was probably better than mine; obviously, he had been well educated. Souzan struggled but could understand most or gave the impression that she did. What surprised me most was how much Amina seemed to understand; she must have received a good education before her capture. I wondered why she gave me the impression that she didn't speak English in the Bedouin tent. The time in their garden that afternoon flew by, and we were saying our goodbyes in no time at all.

"Margaret, could you take Amina shopping in Damascus?" Yoran asked before we all parted.

"No, Baba; I am afraid," Amina said, shaking her head.

"I will come as well; if it would that make you feel safe?" Ali butted in.

"I would like to come as well," I hastily and enthusiastically added, not wanting to miss a chance of seeing Amina again.

We all looked at her, waiting for a response. "Thank you," she said finally and smiled, but then her smile dropped. "But we have to keep close," she said shyly, "Is that okay?"

"You will have the full expertise of the Syrian army, escorting you, together with my wife and friend," Ali joked.

It was the first time Ali had described me to others as a friend. I wondered whether he meant it or it was just a part of his joke.

I could understand why Amina was so frightened of going out without her parents for the first time after her ordeal. It would test the family as she had never been out of their sight since her return. I presumed that Yoran, being a doctor, understood that the sooner she tackled her lack of confidence, the better for everyone.

Chapter 14

Amina is Gaining Confidence

It was arranged that we would collect Amina from her parent's house. I remember that day so well. We could all see how timid Amina was, venturing out into a big city where there would be crowds of people. Ali drove, and I sat beside him as we entered the city centre. I could hear the girls talking in the back, mainly in English, with a few Arabic phrases. Margaret was trying to help Amina decide what she wanted to see. High on her list were buying a mobile phone, learning how to use it and buying some books. As we walked around the souq, Amina and Margaret linked arms. They walked in front of us, unusual in a country where it is custom for women to walk behind the men, but such customs would never worry Margaret. Step by step, Amina was getting more confident. She was continually stopping, looking and pointing through shop windows. I could almost see her brain computing all she could see, looking in the window, then at the shop's name and registering it for the future. After a while, Ali suggested we take a break for refreshments in a small coffee house. We sat around a table, and for my benefit, they spoke English as much as possible. What Amina couldn't understand was quickly translated into Arabic.

"Are you still scared?" Ali asked Amina.

"Yes, a little," she replied.

"Why don't you and Margaret do a little shopping on your own?" Ali suggested to Amina. "We will observe you from the coffee house."

"Come on," Margaret encouraged. "You will be safe with me." Margaret stood up, offering Amina her arm.

Amina looked apprehensive but nodded in agreement. "Okay, but you will watch us, Ali, please?" Amina asked.

As they left, I watched them walk away, arms linked together as friends. I realised that Amina had missed so much of growing up and thought, though scared, she would also be excited, if not overwhelmed.

I said to Ali, "They seem to have developed a friendship and understanding so quickly."

Ali replied, "That's Margaret, she hammered me into shape, and I didn't feel a thing."

Their leaving gave Ali and me time to talk about other things.

"I am on the Conch Oil payroll now, Ali, thanks to you."

"I know, that's good; we can spend more time together."

"I was an only child, perhaps the reason I don't make friends easy; what about you, Ali?"

"I came from a large family, and that's why I don't make friends easily, but that's for another time."

"I've seldom found someone to be a real friend with," I said, a little embarrassed.

"Me too," Ali replied, "it's not easy for me either, as most of the soldiers I mix with are quite religious."

"You have no worries about me on that score. I don't believe in any god; there are so many, I find it hard to choose one."

"Me too. Perhaps it's because I enjoyed my time in England, and I loved the freedom and the lifestyle there."

"Yes. It's very different here, and to me, it's still a novelty, it's not permanent, and I haven't started to miss Blighty yet."

"I wish that Syria would modernise, rid itself of religious constraints and bring itself into the modern world."

"Don't you think it suits the government to keep the status quo, one rule for them and one for the rest of us?"

"Sadly, I think you are right. Unfortunately, they have all the wealth and power."

"Every country is the same. The rich get richer, and the poor get poorer, but in Syria, the poor can't get any poorer, can they?"

"No, they can't. It's getting worse, and we're not a poor country anymore. We are oil producers. There's enough money for everyone."

"Are you concerned there is going to be civil unrest?"

"Yes, and not just me, the government is concerned as well. That's one of the reasons we are at the refineries."

"When you told me before about 'various factions' harming the refineries, I didn't realise you meant your own people."

"It's hard to come to terms with," Ali said, nodding.

"Did the trial blow your cover? How will it affect you?"

"Not really. Conch Oil and the government have decided that the protection should remain the same for now. The original instructions were not to get too friendly with foreign workers. Everyone was still under suspicion, regardless of their country of origin, so nothing has changed."

"But all the workers now know who you are. Surely your cover is blown?"

"Look, it's not as simple as that. Government intelligence is aware that various fundamentalist factions are networking and growing in strength within Syria."

"For what purpose, Ali? What do they want to achieve?"

"Their aim is to oust the present government and replace it with a caliphate."

"Ali, the government is not just one man, though – a dictator. It's a complicated machine that looks after all the people, not just a few."

"Yes, I know that, but the religious fundamentalists seem to want to go back in time, remove the dictator and replace him with another of their own making."

"Ali, you know what I always think is weird about these people? They use modern weapons and technology to their own ends. At the same time, they don't believe in education or modernisation."

"I agree with you, Allan; a bow and arrow won't stop a tank."

"Or a prayer, Ali, regardless of religion," I added.

We discussed what he had seen regarding some of the European staff's behaviour at the refineries, what he witnessed himself and what I had told him. He said, "The world over, it's the same without checks and balances; people will move the boundaries if they are not pegged down."

I had shared with Ali how most of the workers were skiving and that I was expected to fabricate false charts, and we had both agreed that it was wrong. But he also believed that those corrupt or not fulfilling their roles should be booted out.

"What about me, Ali? I'm not doing the job I was hired to do, either."

"Conch Oil have something in mind for you," Ali said.

"How would you know that, Ali?"

"It will come clear in good time; Conch Oil realise that things have to change."

"What would that be then? If you know something, don't you think I should be the first to know?"

"Sorry, Allan, all in good time. I have said too much already, so please don't mention what I have just said to anyone."

"Ali, you obviously know what's going on; do the powers above know about our friendship? How does that affect you? Wouldn't they see it as a conflict of interest?"

"All will come to light very soon, don't worry."

"But should other members of staff be worried?"

"No, they shouldn't be. That is, unless you tell them, which you won't, will you?"

"Of course not; everything is between the two of us."

"Here they come. Time to change to another subject, I think," Ali said.

Ali had been keeping his eyes on the shoppers, who were now returning, excited and laden with bags. Our conversation switched to the purchases the girls had made and they told us how wise they had been with their bartering. Apparently, everything they had bought was a bargain and justified on price alone.

"We almost missed this one," Amina chanted.

"He let us have it so cheap," Margaret countered.

"It was the very last one," Amina said, smiling.

Ali and I caught each other's eyes, sharing our amusement. I thought we were both thinking the same thing, that perhaps the seller had hundreds of 'last ones' stored away. We watched the girls convince themselves how clever they had been to snap up their bargains and beat the sellers into submission with their superior female intelligence.

Margaret and Amina appeared to instantly form a friendship that grew over the coming years; for Amina, it must have been like having an older and wiser sister. For Margaret, Amina was a companion and friend and someone she could help. Margaret loved being able to pass her knowledge on.

On the way back from taking Amina home, Ali suggested that I stay with them at their home in Damascus for a while before returning home to the UK. Ali had something on his mind.

"Stay as long as you like; it's up to you," he said.

"You are welcome; it would be helpful to have another man about the house. I might get some jobs done."

My visa was valid. I could change my departure flight, so nothing stopped me from staying on for a little while.

"That's sorted then," Ali said. "I have some leave owing to me; let me know how long you want to stay."

"It would be nice for me too, as I have time off most days and have evening lectures, so you could be companions for both of us," Margaret said and nodded. It would be a good idea.

"I wasn't looking forward to another month in a Travelodge on my own again; are you sure?"

"Of course, we are," they replied in unison.

"Silly boy," Margaret added.

"Well, thank you very much. Would a couple of weeks be too much?"

"We said as long as you like," they both said at the same time.

I was curious about what was on his mind but left it there.

Chapter 15

Discussions with Ali

We discussed many things to pass the time away during my stay with Ali. Still, he pressed me on the refinery issues, mainly some evenings when it was just Ali and me, over a glass of whisky. Ali understood the basic idea of why planned maintenance was essential. I explained that it was easy to clear up unimportant maintenance, like repairing a dripping tap, as it required little effort and was visible. Other tasks that are not visible but critical have to be recorded to establish compliance. Some tasks were covered by legislation and mandatory. Some were an exceptionally high priority because negligence could cause harm to persons, plants or production. The most crucial aspect was to keep records of actual work done and the condition of the plant. My preferred way of handling the maintenance is to have two separate dedicated teams. One team concentrated entirely on Planned Preventative Maintenance. The second team on purely Breakdown Maintenance. The supervisory teams were dedicated to one or the other. The workers could be moved as required at the discretion of the supervisors to suit the circumstances and whether planned or breakdowns were the priority. It was all about motivating the workforce to take ownership of the plant. That's why I thought trained Syrian nationals were the best bet, as it was in their interest.

We also discussed how unsuitable candidates, like Doug, were employed. My impression was that the contract company was interested in their commission rather than the worker's suitability. I explained to Ali that Matt and I had gone through a technical interview followed by a thorough medical, whereas I didn't think that was the case with John or Doug. Perhaps the contract company thought they could slip in the occasional unqualified worker, or 'chancer', as Matt would describe John and Doug, and get away with it.

Ali was aware that maintenance must start from day one, but the plants at Al Farat had no planned maintenance at all, just repairing breakdowns. As the plants were still newish, maintenance was not seen as an issue, but soon would be. Paying ridiculous amounts of money to employees who do nothing was not the way forward.

I went into detail regarding my instructions from Bente regarding the false charts. The charts provided no actual evidence of work done. They would be scrutinised if anything serious happened, like a major incident. Even then, it would require the expertise of those investigating to realise that there had been a cover-up. I explained the standard practice of having two separate budgets for new projects and equipment. Repairs were always more affordable if a well-planned maintenance system was in place. Whilst discussing the issue, I realised the revenue budget must be significant.

If it wasn't fully used, it would be reduced the following year. Most managers work hard to maintain their funding levels. How was the budget spent, and what little work was done? I concluded that someone there must be responsible for creative accounting or, in other words, corruption. I suggested to Ali that a proper audit be completed to establish where the money was going. We spent many evenings going through the plant's requirements regarding good supervision, training and procedures.

Ali had once mentioned to me that he went into my room every day, which had bothered me at the time, but I hadn't felt close enough to him to ask about it. Concerned. However, I had placed a hair discretely across the door jamb, and it had always been intact on my return. This was proof that no one but myself entered my room, and what he had told me was incorrect. Now, I had the confidence to ask Ali what he had meant. So I looked directly at him and asked him outright, "How do you get into my room every day because it's not through my door, is it?"

Ali looked at me directly with a confident smile. "Not only am I in your room every day, but I am also in your office. I see and hear everything that goes on, everywhere."

It then dawned on me that surveillance cameras were placed strategically on site. I felt angry and raised my voice. "Ali, I thought we were friends, but you were fucking spying on me all the time, weren't you?"

Ali smiled and shrugged apologetically. "The only reason you are in my home, Allan, is because I spied on you."

"Shit, Ali, fucking shit, I don't know what to think."

"You should think that you have my trust, unlike the rest of the staff who don't. I am your friend. How the hell did you think it was so easy for you to be transferred to Conch Oil? Think about it."

"Shit, shit, Ali! You watched everything I was doing? You probably know how many sheets of toilet paper I use to wipe my backside."

"Not quite; you do have some privacy, Allan. And the reason I asked you to stay here with me instead of going home on leave was out of respect and also to learn from you."

"But, Ali, you were asking me questions you already knew the answers to; that's bloody sneaky, isn't it?"

"Not really. I was double-checking and confirming your honesty, that's all. I repeat again, Allan, you are under my roof as a friend, and I don't make friends easily."

"I just wish I had known, that's all."

"Allan, how would that have worked? If you knew what was going on, you might have changed your behaviour and not been open, and we would not be friends, would we?"

"Okay, Ali, you win, as always. I don't like it, but the outcome is that we are still friends, I think."

"Maybe you overthink. Have another scotch."

Ali poured a couple of whiskies, we clinked glasses, and Ali toasted, "To my friend!"

"Without doubt, I think," I replied, and we laughed.

Ali smirked. "By the way, it was three sheets of toilet paper on average." He looked at me for my reaction before adding, "Only joking."

"How do you do the surveillance? Where are the bloody cameras? So I can flick you the 'V' sign every now and again, you sneaky bugger."

"You would have found them had the fire alarm maintenance been carried out every now and again."

"Right, Ali, I am really going to fuck you up, and it's going to be on my next planned maintenance schedule now."

Ali was now laughing openly at my frustration. "Well, that's one way of getting things done," he bantered.

"Can you install the surveillance cameras in the emergency lighting system next? They need a good going over."

"I am always one step ahead of you; perhaps I could advise you on your useless planning boards. Bente would be pleased." Ali then poured another large whisky each and toasted, "To my trusted friend."

We clinked glasses.

"So you relied on poor maintenance to do your sneaky work, then?"

"Well, it was obvious from the beginning that tossers were running the place."

"Really, Ali, you knew everything all the time?"

"Yes, well, almost everything."

"You must have thought I was nuts, day in and day out producing rubbish."

"Allan, you have to remember that I have been in the army a long time. Some of the stupid things I have been told to do would amaze you, but orders are orders, crazy or not; you just have to carry them out. It's called discipline."

Chapter 16

Socialising

Margaret was spending a lot of time with Amina during the day. Their friendship was easy to see, as they were like sisters, and both were wise in different ways. Amina was getting more confident as time went by. Margaret was probably the perfect match to encourage Amina in the way things could be. To be confident, speak her mind, and walk beside people, not a few paces behind.

"You're as good as the next person," Margaret would tell her.

Margaret also had a wicked sense of humour which puzzled Amina initially. As time went by, Amina was learning to become just as witty and assertive as Margaret.

Margaret became a good friend to me. Sometimes, we spent time in each other's company when Ali was busy at work. Margaret had studied history at Oxford University, so it was natural for her to be interested in the history of Aleppo. "The more you see, the more you are overwhelmed by the city's beauty," she would often say. She would often relate interesting historical facts about Syria and, in particular, Aleppo.

Sitting on lazy afternoons on their balcony, which overlooked a small shared courtyard, we discussed Syria's history. Amina was also often the topic of conversations, including her past and how it might have affected her. Margaret explained that Amina thought she would always be considered soiled and was unlikely to marry. It was hard to shake these thoughts off. As part of the traditional Arabic betrothal of marriage, the bride must be completely pure. Amina felt that having been held hostage would cast doubts on this purity.

Margaret went to some lengths to explain Syrian customs related to marriage. In Syria, the groom pays the bride's father a dowry. The value of the dowry is based on the value of the bride, which is assessed by the female relatives of the groom, similar to how a horse breeder assesses the quality of an animal before purchase. The families usually arrange betrothals with prospective partners at quite a young age. The female child matures into a young woman. If especially beautiful, someone more prosperous (and usually older) may offer more than the original betrothed 'groom', and a new arrangement is made. The female has no say in the matter, even if she wants to marry her original betrothed partner.

Margaret told me this would not be the case with Amina. Her parents were modern Muslims. Her parents would have guided her to find someone suitable, but the decision would always have been hers. Margaret explained that Syrian women don't flirt or meet the opposite sex outside of the family. Margaret had discussed the topic of marriage with Amina, and Amina had already addressed the issue with her parents. Yoran and Souzan agreed with Amina that her happiness came first. As she had been away for such a long time, it would be difficult to find an appropriate suitor. We talked about Syrian customs, marriage and Amina for a while. As the conversation progressed, I became more intrigued about Amina and said, "She will find someone; she is a real gem."

"Amina asked me about your feelings towards her. I told her, wasn't it obvious?" Margaret was looking serious.

"Is this one of your wind-ups?"

"Really, darling, do you think I could be that thoughtless?"

I still couldn't be sure of her expression. Unsure of whether it was a wind-up, I changed the conversation slightly to avoid being drawn into her mischief. "Amina, though so small and graceful, is a little clumsy; she often accidentally bumps into me."

"You are a silly boy; sorry, the wrong word, stupid is more like it!" Margaret's face was definitely mischievous now.

"Me, stupid, why?"

"Don't you realise it's her only way of making physical contact with you? Next time, when in her company, look at her eyes and see what happens next!"

"I tried that once, at the Bedouin camp, and she turned away."

"I wonder why?" Margaret said. Her incredulous expression now made me feel stupid.

"Margaret, there's another thing that puzzles me."

"Only one, you surprise me," Margaret butted in.

"I am trying to be serious. In the Bedouin tent, I talked to her, and she behaved like she didn't understand me."

"Well, why do you think that might be?"

"I wouldn't be asking if I knew."

"Allan, to put you out of your misery, I will tell you why. You should be capable of working it out for yourself, though."

"Margaret, I am not psychic like you."

"Well, you must have noticed the guard outside the tent, yes?"

"Yes, of course."

"Do you think he understood English?"

"Probably not."

"Well, what do you think he would have done if he had heard you two talking in English?"

"I don't know."

"Well, he could have thought she was trying to help you, yes?"

"I never thought of that."

"So, Allan, she was trying to protect herself and you from punishment."

"Of course. That also explains why she only whispered her name when I asked. Bloody hell!"

"She feels guilty for that deception."

"That puts a different light on it. I am stupid."

"Well, you have got something right, at last," Margaret replied, laughing. She then added, "The big question is how do you feel about her?"

"She is out of my league, in my wildest dreams."

"Allan, you don't listen; I have already told you how she feels about you."

"You are playing with me; you are not serious, are you?"

Margaret then touched my hand and said, "Look at me. I am being serious. What is it about you men? Why can't they tell what is obvious."

"Dare to dream comes to mind, Margaret; I have had my confidence shattered recently by a woman, and I'm scared to let my defences drop."

Margaret smiled and said, "As they say, a faint heart never won a fair lady."

"Okay, don't laugh; I haven't been able to get her out of my mind. You've just made it a lot harder; happy now?"

"Very much so. I think a glass of plonk is on the cards to celebrate your awakening; there's a bottle of white in the fridge if you don't mind."

After lunch, the following afternoon, we were sitting on their balcony when Margaret asked me a favour. "You couldn't do me a favour, could you?"

"No problem, whatever you want," I replied.

"Could you meet Amina in the Al-Hamidyah Souq this afternoon? Something's just come up."

"No problem, but can you contact her to check if she would be okay with that?"

"Not really; she's probably on her way, and I wouldn't like to disappoint her."

"But she will be disappointed when I turn up, won't she?"

"I don't think so; she might be pleasantly surprised," Margaret said with a warm smile.

So I met Amina in the coffee house within the souq as instructed. I was met by a very puzzled face that turned into a lovely smile when I explained why I was there. The Al-Hamidyah Souq is tiny and bustling, and it would have been relatively easy for us to become separated. So I offered Amina my arm, which she took reluctantly and with embarrassment at first, although she soon seemed more comfortable.

We walked around the market stalls; all sorts of merchandise were on display. Produce was separated into categories, whether spice or silk. We didn't have to go very far to compare quality and prices. Bartering was part of the enjoyment of shopping in souqs.

Amina certainly enjoyed this part, and I was amazed at how much time she spent over haggling for so little profit; it could take fifteen minutes to gain so little. Each transaction was a victory, and after each win, she took my arm as we walked away. It seemed a natural thing to do. We rested in a small café where she opened her shopping bags to examine her prizes. I remembered what Margaret had suggested, and I looked directly into her eyes; she looked back into mine. It was like she was talking with her eyes. My feelings were so intense, and I knew then that something extraordinary had happened between us.

"When do you return to Al Farat?" Amina asked, looking away.

"In about a week," I replied. "Could we meet again?"

She looked surprised. "I hope so. You could come to my house."

"Would that be all right with your parents? Have you asked them?" I said, surprised.

"It was their idea; they are having a garden party with friends and relatives to celebrate my safe return. Could you come?"

"Yes, I would love to," I replied without thinking and was surprised by the invitation. I felt a little excited and hoped it showed.

I wasn't sure what the protocol was for saying goodbye to a single woman in Syria. Was it shaking hands or kissing cheeks? I waited for Amina to make the first move. She looked at me, touched her head and put her hand on her heart, so I thought it best to imitate her actions. She hailed a taxi and was gone. I was left pondering what had just happened.

Chapter 17

The Garden Party

We all met at Yoran and Souzan's house for the garden party as arranged. Several neighbours and friends of the family were there, and Ali and Margaret, of course. We were all seated on the majlis positioned under the shade of the trees. Yoran barbequed pieces of meat placed on a large tray on top of a mountain of rice flavoured with various herbs and spices. We were eating the traditional way, with no utensils, just plates. The skill was to roll the meat and rice in tiny torpedoes using the right hand only and pop them into your mouth. Trays of pastries were brought out by Amina and her mother and placed in front of us. The pastries were filled with the fruits from their garden and were delicious. Yoran served Belgian beer and homemade red wine. Fully sated, we relaxed and chatted. For my sake, it was mainly in English. I tried to join in with the odd Arabic word or phrase without embarrassing myself too much.

As the evening went on and the visitors started to dwindle, a small group remained: Yoran, Souzan, Amina, Ali, Margaret and myself. Yoran asked me to join him inside the house; we sat in the same room where we had first met.

"Sit down, please; we need to talk," Yoran started the conversation.

I felt like I was back in my school headmaster's office and was about to get a reprimand for my demeanours, so I nervously waited for Yoran to speak. I thought he was going to warn me off for the way I was looking at his daughter.

"I know how Amina feels about you, and I think you feel the same way about her, so please stop me now if I am wrong."

I was shocked, and it took a little time for me to realise what he had just said. "I can only speak for myself, and I hope what I say doesn't offend you. I have no idea what feelings Amina has for me. I am drawn to her like a magnet; it's hard to explain my feelings." I waited for Yoran's reaction, which I couldn't read so I continued. "Yoran, how do you know how Amina feels about me?"

"Because she's told me."

"Yoran, I'm surprised that you talk about such things with your daughter."

"All I desire is her happiness. I understand you haven't known each other very long. But far longer than a traditional Syrian couple would. These marriages are arranged without their knowledge, so they don't get to know each other at all until after they marry."

"Yoran, you do realise there is an age difference?"

"Nobody is perfect," Yoran replied, laughing.

"That's very true in my case."

"I don't want Amina marrying someone who would treat her as a possession or unequal. She needs to be with someone who respects her and lets her grow," Yoran explained.

"Yes, I agree wholeheartedly."

"You have been through things together, far more than a typical betrothed couple in Syria."

"Yoran, are you suggesting what I think you are?"

"Yes, I am, and as far as a dowry is concerned, it's not necessary."

"Yoran, I am thinking about what you have just said. I think it's far too soon to broach the subject for several reasons. I am a non-Muslim, older, and a foreigner."

"I don't care about religion; being a good person is more important. Age is a number. My child's happiness far outweighs everything, and regarding being a foreigner, what difference does that make?"

"But you know so little about me. How can you be so sure I am the right person for Amina?"

"I know more about you than you think I do," he said with a contented smile.

I knew the only person who knew anything about me was Ali. "Obviously, you have been talking to Ali about me."

"Maybe, I have talked to Ali a little."

"A little? Is that enough for you?"

"Believe me when I say I know enough about you. Can we leave the matter there?"

I didn't want to be rude or question him any further, so I decided to let the matter drop. "You're a good father. I'm sure you're thinking of your daughter's interests."

"That's the best and only way, as far as I'm concerned."

"Yoran, I'm not sure of the customs in Syria. What do I do next?"

"Well, in the village I come from, the engagement was simple. When Amina was a child, I told her many times how I proposed to her mama, and I think she should remember. All that is required is for the man to present a silk scarf filled with coins to the girl. If the girl opens the scarf and accepts the contents, they are considered engaged."

"That's easier than going down on bended knee in front of people."

"How do you feel about doing that in front of my family and friends this evening?"

"Excuse my language, but bloody hell. I never expected this, just the opposite, in fact! I thought you got us on our own to warn me off! Okay, I'm up for it. The worst that can happen is that she turns me down!" I nervously replied.

Yoran went to a small table, opened a drawer and pulled out a silk scarf. I pulled out coins from my pocket and placed them inside the scarf and folded it. I thought, *shit, is this really happening?* We rejoined the rest outside. I could see the apprehension in Amina's face as I walked toward her, holding my hands behind my back. I sat down opposite Amina, looked into her eyes and handed her the scarf. Amina looked bemused and accepted the scarf and opened it. She saw the coins. She looked at them confused at first, then she seemed to realise what they meant and smiled. She looked at me to check she had understood what was happening. Her eyes filled with tears, she nodded, and everyone knew her answer. Yoran took me to one side and told me to leave and say goodbye to everyone.

"The next time we meet will be at the wedding ceremony," he explained. He then embraced me as a friend, kissed both cheeks, shook my hand and said goodbye.

"Did that just really happen?" I asked in the car, driving back to Ali and Margaret's. "If I'm dreaming, wake me up!"

"We were there. It's not a dream. Like a lamb to the slaughter," Margaret laughed.

"You can't get out of it now," Ali said, laughing with her. "We both witnessed the offence of punching well above your weight."

"Your punishment is having to spend the rest of your life with Amina."

"Sorry, I'm still in shock. What happens next?" I asked, hoping to get a serious response.

"We're both so happy for you; it's a shame you were last to know, though," Margaret said, turning to me with a genuine smile.

"Ali, what happens next?"

Ali explained that it was customary for the bride and groom to have no contact before marriage after a proposal. There were rules and laws in Syria regarding different nationalities getting married, as he had found out at his wedding. It was easier when the man was Syrian. My marriage as a non-Syrian to a Syrian national would need the Ministry of the Interior's consent. But he was sure that it would be all right because I was employed as a key worker for the Al Farat Oil Company. Going back to Al Farat wouldn't be a problem, and I would leave everything to them to arrange. Hopefully, by the time I had completed my next tour, all would be ready.

Chapter 18

Return to Al Taim

My leave in the UK was short and entirely centred around my children. I didn't tell them or anyone else about Amina. It would be impossible to justify, as I found it difficult myself. I felt guilty that something so important to me was a secret from those I cared about most. So returning to Syria was a surreal experience, completely different from my previous trips. I was looking forward to it this time, rather than dreading the loneliness. Amina was always in my mind and Ali and Margaret's company.

I returned to Al Taim for my next month's contract and continued installing the so-called maintenance programme. It seemed strange to be back at work, wasting my time, as usual, hoping that things would change. The only break from boredom was the visits with Ali in his room. On one visit, I was surprised because the curious picture frames which used to be placed face down were now on show. I had presumed that they were private and for his eyes only. The photos were of Margaret and Ali together. There was no one else in the photos, which was a surprise as I had presumed some would be of his family. My curiosity got the better of me.

"Why no family photos?" I asked.

"I am the black sheep of the family; they disowned me some time ago," he replied.

"For what reason?" I asked. "What have you done that's so bad?"

"The simple answer is that I am not a good Muslim, well, not good enough for them. They disowned me in the end for marrying Margaret, amongst other things."

"Bloody hell, Ali! I had no idea. Do you ever see them?"

"Never. I tried, but there's no point."

"Are they that devout, then?"

"You could say that, but I would say extremely devout, to the point of being extremists."

My eyes were attracted to the photos, some taken in Oxford, where they were married at a register office. All the pictures depicted a happy couple, obviously non-Muslim. I could now understand why they were not openly on show. There was still one photo face down.

"If I'm being too nosey, tell me to piss off, but why is one photo still face down?"

"Well." Ali paused. "The photo is of Margaret. I am not sure how it came about, but her eyes follow me around the room. It must be some accidental trick of the camera, as wherever I am, her eyes stare at me."

"There are some famous paintings that appear to do the same thing, but it could all be in your guilty head."

"Maybe," Ali said, "but I don't think so. Hang on, what guilt?"

"Punching above your weight! Touché! Can I have a look, Ali?"

"Sure, but don't blame me if it spooks you."

I walked around the room.

"It's spooky, bloody spooky; she's watching me," I agreed.

"It comes in handy sometimes. I can talk to her, and she listens, with no smart-arse answers."

We both laughed.

"We have all been at the end of Margaret's cutting, witty remarks."

"That's what she braggingly calls them; I still never know which way to take them after all these years. Mind you, she still wins the argument when she's not here."

"But she is funny, and it's all said in good humour, don't you think, Ali?"

"She gives as good as she gets and a bit more," he replied.

On another evening session with Ali, he brought the conversation around to the running of the refinery. "Just to let you know, but keep it to yourself, all of the Conch Oil contracts are being reviewed."

"Why now?"

"Al Farat Oil Company knows that all is not as it should be."

"How come?"

"The visit from the Ministry of Energy inspection didn't go as well as Bente thought. The minister is no fool; he played dumb."

"I noticed he was giving me strange looks as he walked around the office as he checked each wall chart. I thought it weird at the time!"

"Well, he is a qualified marine engineer and was only acting like an idiot."

"It would be easy for anyone with a bit of knowledge to see what I mocked up was a load of crap."

"His visit will eventually lead to a complete rethink of how the plants are run and by whom."

"That would be a good idea, as carrying on like we are is stupid and dangerous," I remarked.

"He is fully aware of the position you have been forced into and how uncomfortable it is for you."

"How?"

"Because I told him, okay!"

"I have no issue with that, thanks."

"I have influence with the Al Farat Oil Company and could find a position there for you. It's up to you."

"Thank you."

"No problem. Your honesty and confirming what I already knew will hold you in good stead. The Syrian trainees also told him that you were a good man."

"I enjoyed their company. Even they could see what I was up to. I think the long-term solution is to train young Syrians and encourage them to do things the correct way."

"The minister is talking with Al Farat Oil management about setting up a training school. Are you interested?"

"Yes, I would be. That is the best way forward. On-site training backed up by theory."

"I thought you would agree, and it would suit your present circumstances. I have already arranged it."

"Do I have a say in it?" I asked sarcastically.

"Yes, you do; it's completely up to you. Remember, though, what I said about the plants being under review."

"Sorry, you have taken me by surprise. A bit of a shock, that's all."

"I know. I was being presumptuous, but it would be better for you in so many ways."

"Thanks, Ali; if there is an interview, I would certainly be interested."

Ali's influence with Al Farat Oil Company and the energy minister accelerated the interview process. The interview was for a position at Aleppo University, provisionally setting up a school for trainee engineers. I accepted the offer, including good accommodation with excellent terms and conditions. It included a standard forty-hour week, a generous leave package and a company car. I insisted that my salary was paid in pounds sterling into my UK bank account. It was far more stable than the Syrian pound and in line with my previous arrangement. Al Farat Oil Company was providing finance for the training school, so this was not an issue. The start date was immediate. I said my goodbyes to the staff at Al Taim and contacted Matt to tell him, 'sorry, but you are on your own now.' He told me that he had had enough and that this was his last trip; I asked for his contact details to keep in touch. He wished me luck. I wondered if he was interested in joining me on my new adventure. He declined as he had a wife and family and the time away from them was an issue.

What was really happening was Ali was showing me true friendship, although he probably wouldn't have admitted that to himself or me. I had been accustomed to the Arab psyche before in Saudi Arabia; maybe it was still within him, even though he portrayed himself as a modern Arab. Perhaps, Ali had to prove to himself first that I was worthy of being his friend. If so, I had passed the test. I remembered how awkward it was in Saudi Arabia when I was considered a friend. How they couldn't understand my refusing to hold their hands. I recalled how our greetings changed from a token kiss on both cheeks to a full embrace as I got to know them more, which I found embarrassing. It made me anxious about my next meeting with Ali. I couldn't imagine how I would respond if Ali embraced me in the full traditional Arab fashion as a friend. There was no need to worry, although I noticed slightly more body contact at our next meeting. I comfortably dealt with it, but there had been a change in his actions towards me, confirming Ali was my friend. We spent more time with each other, mainly playing chess and backgammon in the evenings. Ali was good at chess. I always think you have to be a little evil and have a no mercy, killer instinct to play chess, which I didn't have, but Ali had in abundance.

Chapter 19

Marriage

Ali often visited my apartment, usually at weekends. Margaret would sometimes come as well, sometimes on her own. Neither ever came empty-handed. They were welcome visitors; the eight-hour working day left a lot of time on my hands; even though I stayed on in the evenings or brought work home, it still left me a lot of free time. They always came bearing gifts for the apartment; Margaret's gifts were mostly with Amina in mind.

We discussed the Syrian marriage ceremony and what was required. The marriage would be registered in court via a legally binding contract called a Kitab, usually preceded by an engagement ceremony called a khetbeth. A khetbeth would not be necessary in our case as only one family was involved, and there were only a few friends to invite. After the wedding, it was decided a reception would be held at Amina's parents' house. Usually, these parties would last for a couple of days. It was agreed that drawing attention to the marriage would not be a good idea, as it wasn't typical for mixed-race or mixed religion marriages. After the reception, we would depart to start our new life together. Ali confirmed the arrangements with Yoran and Souzan. I had no contact with Amina whatsoever and decided not to use my mobile phone, as it didn't seem appropriate. As much as possible, the wedding would be traditionally Syrian. Like strangers, we would meet at the court, and the wedding would be formal.

Amina dressed in a traditional red Syrian wedding dress, and she looked stunning. We were both a little nervous, with bride and groom jitters. We only spoke to officials when requested and not to each other. After the ceremony, we gathered at Amina's parents' home for a small reception in the garden.

I had previously asked Margaret to tell Amina that we would be honeymooning for a week and to pack clothes for all occasions. I was taking Amina to the Zenobia Cham Palace Hotel in Palmyra on the night of our marriage. Margaret only told Amina that it would take a few hours to get there.

The first time we were able to show each other any affection openly was in her parents' garden. It was awkward at first, walking hand in hand as newlyweds, knowing so little about each other, but at the same time, ready to learn so much.

We mingled with the small party, including a few close friends of Amina's parents and their neighbours. There were lots of handshakes and kissing, Arab-style. I approached Ali, who was talking to a man I hadn't seen there before. They were both dressed in pure white thawbs; most other men were similarly dressed. I wore a traditional Western suit and felt a little out of place. They turned towards me as I came close. It was one of those déjà vu moments when the knowing look on a stranger's face stopped me in my tracks.

"I would like to introduce you to Emre, the minister for energy," Ali said.

"Nice to see you again," Emre said, extending his hand out politely.

"What are you doing here?" I asked clumsily as we shook hands.

"I am an old friend of Yoran's; we were brought up in the same village and went to the same university. We have always kept in touch."

I was floundering now and felt the need to apologise for the scam. "Sorry about the deceit."

"There's no need to apologise; I knew what was going on."

"But I was still involved."

"You had no choice, did you?"

"I told Ali I didn't like it, and I know that he spoke to you."

"Ali not only spoke to me, but he also sent the videos of your discussions with Bente; what a prick he is. Sorry for my English."

"A pretty accurate use of the English language, I would say."

"Not that I needed the videos because the wall charts told me everything."

"How's that? What did they tell you?"

"Well, to begin with, they were all new, far too clean, no mistakes, no rubbing out to change data, everything was up to date. This wouldn't happen with typical day-to-day worksheet entries. Nobody is that perfect."

"Fresh off the press, so to speak. Bente wanted them clean and sparkling. He thought that would impress you."

"I noticed that they were certainly very bright and colourful, but the one thing that stuck out like a sore thumb was there was no planning chart for remedial work."

"I know, I didn't have time to do that. It would have meant cross-referencing nonsense from one chart to another nonsense chart. There's no way I had time to do that, or the inclination, as I was already brain-dead."

"The other thing was one person can't run a planning office properly for a workforce of that size."

"I know that more Syrian trainees is the answer."

"It must have been hard taking that shit from that prick."

"It was soul-destroying. Thank you for helping with my new position. I am very grateful."

"Ali sent tapes of you and the trainees. I liked the way you interacted with them. Now, please, it's a new start: it's your wedding day!"

"Excuse me! I must get back to Amina, but thank you for all your non-intervention," I said, smiling.

I shook Emre's hand. I knew he was probably responsible for my new job at the university, amongst other things.

We packed the car with our luggage, bade farewell to everyone and started the journey to Palmyra, the start of our new life together. We talked little on the trip, as the roads were not that good after we'd left Damascus, so I needed to concentrate. I occasionally touched Amina's hand for reassurance.

"Where are we going?" she asked curiously.

"I hope it's a pleasant surprise."

"I trust you," she said and reached for my hand again.

The time Amina had spent with Margaret had improved her English. All Margaret's Syrian history books were in English. Amina was schooled in English as a child before the kidnapping, which may also have contributed to how quickly she learned. Their conversations may have helped Amina become more confident. She was also strong-willed, which gave me confidence that she was sitting beside me because she wanted to be there.

We stopped for a rest at the Bagdad Route 66 café. From the outside, it looked like an ordinary ramshackle unfinished house. Inside, it was completely different; it was themed with genuine Syrian historical artefacts on the walls, carpets on the floors and cushioned seating everywhere. The owner was a Bedouin and had designed it in the style of a Bedouin tent. I could see it brought back memories of where we had met; she smiled at me as she looked around.

We arrived at the Zenobia Cham Palace Hotel in the early evening. On arrival, we were greeted by Ahmed, who had worked at the hotel for over sixty years, starting as a dish washer, he later told us. Ahmed was so proud of the hotel, and nothing was too much trouble for him. A porter took the luggage to our room while we were checking in. The room Ali had booked was the best they had, with superb views from a veranda overlooking Palmyra. The view was stunningly beautiful. The room was quite large and fitted with quaint antique furniture. Ahmed later recounted the names of all the famous people who had stayed in the room. Amusingly, the room number was 101. In the UK, 'room 101' is where you put things you don't want, which was the opposite for me.

At last, we were alone, and I could sense that Amina was a little nervous, as I was too. I suggested that we shower, change, and go out for a walk and refreshments. We discretely prepared ourselves for the evening and walked out of the hotel to a restaurant recommended by Ahmed called Cassa Mia, a small, quaint but innovative restaurant and cocktail bar. The maître d' escorted us to a table that overlooked Palmyra. Amina was interested in the word cocktail, which she had seen on a flashing sign above the bar.

"Surely you don't eat cocktails, whatever they are?" she asked.

"No, you don't eat them; a cocktail is a drink usually taken before or after a meal."

"Why didn't they give them a better name?"

"I've never thought about it; to me, cocktails have always been cocktails."

"Well, what are they, then?"

"They usually contain alcohol in the West, but you can have one without. There are many different types with different ingredients and weird and contrived names designed to make them sound attractive and inviting."

"Can I try one?"

I ordered two Mojitos, one with and one without alcohol. While we studied the menu, Amina occasionally asked me to describe the ingredients of the different meals available. We ordered our food, and the cocktails were delivered. I sipped mine, and Amina sipped hers. She was pleasantly surprised. "Can I taste yours," she asked.

"If you want to. Are you sure? It contains alcohol."

"Why not?" She took a few sips. "I prefer yours; it's a lot nicer."

We were thirsty, so I ordered two more, and she insisted that she wanted the same as me.

After the meal and cocktails, we left the restaurant a little less nervous than when we had arrived. As we walked to the hotel hand in hand, I could feel Amina's grip tightening. I had the feeling that she was indicating to me everything was going to be all right. We both made ourselves ready for bed. Amina prepared in the bathroom. I got into bed and waited for Amina to join me. The bathroom door opened, and she slipped into bed beside me. We both lay there for a short while, not moving, I could hear her trying to control her breathing, and she could probably hear me doing the same. Our hands touched, and slowly, we moved closer. It was as though we both knew when to move; we moved simultaneously until our faces touched and then our bodies. Though experienced in love-making, these feelings were entirely new for me. I was lost, and everything that happened felt natural. We lay together and slept together as one that night, and in the morning, when we looked at each other, no words were necessary. We were right for each other.

I ordered a breakfast of traditional Arabic food – bread, honey, cheese and eggs – which we consumed on the veranda while discussing what we should do during the day. We decided that a guided tour of Palmyra would be good. I arranged the tour with Ahmed. He told us we were lucky because the curator, Khaled al-Asaad, was doing a guided tour that day.

We met with Khaled as agreed at the front of the hotel. Ahmed provided packed lunches, so we were set for the day. Khaled was well into his seventies, like Ahmed. He was born in Palmyra and had lived there all his life except for when he was studying archaeology in Damascus. Khaled and his driver sat in the front of the Land Rover, and Amina and I sat in the back. Khaled was enthusiastic and articulate in describing the ruins and what each building was used for when built. It was far too much information for me to take in all at once. I could tell the facts were stored deep in Amina's head, and she asked many more questions than I did. Khaled explained he had removed artefacts for safekeeping, and some were stored in a museum on site. Palmyra was once the most important city globally. It was ideally located on what was known as the 'Silk Road'. It had initially been just an oasis in the middle of the desert. As trade increased throughout the world, people of all nationalities flocked there to live. Overloaded with information, booklets and pamphlets to read later, we were dropped off at the hotel and made our way to our room. Amina said she was tired, so she showered and lay on the bed. I followed suit and soon realised that she wasn't tired at all, and it would become a pattern of the stay at Palmyra: afternoon delights. When we fell asleep in the late afternoon, she would fall asleep with her head resting on my chest. Our breathing and heart rate would synchronise. It reminded me of the feeling when a child falls asleep in your arms, the incredible sense of another human being trusting you completely.

"Do you love Palmyra?" Amina asked me one morning.

"Yes, I do, very much."

"Are you being unfaithful with me on our honeymoon?"

"What could possibly make you think that?" I asked, puzzled as to why she might think that.

"Well, Palmyra is known as 'the bride of the desert,' and you are sleeping within her, aren't you?"

"Very funny, haha. I didn't know that." I paused to think of something to outwit her. "Do you love Palmyra too?"

"Well, of course, I do; who wouldn't?"

"Then what describes a bride that's in love with another bride?" I replied, making the gotcha sign in the air.

"Haha, clever boy!"

During the days that followed, we spent most of the daylight hours touring the spectacular ruins of Palmyra, sometimes on ponies rented from a local boy. He was dressed similar to those on the banks of the Euphrates. Amina spoke to the boy before selecting a ride for each of us. She always checked that my mount would be docile. When Amina mounted her pony, his ears pricked up, and mine remained drooped as though bored, perhaps from disappointment. Amina rode confidently, and her pony moved on her commands as she dug her heels in or tapped it with the reins. Mine just followed hers as though being invisibly towed with me hanging on. We rented camels for the day with a guide; this was essential for me but not for Amina. She was accomplished and encouraged her camel to sit, walk or stand. In contrast, my guide did all the work for me.

Riding through the ruins of Palmyra on the back of an animal following the tracks of those 2000 years ago was a profoundly moving experience. We had maps and drawings of Palmyra when it was a fully functioning city. The scale and size of its buildings, roads and arcades were more than impressive; how it had been built without modern-day equipment fascinated both of us. In the evening, we sometimes dined at the restaurant hotel, which had panoramic views of the desert. The food was typical for the region, mainly salad, fruit and vegetables with some meat, which I would describe as adequate. Our time in Palmyra flew by; when we were not exploring the site, we had plenty to occupy us, getting to know each other.

Amina read all the information provided in both Arabic and English. She questioned me about the English language. Words I took for granted didn't make sense to her, nor to me when I tried to explain. I explained to her that there are so many words that are spelt the same and mean entirely different things, and there are words that sound the same but are spelt differently.

"Why are some letters within words silent?" Amina asked.

"It doesn't make sense to me either, Amina," I often replied to her questions. It brought back memories of my Saudi Arabian trainees, who were schooled in English. They frequently asked me questions, and I soon realised that many of my explanations were wrong. This only encouraged them to ask more so they could have a good laugh at my expense.

It often annoyed Amina if I laughed when she pronounced a word wrong or used the wrong word. Sometimes she would learn the meaning of a word and ask me to explain it. When I explained it all wrong, she would ask who was the stupid one now and laugh as she made an imaginary mark in the air with her index finger.

On the last but one day of our honeymoon, we drove back to the hotel. As you do when driving along a route without any interesting features, I was sort of daydreaming.

"Did you see that article about dirigibles coming to Palmyra," Amina asked?

"Well, they have to go somewhere," I replied.

"What do you mean?" Amina looked puzzled.

"Well, they can't help it, can they?"

"I don't understand what you mean; please explain?"

"Just because they have fallen on hard times, it's not their fault, is it?" I replied in a conciliatory tone.

"Sorry, I still don't understand; please tell me more?"

"It's quite simple; people shouldn't be blamed for being poor. Giving them a leg up getting a job is a good thing, isn't it?"

Amina laughed; her whole body was shaking. "Could the cause of their fall be inflation, maybe?"

"Yeah, something like that, perhaps," I said confidently.

"Maybe their bubble had burst?" I could see tears rolling down her cheeks, and she was laughing uncontrollably.

"Maybe! What's so funny?"

"Stop it! I'm gonna pee myself," she retorted. She then made an effort to control herself, which failed as she burst out laughing again. Her infectious laugh caused me to laugh uncontrollably too. I stopped the car and looked at her. We were both crying tears of laughter by now, but I still didn't know why.

"What is it?" I blurted out.

She burst out laughing again, slapping her thighs. "Give me a minute," she asked, wiping away her tears.

"I'm glad I've made someone happy," I said, still confused.

"You say the silliest things without thinking first."

"What have I said that's daft enough to give you an uncontrollable laughing fit?"

"If you don't know the meaning of a word, why did you guess? That is silly!"

"Well, what is it then, know-all, and how do you know?"

"I know because I read an article about them in the hotel."

"Well, there are a lot of poor people around Palmyra. What does it say about them?"

"Well, they are going to take the tourists for a ride."

"Here we go again, blaming the poor."

"No, they are giving the tourist a better view of the site."

"What, like more camels, horses or trucks?"

Amina, struggling to control her laughter again, continued. "No, not that. They are going to give an aerial view of the site."

Then out of the blue, somewhere from the back of my mind, popped the image of an air balloon. "Air balloons," I said and immediately felt foolish.

"Yes, at last. I do love you, you know, even if you are not very bright."

Amina spent much time testing herself over the meaning of words while reading, sometimes with a dictionary at hand. Sometimes, it was quicker to ask me but not as reliable as getting the correct definition. She would always confirm later if my explanation was valid and tell me if I was clever or not.

The honeymoon in Palmyra ended, and there was a definite change in Amina. I was learning so much more about her. She was like a sponge soaking up information, reading and learning about all sorts of things. She questioned me about my life in the UK and my family relationships with genuine interest and concern. I told her that I had made my home in Syria but would like to take her to Wales. After saying our farewells to the hotel staff and a special thank you to Ahmed, we drove back from Palmyra to Aleppo. Amina insisted on filling in the guest book, taking great care to thank all the staff for our wonderful time there.

Chapter 20

Making Home in Aleppo, 1996

The journey from Palmyra to my apartment in Aleppo took about four hours during daylight, so we departed after breakfast. We decided the best route would be Homs to Deer-ez-Zur, along the Euphrates Road to Rakka and Aleppo. We had packed lunches with the intention of not stopping other than toileting and fuel stops. We would possibly be passing scenery and landmarks that would have been unpleasantly familiar to Amina. As we were driving through some areas which Amina recognised, she fell silent. As soon as we entered places and sites she hadn't seen, she became less pensive and started chatting, mainly asking questions about my work and where we would live. Would we live close to Margaret and Ali, would we see them much, how often we would go to Damascus, and could her parents' visit.

So much had changed in such a short time. I went from an insular individual drifting through life to being a married man with all the responsibilities it brings. I could imagine friends and family back home exclaiming, "You won't believe what he has gone and done now! He has only gone and married an Arab!"

There was a lot of pointing and nodding at interesting landmarks. Some parts of Syria are so beautiful, although many areas are desolate and uninviting. Where people had settled, beauty had been replaced with ugly concrete buildings and discarded rubbish everywhere. As we passed through dull and uninteresting landscapes during the journey, Amina would ask questions again about the English language. Sometimes I think the questions were to catch me out or just for a bit of humour.

"What word has five letters, four of which are silent?" she asked.

"You tell me!"

"You really don't know?"

"Go on then!"

"Queue! And what I find very strange is that the word 'cue' is pronounced the same and only has two vowels."

I laughed and nodded in agreement. "It's weird; don't try to make sense of the English language!"

"Where does the word 'cocktail' come from?"

"I don't know, but you will tell me, won't you? Sorry, please go on; how did it come about?"

"Well, the barrel drain tap is called a 'cock', and the dregs are the last of the barrel hence 'tail', put them together, and you have a 'cocktail'."

"That makes a lot of sense, so the bar owner can maximise his profits using throw-away waste and selling it. That's enterprising; how do you know these things?"

"Because I check words in a dictionary

"You researched this word because you thought it didn't make sense, and you needed it to make sense, correct?"

"Yes, I have so much to learn, and it irritates me if I can't understand the meaning of something."

"I am glad I'm not the same, or I would be irritated all the time."

"True, you have so much to learn," she giggled, with a look that reminded me of Margaret.

I was beginning to understand that she was trying hard to catch up on her missed years of schooling. I remembered what her father had said: she wasn't going to be anybody's fool.

As we travelled through the poorly constructed small villages, we discussed how 2000 years ago, they could build things as beautiful as Palmyra. Yet, nowadays, so many modern buildings are ugly and decayed fast.

We arrived in Aleppo in good time. I decided to drive through the town's hustle and bustle to give Amina an idea of her new home. The first thing you noticed was the traffic noise and horns blasting for no apparent reason. Other vehicles appeared to be trying to remove the paint from yours without actually touching it. It was utter mayhem, just like Damascus. You might get used to it, but it was never enjoyable. We drove through Aleppo past the ancient citadel and the souq.

"Old yet beautiful, just like parts of Damascus," Amina remarked.

"Yes, it is, but it's a shame that the modern buildings have been built with little thought."

"Yes, ugly and cheaply built, showing more signs of age than the older ones."

"Makes no sense to me either."

We arrived at my apartment. Amina inspected it as any woman would. I could see the approving and disapproving expressions on her face as she moved from room to room. It is considered rude in Arabic to disapprove openly. Still, I detected what she liked and disliked from the things she openly approved of. I was prepared to accept her ideas as it would be her home too. Soon after we had refreshed ourselves, Amina began to make suggestions for improvements. I had expected her to do this as, after all, it was an English man's bachelor pad with no feminine or Arabic input. Amina conceded that eating at a table was far better than sitting on the floor as she was used to. Still, she preferred a majlis seating area for comfort and entertaining friends. I chose to sit in a comfortable armchair rather than on the floor and told her so.

We drove to the Al-Madina Souq the following morning, where we had breakfast and walked around the historic buildings. It was mostly new to me as we walked from stall to stall; she was attracted to mainly new things. Amina bought various foodstuffs and passed them to me to carry like a beast of burden. I suggested that she purchase anything she wanted for our home, within reason. She replied, "I don't need anything at all." However, slowly but surely, things appeared in the apartment after Amina and Margaret had been out shopping together. Sometimes I didn't notice the new additions straight away. When I inquired if something was new, her usual reply was, "You must be blind; we've had it for ages." I think this was a tactic learned from Margaret, so I never really knew what was new.

When I went back to work, I was delighted that Margaret and Amina spent so much time together. At the weekends, the four of us relaxed together, dining, playing card games, putting the world to rights, or simply enjoying each other's company.

As time went by, it became apparent that Amina needed to challenge herself; she needed to be stretched and tested. Reading and learning at home wasn't enough. Being a housewife was not fulfilling, so we discussed what she could do. The choice was limited, so we brought up the subject one weekend when Ali and Margaret came over for an evening. Margaret suggested that Amina enrol at Aleppo University for further education, maybe in English language or Syrian history, as she and Amina were interested in both.

"I could set up an interview for you?" Margaret suggested.

"Let me think it over first, and I will let you know," Amina replied tentatively.

"Amina, you are very clever, don't doubt yourself. I will put the ball in motion and see what's available if you like."

Amina was accepted and enrolled as a full-time student studying English. I was proud of her.

"You're too clever by half. Soon your English will be better than mine."

"Your Arabic is better than your English. It's a shame your Arabic is so poor," she replied with a sparkle in her eye.

Ali and Margaret interacted as equals, which influenced Amina to become more confident. Amina presented her perspective when we had discussions, like the rest of us, either disagreeing, conceding or failing to agree. Our talks always ended constructively, with one or all of us learning something.

Ali had the knack of restarting a debate, taking the exact opposite side of his previously won argument.

Using the points we had made, but more convincingly, to prove his previous stance was incorrect. When asked why, he replied, "Because I can." We became even closer as friends, playing the usual games after dining and talking long into the night on various subjects.

One evening in February 1998, I arrived home from work to be greeted by Amina.

"Please sit in your chair; I have something important to tell you," she said nervously.

I could see she was excited as she knelt down before me. I thought maybe she had just passed an exam or something. She looked directly into my eyes and spoke slowly. "I am going to present you the greatest gift anyone could give to another."

"I don't need a new car," I said jokingly.

"Don't be stupid. I am serious. The gift is our child."

I was overcome with emotion; we embraced and congratulated each other for being so clever. When the initial excitement was over, I began to think practically.

"We need to find ourselves a good home with outside space, a nursery, and away from the hustle and bustle of town."

That evening, while Amina was reading a book, probably about babies, I reflected back to the first time I was told soon I would be a father. It had been a completely different experience from what I was feeling now. I was twenty-one and had been courting Jane for a while. One evening, she told me her periods were late; I didn't think much about it as it wasn't the first time. A month later, she confirmed she was pregnant, and we had a discussion. I decided to stand by her, whatever she decided. In the Midlands, at that time, it was a reasonably regular occurrence. Courting couples that planned white weddings in a church settled for register office marriages because a bump in a wedding dress didn't look right. White weddings also took longer to arrange, allowing the bump to become more prominent. In contrast, a register office ceremony was quicker, cheaper, with a smaller gathering. So that's what we decided. I had to face the music with her parents, who never liked me. I knew they thought she could do better; they were never friendly to me. When I went around to their house after Jane had shared the news, I expected a roasting, but instead, they were suddenly friendly with me. I soon realised why; they were scared I would do a runner.

When I told my mum and dad what had happened, my mum had been quite harsh. "I am not surprised the way you pair carry on," was her first comment.

My father had been more supportive. "I don't like her; a bit stuck up in my opinion, but I will stand by you, whatever you decide, son."

The next step was to get both sets of parents together, so a meeting was arranged at the Hudson's house. Their house was almost identical to ours and also built just after the war: two square reception rooms downstairs, comprising the front room and kitchen. A door on the right led straight into the front room from a small hall-cum-stairwell. A door on the opposite wall led directly into the kitchen. The James family, which included only Mum, Dad and me, were invited into the fully furnished front room with comfortable furniture and other luxurious trappings. A sofa was positioned as a guide through their pristine front room to the kitchen door; newspapers were placed on the carpet where we were likely to walk. I could see Dad clumsily trying to avoid them. We were escorted through the comfortable lounge into the kitchen and told to sit around the table.

"Do you know you've left a light on next door?" Dad said, being the first to speak.

"Yes, it's for effect," Mrs Hudson replied.

I could see Dad's brain working. I was hoping he wasn't going to ask, 'effect for who'. Being on his best behaviour, he said nothing but raised his eyebrows at me. The intended arrangements were made that day, and the Hudsons were invited to the James' house the following week. Before leaving, they showed us around their lawned garden, with imitation Greek ornaments scattered 'for effect'.

"Did you see that front room? It's just for show. It's never used, a waste of space! Keeping a light switched on in an empty room is bonkers," Dad said on the walk home.

"I wonder what they will make of ours," Mum said.

"I don't care a toss; at least it's used. Did you see their garden? What's the point of that? It's just for looking at; it must cost a fortune in plants. More money than sense, that lot."

We had a very comfortable kitchen which we lived in. I was an only child, and there was plenty of room for the three of us. The front room was my playroom as a child; as I grew older, it became the place to store stuff. I kept my bike in there. It made sense to keep it safe and dry. On rainy days, my mates could come round, and we could play games. Dad stored his tools there, safe and handy. He also had a darts board; he was a stickler for detail as an engineer and fixed it at the right height with a proper oche screwed to the floor. "Measured to within a gnat's cock," he would brag.

He also made a proper scoreboard from a natural roof slate. Dad often invited his mates round for a game of darts. Hence there were also crates of beer and a few deckchairs in there. Our back garden was more like an allotment, with all sorts of vegetables growing. He often proudly gave home-grown produce away to the neighbours.

"You'd better clean up the front room. The Hudsons are coming," Mum instructed as the visit drew closer.

"Okay, it won't take me a minute," Dad replied. "Do you want me to leave the light on when I'm finished?"

Mum laughed. "Maybe the light over the dartboard for effect?"

"Will do," Dad replied, grunting as he folded the deckchairs and dragged the beer crates into a corner.

The Hudsons arrived, dressed like they were going to the theatre. I showed them quickly through the front room into the kitchen, and we sat around the kitchen table. The smell of aftershave and scent was overwhelming. The arrangements were agreed upon. Dad insisted we paid half of everything. The usual practice was that the bride's parents paid for everything, but Dad would have none of that; 'we pay our share' was his motto. The Hudsons seemed grateful. Dad then proudly showed them around his garden. They didn't comment, but we could tell they disapproved.

In the kitchen, Dad asked Mrs Hudson, "Would you like to take some vegetables back with you?" Before she could reply, he brought an orange box of potatoes out of the pantry.

"We only buy Egyptian; what are they?" Mrs Hudson replied, looking at them.

"Maris Piper, the best you can get," Dad replied.

I could see Dad was displeased.

"No, thank you, we have plenty," Mrs Hudson replied, perhaps because they were still covered in dirt and she wasn't used to that.

When they left, Dad was furious. "Son, I don't like them. They're not my type. I hope you don't regret marrying this girl. They probably think potatoes grow in polythene bags!"

"Fur coat and no knickers, that one," Mum said, referring to Mrs Hudson.

I never told Amina any of this; she would have found it hard to understand. I was finding it difficult myself. I was a different me back then. I missed my parents, who both died pretty young. I think I was spoilt with love because I was an only child. They told me I was a surprise and came to them when they least expected a gift. They gave me the values I still have today. I was taught right from wrong to be truthful and careful with my pennies so the pounds would look after themselves.

Over the next few months, we searched for a house on the quiet western side of Aleppo. We found a place in a good area that we both liked, and it had a garden. We took out a bank loan to pay for the shortfall. I earned a good wage, so it wasn't a problem. We settled into our house, which gave us something to do during the latter stages of her pregnancy. Amina occupied herself turning our new house into our home with some help from me. The birth of a baby girl blessed us in January 1998. Amina had already chosen the baby's name: if it was a girl, Amara, and for a boy, Amal. It is traditional in Syria for first names to have meanings.

"'Amara' means kindness and grace, and 'Amal' hope and inspiration."

"So, what does your name mean?"

"It means peace, but I thought you knew that. What does your name stand for?"

"I don't know, nothing probably. I have never given it a thought."

"It means harmony," Amina. replied.

"Well, I didn't know that! So we have you as peace, me as harmony, and baby as grace: all we need now is a baby boy called Amal, and then we have hope."

Soon our hope was born, in December 1999. Amara was the image of Amina: delicate, pretty, with jet black hair and brown eyes, and she was bright, clever and full of energy. Amal took after me; he was fair-haired, not delicate in any way, noisy and into everything. They both had Amina's golden alabaster skin tone without a blemish.

One night I remember well, was when we had Ali and Margaret around for the evening. After maybe too much wine, I played a little game with myself. I often did this, imagining who friends most resembled if I had to describe them to someone else. I thought Margaret resembled Elizabeth Taylor in many ways and told her so. She was pretty flattered by the suggestion, and it showed.

"Why?" she asked. "Tell me more."

"Well, she is beautiful, intelligent, with blue eyes, black hair, and has a wicked sense of humour." I then waited for her smile of approval and added, "She is also a bit of a handful."

"Thank you," Margaret said. "I am very flattered, but not sure what you mean by a bit of a handful; I hope you are not implying I'm difficult. What about Ali?"

"Ali! That's a hard one, except for the gap in Omar Sharif's front teeth; he is the image of him, don't you think, Margaret"?

"I can see why you would say that, but surely it has to be his dark, seductive wicked eyes as well, don't you think?"

Ali purposely flashed his white teeth. "Tell me more! I am enjoying this," Ali joked.

"Well, you are tall, dark, handsome, intelligent, caring, always win at backgammon when playing for money. Look handsome in a uniform, gullible, and you believe this bullshit," Margaret bantered. She made a number one with her index finger in the air.

Ali didn't say a word but just nodded in complete agreement while obviously trying to think of a suitable quip.

Margaret studied Amina. "I think Amina is the image of Audrey Hepburn."

"I couldn't agree more; what do you think, Amina?" I asked, looking at her for a response.

"I haven't a clue what you are talking about," she said, looking annoyed. "Who is she?"

"Only recognised to be the most beautiful woman ever," Margaret explained.

"Surely you mean the second-most?" Ali checked, looking at Margaret.

"Thank you, darling. I didn't know you cared," Margaret said, smiling.

"Oh, sorry, darling, you didn't imagine I was thinking of you, did you? I was actually thinking of Souzan," he retaliated, flashing a smile, obviously content to finally score a point against Margaret.

"I don't like this silly game," Amina said, embarrassed and blushing.

"Audrey Hepburn also did a lot of charity work and was intelligent and highly respected," Margaret said, trying to appease Amina, seeing she was annoyed.

"I don't know any of the people you are talking about; are they all dead?"

"They're famous film stars," we replied in unison.

"Okay, then what about you, Allan? You started it. Which film star does he look like, Ali?"

"Paul Newman, maybe," I said.

Margaret and Ali laughed loudly and then started whispering together. Finally they nodded in agreement. "Anthony Hopkins," they chanted together.

"Thank you, both. I presume you mean as a young man, not as he is now."

"That's settled, then. Tell me, if we are all similar to beautiful, successful film stars, what are we doing here?" Amina asked jokingly.

"Even the rich and famous like to see the rough side of life," Ali argued.

"You think this is rough! Try being a Bedouin," Amina said, ending the conversation.

"Time for another glass of wine, I think," Margaret suggested.

Chapter 21

Vacation to the UK, 2003

Amina had often discussed my previous life in the UK and my children there. Amina was interested in what went wrong with the marriage and why I was divorced because I had children. It was unthinkable to her that the children were not more important than the marriage. She was interested in the children and often asked whether I missed them or they missed me.

"Of course, I miss them, but it's complicated," I always replied.

"It's not complicated; you should see them growing up. My parents missed that, and I missed them too, so I know what they are feeling and what you are as well."

"After a divorce, children shouldn't be used as a weapon inflicting anguish on the other parent."

"But you both have equal rights; they are your children."

"Sometimes, it's best to take a backward step rather than place the children in a loyalty battle. I feel it's far better to let the children make their own minds up."

"But you have to let them know that you are always there for them."

"As they grow older, they can make up their minds and hopefully realise that my actions were in their best interests, not mine."

"Okay, but they have to know now, not later. It's so important; you have to understand, I know what it's like for them."

The letters I sent to my children included Amina's contributions, which increased as time went on. At first, I wrote letters and sent pictures of us and Syria, where we lived and places of interest. I encouraged Amina to add her own messages as well. Amina was curious because both were blond like me, and I told her that their mother had dark hair. They looked very formal in their school uniforms and appeared more sophisticated than Syrian children of the same age.

Amina wanted to know all about them and insisted we meet them. However, she was a little apprehensive about travelling to the UK, having read it was an immoral country. Margaret persuaded her it wasn't, and our children would be fine with her parents for a couple of weeks. Amina was able to apply for a spouse visa, allowing her to stay in the UK for two years, nine months. She was very anxious about meeting my children. I explained they were nothing like Syrian children of the same age. Helen was seventeen and would behave more like an adult than a girl of the same age in Syria. My son, Paul, aged sixteen, would probably not be very communitive, as typical for a boy of his age. I told her not to worry because Helen could talk the hind legs off a donkey. It was the first time Amina would be travelling to a non-Arab country. As usual, she spent time reading about what to expect to be prepared.

It shocked her when we landed at Gatwick; even after her research, everything appeared different from what she had expected, including the weather and the people. She said later that she thought people would look at her because she was different, but nobody did. She told me everyone seemed preoccupied and unaware of their surroundings and almost walked into her all the time. She realised that everybody was only interested in themselves and paid little attention to anyone else.

Helen had booked a four-bedroomed cottage at Freshwater East, close to Pembroke town, for our holiday. It was in an ideal location, close to the beaches and the town. Their mother had given permission for Helen and Paul to stay with us. I was surprised she agreed to this with little fuss; I thought she must be mellowing as she grew older. It was the school holidays so we would have plenty of time to spend together and the weather would be pleasant. Apart from when the kids were young and had family holidays, this would be the longest time we had spent together. I hoped that the kids would like Amina. It was hard for me to judge whether they would get on well or just tolerate her. I knew that Amina would do her level best to ensure that she would not cause issues, as it was not in her nature. I also knew that she would endeavour to make sure everything would go as smoothly as possible. So, with both excitement and apprehension, we met at the cottage as arranged. For Amina, meeting my children went smoother than expected. I wrongly assumed that the slight age difference would be a problem.

To begin with, they were very curious. Perhaps they were a little worried that their father had behaved recklessly, marrying a young Arab woman. Their mother may have tried to influence them, but they were now at an age to form their own opinions. After a short time, they were intrigued by her, how she spoke in perfect English, how well-mannered and how genuinely interested in them she was. There was very little difference in their height when they stood together. I wondered whether they were getting on so easily because they were face-to-face. I quickly became redundant as both the children were far more interested in her than me. Even Paul joined in the conversation and appeared interested; this was a first. I hadn't discussed how we met or the circumstances that led to it, as that may have alarmed them. So, I told them we met through work, and after a while, it was like they had known each other forever.

In Aleppo or Damascus, when we went shopping at the weekend, Ali and I would sit and have a coffee while waiting for the shoppers to return. Now it was Paul and me, passing the time away while the two girls were shopping. Shopping with Helen was an utterly different experience for Amina to her shopping trips with Margaret. Of course, Margaret and Helen differed in age and personalities. Helen was like a whirlwind and knew precisely what she was looking for, unlike Margaret, who tended to browse and was very selective.

Amina was puzzled why I gave up my life in the UK to work in Syria. I explained that it seemed a good idea at the time, and it suited my circumstances. I reminded her if I hadn't, we would never have met.

One of my 'must-do' things was to meet up with my old mate, Derek, and his wife, Liz. I had kept in touch, so he was aware I had married Amina. He probably had a preconceived idea about her, as no doubt all my ex-workmates had. I was so proud of her; I suppose it was some sort of vanity driving me to show her off as a prize. I also wanted it to be known that I had done well.

We met one evening for a drink at a local pub. I can honestly say I didn't expect the reaction I got from them. Derek was really taken aback and seemed a little nervous when he introduced himself and his wife. He was talking slow and deliberately in his Pembrokeshire accent as though he thought Amina wouldn't understand. He was naturally shocked when she spoke so clearly and confidently with a better command of the English language than his own. I noticed how Liz looked at her; maybe she was trying to work out how old she was. We got on well and didn't talk about old times very much, as they were more interested in what it was like in Aleppo.

"I can't wait to tell the blokes at work," Derek said as we were leaving.

"There's someone else I want to tell," Liz said, giving me a wink and a knowing smile.

Over the coming years, Helen and Paul joined us twice for holidays; they enjoyed the different culture here, to begin with, as everything was vastly different. The novelty did wear off as they came in the scorching hot summer months; the absence of swimming pools or beaches may have been a possible reason. They were at the age where friends of their own age were more enticing.

Amina did join me one more time on short breaks in Wales; as Amara and Amal got older, she decided to stay at home and care for them.

Amina would often tell me that Helen had phoned during the day and relay what she said in detail. I am not sure that I was told everything; I thought maybe Helen was using her as a big sister and phoned when she presumed I wouldn't be there. I called Helen and Paul once a week to catch up and ensure they were both okay. The conversations mainly were regarding how well their studies were going.

I realised it was vital for me to see them in person as often as possible, so once a year, I took a break in Pembroke when work permitted. It became apparent that they had a lot going on in their young lives, so I saw them often, but not as much as I would have liked.

* * * * *

One of the memories that still sticks in my mind is our first visit to Broadhaven Beach with Amina. The weather in West Wales was often a bit hit and miss, so the locals made the most of it when the sun shone. My kids were no different. With the promise of a warm, sunny day, we agreed on a trip to Broadhaven Beach. It required a bit of organising: windbreaks, towels, food, drink, and beach toys had to be packed and carried some distance to get to the best spot.

"I'm in charge," Helen announced excitedly. "I'll pack the towels, sun cream, etc. Paul, you are responsible for entertainment. Dad, you are responsible for food, drink and carrying anything heavy. We girls are responsible for enjoying ourselves. After we have been for our swim and got dry, we expect the food and entertainment to be ready and prepared by you men. That's correct, isn't it, Amina?"

"Yes, of course," Amina replied meekly. "I will just watch you swim, as I have no costume."

"No problem. I have plenty. Pick one of mine," Helen said with enthusiasm.

"The women in Syria bathe fully clothed alongside the men wearing swimming trunks," Amina said quietly.

"Surely not! It's so hot in Syria, and you can't swim fully clothed, can you?"

"I wouldn't know. I have never been swimming."

"There's a first time for everything," Helen said happily.

"Can I just watch, please?" Amina begged.

"No way! You have to join in the fun."

Helen managed to coax Amina to try on one of her more modest one-piece swimming costumes. I knew that this was a big step for Amina, not to be fully clothed in front of people. On the day, she was openly nervous and wore the swimming costume under her clothes. Helen persuaded her to borrow a pair of jeans and a T-shirt. Getting her to wear them was difficult. Helen pointed out that she would blend in with the crowd more. Amina looked utterly different in Helen's clothes, and I noticed she spent a lot of time in front of the mirror. I think she was trying to justify why she was wearing clothes that showed off her feminine shape. I'm not sure if she liked what she saw; I definitely did. Amina drew the line at wearing shorts like the rest of us but appeared pleased that she had agreed to wear Helen's clothes. We parked in the car park overlooking the beautiful bay. We stood for a while, admiring the view and selecting a quiet, wind-protected spot.

"It's so beautiful and clean; nothing like the beaches in Syria."

"What are they like in Syria, then? With all that sun and sand, I thought that they would be lovely."

"The coast is only about 100 miles long, and the beaches are horrible. They should be beautiful but are spoilt with litter and not suitable for bathing."

My favourite memory of that day was the three of them walking down the beach to the sea in their swimming costumes. They walked into the water, holding hands, with Amina in the middle, placed there by the kids on purpose to stop her from escaping. Then suddenly there was an almighty shriek. Amina turned around towards me. I was some distance away, waiting in anticipation.

"Really, you can't be serious?" she screamed.

"Don't be a wuss," I shouted, waving my hands in a pushing movement indicating she should follow the kids. They were already swimming and shouting back to her.

Amina stood like a statue, confused. "I'm a wuss? What about you?"

So I ran into the sea to join them, splashing as much water as possible, trying not to show the shock as the freezing cold water hit my body. "This is lovely, isn't it?" I shouted.

"No, it's not; it's bloody freezing," Amina shouted.

"Language," I admonished, laughing.

I coaxed Amina deeper into the sea, trying not to show how cold I was. "It's lovely once you get used to it," I encouraged.

We gently walked into the sea up to her chest height. "It's lovely when you get used to it? How long does that take?" Amina asked sarcastically.

Then a rolling wave crashed into us, knocking her over and almost submerging her. The kids were swimming around us and splashing in an attempt to encourage her fully into the water. I tried to encourage Amina by diving under a wave. She was unconvinced, so we all raced out of the sea and wrapped ourselves in towels.

"Why did you leave this for Syria?" Amina queried through chattering teeth.

At the time, I thought she was being sarcastic about the weather and the cold sea. I later learned that she was really struggling to understand why I had given it all up. As the holiday drew to a close, Helen and Amina were spending more and more time together. Helen was intrigued by Amina's eyes, make-up, clothes and dress. Likewise, Amina was just as fascinated by Helen's clothes, jeans, blouses and casual look. Amina's clothes were elegant, long and covered most of her body. Sometimes they would come downstairs in each other's clothes, giving us a fashion show. For some reason, to me, they both looked better in each other's clothing, perhaps because I had not seen either dressed that way before. Helen tried to appear to float gracefully across the floor when dressed in Amina's clothes, but couldn't quite pull it off; it was hilarious to watch. Both the kids tried to sit and rise from the floor in one graceful movement like Amina, which was hysterically funny. Sitting and rising just using the balance of your arms seemed alien to us. Yet old and young in Syria managed it effortlessly. The kids persuaded Amina to cook a typical Syrian meal. Though the ingredients were not going to be identical, we did our best to find substitutes.

"If we were going to eat Arabic food, it should be as authentic as possible," Amina insisted.

That evening, we all dined on the floor around many dishes, eating only with our right hands. That was funny too. I told the kids the best way to do it was to sit on their left hand.

Before we left for our home in Syria, they told me they both liked Amina, which really didn't need saying as they got on so well together.

Helen asked, "Would it be possible for we to join you for a short holiday soon?"

Paul joined in and said, "Me too. I would love to come."

Amina replied, "That would be lovely, anytime. Just let us know when."

I looked at both of them and asked, "What would your mum say?"

Helen replied, "Dad, she has changed quite a bit; it shouldn't be a problem." Paul nodded in agreement.

Amina butted in and said, "That would be great; you will be able to see your sister and brother in the flesh."

I said, "When you know when, just let me know, and I'll book the flights and visa. That's settled, then."

"You're a lucky man, Dad," Helen whispered in my ear when we hugged.

Paul talking to anyone was a novelty; he openly showed his approval of her by talking to Amina. I was delighted at how well the visit had gone; not only had they accepted Amina, but they had accepted me too. We said our goodbyes in the Arabic way, kissing on both cheeks. Paul had to be coaxed but shyly managed it.

Chapter 22

Returning Home

"I could live here," Amina said as we drove to Heathrow for our return flight to Aleppo.

"Why, what's changed your mind?"

"I feel safe wherever we go; nobody is watching or judging me. I feel like a bird let out of its cage, its freedom. That's what I feel; freedom. Not being watched and judged continually. What I wear and how I behave is up to me. I don't have to conform to someone else's standards, and I can be myself."

"I thought you were happy in Aleppo."

"I thought that I was but coming here has made me realise how different life could be. Women have no say in Syria. Everywhere here is clean and not littered. The way you socialise freely is different. I love the country pubs where friends congregate. I love the shops, the restaurants; everything is better here. In Syria, a woman's word is only worth half as much as a man's. A woman is a possession of a man, either her father or husband. Here, women are equal, have equal rights."

"That was one hell of a rant, but some are more equal than others," I said when I could eventually get a word in.

"I know that. I'm not talking about being rich or poor; I'm talking about how women are treated, that's all."

"Women complain in the UK as well; you should know that."

"Well, they ought to spend time in a Muslim country and see the difference."

"Amina, I thought that most of the women in Syria seemed happy."

"Allan, how could you possibly know that? Have you had a conversation with them?"

"I suppose not. Are you happy?"

"I'm happy with you because you treat me as an equal and always have, but that's not the point. Outside our little group of friends, it's completely different."

"We are going to be all right, aren't we, Amina?"

"Of course we are, don't worry."

The journey home went without incident, but somehow things appeared different to me.

Chapter 23

Aleppo: Discussion with Ali August 2012

We were growing more concerned about the conflict in Syria escalating so quickly. To begin with, we thought that things would settle down in a short time, but the opposite was happening. It wasn't just the government against the rebels, as Russia and Iran backed the Syrian government. The rebels were supported by Turkey, the European Union, the USA, a 'mixed pot' of different countries, ethnicities, religions and castes, all with their own agendas. The 'mixed pot' had boiled over, and now the lid was off: the conflict was spilling everywhere, and friends were now enemies.

Over dinner one evening with Ali and Margaret, Ali explained how the conflict was escalating. He had heard through the grapevine that rebel commander, Abu Bakr, was determined to overthrow President Bashar-al-Asaad. As radical allies joined Abu Bakr, Ali was becoming increasingly alarmed.

Ali heard Abu Bakr making a public address. He said, "My fighters are Islamists; the fighters joining us are too extreme. All they want to do is blow everything up.

My goal is to make a new future, not to destroy everything. Some fighters who have come to Syria believe in jihad, holy war, have links to al-Qaeda, and just want a Syrian base."

"Not only are fighters flooding into Syria, but money, too," Ali explained. "Millions of dollars are coming from other pro-Sunni governments, and there is a drive to form an Islamic State. Hardened fighters from Iraq and Afghanistan are creating their commands. It's a real mess. There are twelve different commands, some working together, others trying to gain control. The local people joining the fight often don't know which command they are under. I am frustrated watching the old and new Aleppo being systematically destroyed, but what can we do?"

"It makes no sense to me, and why can't everyone see what's happening?"

"It's being done in the name of idealism or fundamentalism, but whatever name you give it, it's a crime against humanity."

"Neither side is innocent," Margaret joined in. "What a bloody mess."

"There are too many sides," Amina said. "It's got entirely out of hand. Nobody can win; it's not a game. There's no referee, no full-time whistle. The game will only end when they run out of players."

"I couldn't put it better," Ali agreed. "It's an almighty mess whichever way you look at it. Do you know that the government and allies have started barrel and cluster bombing their people, destroying everything? They are targeting residential areas where some rebels are enclaved with complete disregard for the innocent men, women, and children slaughtered."

"Bloody hell, how will it end? Somehow it has to stop, and soon," I said.

"The latest tactic, known as double-tap, is to bomb an area, wait until rescue workers, medics, and others appear, and then strike again. Ambulances and hospitals are the targets. The real heroes are the rescue workers, doctors, nurses; the people who just want to help those in need." Ali looked into our faces solemnly before speaking again. "I cannot take the side of the Syrian Army anymore. Nor be a rebel, and fight against my government, old compatriots or my people, and I cannot just stand by. I must try and do something."

"What can you do?" Amina asked. "You are only one man."

"I have spoken to Raed Saleh; he has formed a national defence team to operate in opposition-controlled areas within Aleppo. They're former teachers, engineers, firefighters, and tailors deployed to help innocent people trapped in the conflict. These volunteers are not mercenaries but a non-profit organisations. I have no children, no family, just Margaret and my friends."

"I want to help as well. I don't know how exactly, but if Ali is helping, I will too."

This was the first time I had heard Margaret speak entirely with gravity, with no flippant remarks; she looked steely serious, and we all went quiet. Amina and I were shocked and didn't respond at first.

"I have volunteered to help with the injured by doing anything I can."

"Is there anything we can do?" I asked.

"Your circumstances are completely different for various reasons, and to be blunt, you will be of little use anyway. You have no training or experience or witnessed the brutality of war. I doubt you could handle the constant terror of being bombed or dragging bodies from the rubble, or even worse, incomplete bodies of screaming women and children. You have no physical fitness or resolve. I doubt if you would last a day."

"Bloody useless, you mean," I said, annoyed by his weak portrayal of me.

"Honestly, yes. There are other reasons, though. You are obviously not an Arab or a Muslim, which would be a red flag to some rebels. You also have a family to consider, and Amal would be a target, as he is obviously mixed-race. Captured radicals would execute him."

I was getting more frustrated by the picture Ali was painting of me and my situation. "What is there that I could do? There must be something?"

"Yes, there is something you can do, and that is get your family out of this mess. Leave Aleppo. Leave Syria. Take your family back to the UK. Protect them; that is your duty as a father."

"Just like that, up and leave our home, lives, and friends? It's not that simple, is it?"

"No, it's not simple, but it's doable; of course, you could stay here and watch everything you own destroyed, including your family. The choice is yours. Stay and be a hero and lose everything you hold dear, or get them to safety."

"What are the risks, Ali? Tell me, as you know everything." I said sarcastically.

"I can help with the plan, but the sooner you act, the better. There is no way to estimate a timeline for anything at the moment."

"Okay, Ali. If we agree to your plan, give us an idea of what is on your mind."

"Well, unlike most of those fleeing Syria, you have the advantage of holding EU passports, which should make it easy at border controls. That's a good start. In a day or so, I should be able to work something out."

Ali and I met a couple of days later; Ali roughly explained the complications involved. "Your safest way out would be seeking help from the Kurds. The Kurds are fighting against the Syrian government and the Islamic State, helped by the Americans and European countries. However, there is a slight problem. Your route out of Syria to the Turkish border is through areas occupied by ISIS. Turkey is an ally of the West but has been fighting against the Kurds long before the Syrian war. So the way out would be to seek help from the Kurds, who will transfer you to American forces to guide you safely to the Turkish border. That border should not be a problem as you have European passports."

"Ali, there is a problem regarding Amina's passport. Her visa has expired."

"No problem. Give it to me; it will be renewed tomorrow."

"How can you do that so fast?"

"Don't ask. It will be genuine, okay?"

Ali's plan was for us to seek the help of the YPJ, a female Kurdish defence unit based in Jindires. He contacted Rojda Felat, the senior commander, through his secret service contacts and explained our position, and she had agreed to help. He had chosen the YPJ because they were all female, made up of different ethnicities and religions from all over Syria. They were persecuted by other regimes; crimes against them included rape, torture and genocide. All the Kurdish forces were well-disciplined, but the female branch of YPJ was even more determined as they had personally been affected by their enemies. Once we reached their protection, we would then be handed to the American Army, who would make sure we had a safe passage through the war zone. The route Ali had selected was Aleppo, Jindires, then through the Turkish border to Gaziantep. Once we had reached Gaziantep, we would be safe and treated like any other tourist in Turkey. The plan was then to drive along the Turkish coast to a small fishing port called Kas.

Ferries sailed from Kas to a Greek island called Meis; the journey would take about thirty minutes. The ferry was known as the Meis Express, which went across daily. Many passengers travelled to get a Turkish entry visa stamp on their passport, allowing them to stay in Turkey for three months. He told us this because the ferry was always busy, and we should blend in with the tourists. None of this should concern us, as our Turkish visas would be obtained at the Syrian border with Turkey. We would stay in Meis until we caught a ferry to Rhodes. From then on, the journey would be easy as we would be travelling as EU citizens for the rest of the trip.

The other option was to fly out from Antalya, but that would mean going through customs. It probably wouldn't be an issue, but Ali thought it would be more prudent to take the easiest, no-questions-asked route onto UE soil. Ali explained he could only plan a little ahead as the situation was very fluid. As long as we were careful and, inshallah, we would be okay.

I discussed the plan with Amina when the kids were asleep, so she would be fully aware of the route if anything happened to me. Amina phoned her parents the following day to tell them of our plan. She wanted their approval as a dutiful daughter and out of respect for them. Amina enquired about their safety; they told her everything was fine, like always. I couldn't help but think they would say that regardless. Amina probably thought the same thing. For Yoran and Souzan, it would be losing their daughter again and also their grandchildren. Hopefully, one day, we would all be together again.

Once the plan was in place, I contacted Helen and Paul to explain what was happening and told them not to worry. They were both becoming increasingly concerned about our situation. They were probably more in the know than we were due to the media coverage in the UK. I told them we were leaving Aleppo soon, and would shortly confirm our flight to the UK.

I also wondered whether Ali was being cruel to be kind. Was he deliberately overstating how useless I was? Forcing me to protect my family's safety? Regardless, I believed it was the best option for us, and Ali was correct to be so brutal about my worth. He spoke out of friendship, not out of malice, and he was probably right about me not being suitable for the horrors ahead of them.

Chapter 24

Escaping Aleppo, August 2012

Once all the plans were in place, we moved as fast as possible. We packed the petrol-engined Toyota SUV with everything we required, with the help of Ali and Margaret. Ali's final instructions were in the form of a list of names, maps and contacts who could help us. His final advice was to stick to the D850 highway and not deviate from it for any reason. The journey to Jindires would take two hours, and his latest intelligence was that it was safe. He warned me not to stop for anything, even an injured child or beggar, as all may not be as it appeared. No matter how tempted we felt to help someone in distress, it might be a trap. Others escaping would do anything to steal your car, food, money or possessions. People were desperate, and some might be ex-fighters. Ali told Amina and the children to sit in the back and cover themselves with blankets, so they were not visible. There might also be sights that would frighten them. The Islamic State and other radicals liked to show their atrocities to encourage others to conform. He also warned me that the ISIS flag might be displayed even though they had moved on, so I needed to be careful. He thought of offering me a handgun for protection, but it would not be wise unless I could use it. I was untrained in killing another human being, so he decided against it

"Once you point a gun at someone, you cannot hesitate, which is how you get killed," he said.

According to Ali, 2am was the best time to travel. We settled the children in the back of the car and said our farewells to our best friends. We hugged and kissed each other as Arab friends do. We all promised to keep in touch. We would meet up again when it was all over.

We made our way out of Aleppo and were soon on the D850 without any trouble. What I witnessed was a mass exodus of young and old fleeing the war zone of Aleppo. Only a short time ago, these were the people who had homes and livelihoods, albeit without prospects. What they had now was nothing but to hang onto life and protect their families as best they could. I reduced my speed as I navigated through the mile after mile of refugees and vehicles overloaded with what possessions could be squeezed in. Others were carrying or pushing their possessions in wheelbarrows, prams, bikes and anything else they could find. As we drove through the hordes of refugees, we had to ignore the children begging for food, their hands thrusting towards their mouths, indicating they were hungry. Some of these children wore blue school uniforms implying they were from the more wealthy population. I wondered how many I had met and exchanged pleasantries with within the souqs such a short time ago. I felt anger against the ruling government for doing this to its people and how the world watched and did nothing. Anger against allies of the Syrian government and those that had joined the protest against Assad. It was no longer the citizens of Syria protesting against Assad's regime. The wealthiest countries in the world had joined both sides of the conflict, along with radicals and mercenaries. The losers in this were the ordinary people who just wanted a little more. If they had realised what they were getting themselves into, they would have probably preferred the status quo.

As I continued to drive, there was clear evidence that it was a war zone. Destroyed military vehicles littered the road, along with possessions of those fleeing and the stench of rotting bodies. I prayed, not to a god, but to myself, that we would make it through safely. The children were fast asleep in the back of the car. Amina was lying down with them, though not sleeping. She kept asking me what I could see. I told her that everything was fine. To tell her the truth was too distressing to me, and it was better she didn't know. I was petrified and hoped she couldn't detect the fear and uncertainty in my voice.

Roughly an hour into the journey, I came to a road section littered on one side with wrecked vehicles. There was only just enough room to squeeze through. I recalled what Ali told me about not stopping for anything. So I drove as gingerly as possible without stopping until I saw a child lying on his back on the road in front of me. I couldn't tell if he was alive or dead. I couldn't run over a dead animal, let alone a child. I wound down the windows to see and hear better as I brought the vehicle to a stop. I couldn't hear or see anything unusual and left my sidelights on to illuminate the road in front.

"What are you doing?" Amina shouted from the back.

"Sorry," I shouted back, "I have to stop."

"Please don't!" Amina pleaded.

"I have to. Cover yourselves up. I'm getting out."

I got out of the car and walked carefully toward the child. As I got close, he opened his eyes. I knew in an instant that something wasn't right. Before I could move, three fighters appeared from behind the wreckage on the right-hand side of the road, with rifles pointing at me. One had hold of me before I could turn towards the car. The other two opened the back of the Toyota. They dragged Amina and Amara out roughly and forced them against the wrecked vehicles. One fighter held the barrel of an automatic rifle under my chin. At the same time, the other two began to remove clothing from the girls. The fighters were laughing and groping them.

I couldn't understand what they were saying. I knew exactly what was going to happen but could do nothing. Amal was now standing next to me. I could feel him leaning into me, his face buried in my back. I could hear him sobbing. Then I felt something hard and heavy forced into my hand; I realised it was a pistol. What I did next was automatic; I had never fired a gun before in my life. I raised the pistol behind the soldier's back, pointing somewhere close to the back of his head and pulled the trigger. There was an almighty bang as the fighter fell to his knees, then a flash and another bang almost simultaneously. The recoil almost broke my wrist. The two fighters turned and faced me. They moved away from the girls, reaching for their weapons on the ground. I held the pistol in both hands, pointed at one of them, pulled the trigger, bang, and then again at the other, and pulled the trigger, bang; both fighters fell to the floor. They were both screaming; blood was pumping out of their bodies. I ran to the girls and pulled them away. I threw the fighters' weapons into the desert. I pointed the pistol at one of the heads of the prone soldiers but couldn't pull the trigger. I remembered what Ali told me: I couldn't do it when it was a choice.

Taking someone's life or losing my own wasn't the option I was presented with; it was protecting my family, and my actions were completely automatic. I had to get my family away as quickly as possible. I bundled them into the back of the car and drove as fast as I could. None of us spoke. The reality had shocked us into silence. After a while, I started to tremble uncontrollably and felt nauseous. I knew I had to put as much space as possible between us and what had just happened, so I fixed my eyes on the road with my foot hard down on the accelerator. I was sweating profusely, yet I was shivering at the same time and felt physically sick. My shoulder was stinging. I put my hand where it hurt, and it felt wet. It was as though I had been kicked by a donkey.

"Pass me a scarf," I asked Amina.

"Why?"

"Just pass a scarf; I'm bleeding."

Amina passed me the scarf. I realised that there was nothing I could do without stopping.

"Amal, climb into the front!"

"Okay, Baba," my son replied.

"Fold the scarf into squares and push it under my shirt. Press down as hard as you can."

"Okay, Baba."

I could feel Amal's hand very gently and nervously do what I asked him. I felt almost instant relief. I could move my arm without any problem. It seemed that I hadn't been badly hurt.

"How did it happen?"

"I don't know," I said. I might have been shot, but I didn't want to alarm the others.

I wound down the window to see if that would help; as I did, I could hear sobbing from the back of the car. I shut the window and began thinking about what had happened. I was trying to make sense of it. My first question was where the gun had come from. It kept coming into my mind, and I couldn't think of anything else; although I didn't want to upset my family, I needed to know now, so I broke the silence.

"Where did the gun come from?"

Amina, still sobbing, spoke first. "It's mine; I brought it."

I tried to control my anger. "Why didn't you tell me you had a gun?"

"Because you would have taken it off us."

"Why, Amina, didn't you tell me?" I repeated, raising my voice slightly.

"Sorry: we all decided not to because it wasn't for you."

"But you still brought one; why?"

"It wasn't for you to use."

"Who was it for then?"

"It was for Amara and me."

"What for?"

"Our protection. I would have used it, to protect us."

"You don't know the first things about guns!"

"I didn't until Ali showed me."

"When did this happen?"

"One day, when you were at work, Ali took us to a quiet spot and taught us."

"Do you think you could have used it to kill another person?"

"If need be. I will do anything to protect my family. I would even kill Amara to protect her; it would be simple to kill myself then."

"You didn't think to tell me, did you? Why not?"

"If I had told you, we would all be dead. You would have got out of the car just now with a gun in your hand; how long do you think you would have lasted?"

"Bloody hell! Whose idea was this? You said 'we all decided'; who is 'all'?"

"You are not going to like this; Ali and Margaret convinced us it was the right thing to do."

"So you did this behind my back! Bloody hell! I don't know what to think. I thought that I was the head of the family."

Amal spoke for the first time and said the most profound thing. He stopped me in my tracks. "If you knew, there would be no family. We knew that, so we never told you."

"I have never fired a gun before, and I hope I never have to again. It was so easy; that's the terrifying thing," I said.

"I have. All of us have. Uncle Ali showed us. He also told us it's a deadly weapon, to be careful, never to point it at anyone. Never to remove the safety catch unless we intended to use it."

"Amal, you took the safety off before you handed it to me?"

"Yes, Baba. If I hadn't, we would all be dead now."

"I am completely lost for words; I am so proud of you all, but angry at the same time."

"Baba, we hoped something like this wouldn't happen, but if we hadn't gone behind your back, we would all be dead now, or even worse."

"I know, I know," I said.

I would have to come to terms with what I had just done. I knew Ali was right. If I had approached the fighters with a gun in my hand, we would probably all be dead now; his decision had saved us.

Chapter 25

YPJ (Women's Protection Unit), 2012

We managed to reach Jindires without another incident. I was now looking for the YPJ green triangular flag with a red star, and soon one came into view. It was now approaching dawn, as the journey had taken longer than expected. I thought it prudent to wait until sunrise before approaching the YPJ base camp. I desperately wanted to get us all to safety.

"Amina get a shirt from my bag," I asked.

"You are a lucky man," Amina said, looking at my wound as she removed my shirt. "It's just a nick; it looks like the bullet grazed the top of your shoulder."

"What bullet?" I asked neutrally.

"Do you think we are thick?" she asked.

"Sorry."

Amina made a clean pad from the tail of my shirt and used another scarf to hold it in position. "There you go, as good as new," she said, kissing me on the cheek. "My hero."

The wait for sunrise seemed to take forever; Amina and the children were frightened and repeatedly asked me to drive closer to the camp. I was also scared that we were being watched by others but knew it would be wrong to approach in the dark. At daybreak, I gingerly drove the vehicle towards the entrance. I heard a shout in Arabic and asked Amina what they wanted. Amina translated.

"They want to know who we are and what our business is." Amina got out of the car and shouted back at them in Arabic. "We are friends of Ali Mansour and have permission to speak to Rojda Felat."

"Get out of the vehicle, remove all excess clothing and bags and leave them in the car," the guard shouted.

I told Amal, as he was getting out, to put the gun under the seat. Once out of the car, a guard shouted to us. Amina told us to unbutton our clothes and pull them over our heads, then turn around. The guard called again. Amina told us to turn around, face the car, put our hands on the bonnet, and spread our legs. Two guards walked over and frisked us from head to toe. Then we were told to walk towards the camp entrance and were met by two female YPJ soldiers. I felt instant relief as we entered the camp, hoping that we were in a safe place at last. I thought, *inshallah*, but my family responded with, 'inshallah', so I must have been thinking aloud.

I was surprised by the camp's size. I was expecting a small gathering of tents, with the odd building. The base was more like a small town with elevated lookout posts and giant satellite dishes pointing in every direction. The first impression was of an orderly and competent barrack town. Everyone we saw was dressed correctly, was clean and appeared to be going about their duties in a soldierly manner. Female soldiers flanked us and led us through the camp into a room where another female soldier joined us; above the door was a sign in Arabic. It took me a little while to work out it was a motto, which, in English, said 'Know yourself, protect yourself'. The soldier questioned Amina, and she answered to her satisfaction. Then the soldier's tone became softer as the children were chatting openly with the other soldiers. We were led into another room where we were served chai, bread and honey, and told to rest.

Later, I was escorted to see the camp commander, Sewsen Birhat; the children and Amina were left happily talking to the soldiers.

"Haven't you got something to tell me?" were Sewsen's first words.

So I gave her the information Ali had provided, confirming that Rojda Felat had agreed to help us.

"Are you friends with Ali Mansour?" Sewsen Birhat asked.

I thought for a while before answering, unsure if this was a trap. My contact was Rojda Felat, and Ali was once a captain in their enemy's army.

"Please answer my question," Sewsen Birhat said sharply.

"Yes, we are close friends," I replied, still not sure if it was a good idea to admit to this.

"Thank you, that wasn't hard, was it? How is my friend, Ali?" she replied.

"Good, very good, in fact." I still thought it might be a trap.

"You look nervous. Don't worry. I know Ali very well."

"Sorry, Ali told me to be very careful, and my contact was Rojda Felat."

"She is my senior officer. I was expecting you, don't worry, you are in good hands."

"Thank you, I was a little worried. Ali is fine, and now a member of the National Defence Team, he has left the Army."

"Yes, I know; he is one of the good ones. You haven't answered my first question: haven't you something to tell me?"

"About what?"

She then held out her hand. A soldier placed a pistol into it. "About this?" she asked.

I realised that it was our pistol she held. "It was for our protection."

Sewsen then removed the bullet magazine. "It looks like it did that," she said, smelling the barrel and counting the rounds left in the clip.

She looked at me for my reaction. I wasn't sure who the fighters I had shot or whose side they were on but decided to answer, "Yes, it did."

"Why are you hesitating to answer my questions? It would benefit us all if you just responded to my questions honestly and without delay."

"Sorry, yes. I did fire the weapon," I said, not knowing the consequences of my answer.

"So it was you. I thought as much; only a bloody amateur could have done that."

I felt guilt and shame at the same time. "How do you know that?"

"We had troops scouting for rebel soldiers; sorry, not soldiers, 'vermin' is a better name. They heard gunfire and went to investigate. It was a mess when they got there: one rat was dead, and two others were bleeding to death. My soldiers cleaned up the area, made sure it was safe and dragged the wreckage off the road to avoid a similar ambush."

I felt a sense of relief that the fighters were the enemy. "Thank you. I just had to get my family away. That was the only thought I had."

"Why did you stop the car and get out?" Sewsen quizzed.

"Because there was a child on the road."

"He was not a child; he was someone trying to kill you and your family. You should have accelerated and got out of there as fast as you could."

"I didn't know, did I? I thought he was a refugee," I replied angrily.

"Didn't Ali tell you anything?"

"Yes, he told me not to stop for anything."

"Yet you did exactly the opposite; if you were in the same position again, what would you do?"

"I can't imagine running over a child."

Sewsen looked at me with incredulity. "We are going round in circles. It was your decision; your family or him."

What she just said was true and shocked me. "If only I'd been given that choice," I said.

"That's why you shouldn't be in a war zone. Soldiers are trained to respond to situations automatically. Making choices gets you killed."

"It all happened so fast. I didn't have time to think."

"Exactly! You didn't, but, luckily, you're alive, inshallah. Why didn't they search you for weapons?"

"They did. I didn't have any."

"Was there someone else there then?"

"No, no one else."

"But you did fire the gun?"

"Yes, I did; Amal handed it to me."

"Where did Amal get the gun from?"

"I don't know; I suppose it was in the back of the car somewhere."

"So they left Amal in the car."

"Yes, maybe because Amal is a child, maybe because he was of no interest to them."

"No, the reason was they were unprofessional. Their minds were on other things. It didn't matter if he was a child; everyone should have been in clear view. Our soldiers would never have made that mistake."

"I noticed when we arrived here that you treated everyone the same. I thought it was a bit over the top, searching the children, but now understand."

Sewsen seemed to be growing a little annoyed now. Her words were less patient. "Just tell me what happened!"

She wanted to hear everything that had happened from the moment we stopped. She commended Amal's bravery and pointed out that Ali had been with us in spirit through his thoughtful planning in advance. When I'd finished telling her, she told me what would have happened had I not used the gun.

"Your wife and daughter would have been brutally raped several times. You would have been forced to watch, and then they would have brutally killed your son in front of you. Then they would have killed you, making your wife and daughter watch. Your wife and daughter would have been used for their pleasure for as long as they survived."

I was glad that my family weren't in the room with us. I was now crying and shaking uncontrollably.

Sewsen ignored my state and continued. "Most of the soldiers here have been through similar things; they cope with it in their own ways. They have in common that they do not regret killing those who killed and tortured their families. To them, it's a duty but never a repayment for their loss; it has become a way of life. They are not seeking justice or revenge; they just want to rid the earth of the vermin who do these things as quickly and cleanly as possible."

I sat there for some time afterwards, reflecting on what I had just been told. Coming to terms with my own actions and the fears for my family would be difficult. I would never share my conversation with Sewsen with any family member.

"I will get a medic to look at your shoulder."

"Thanks, but it's stopped stinging now."

"We will soon change that," Sewsen said, smiling. "One more thing that might make you feel better – the vermin you shot but didn't kill were terminated by our soldiers. They believe being killed by a woman in battle is a disgrace and prevents them from entering paradise. So our soldiers ensure they are seen whenever we carry out this task; it's a little reward for them."

Sewsen was saddened hearing what was happening in Aleppo but was keen to move on to our escape from Syria. "It will not be a simple task to get you safely through the Turkish border. You will have to wait until an appropriate opportunity arises."

She instructed two soldiers to take us to our quarters, which looked like it had been someone's home. We were made to feel as comfortable as possible and treated well but were always under observation. A soldier stood outside, which I presumed was standard procedure. The children were an attraction for the young women soldiers. Some were only a little older but had seen and experienced things no human should. They came from all different parts of Syria, and not all were Kurds. They held a mixture of faiths, but what drove these women mainly was revenge for what had happened to their families. Although they had survived, they had been bargaining chips, sold as objects to be used, forced into marriage, given as gifts or just abused.

When the children were asleep, the women often talked openly about their abuse, the dreadful atrocities they had witnessed and their revenge on the perpetrators. Surprisingly to me, their revenge was simple; it was to remove the abusers from the face of the earth, not to inflict the atrocities they had endured on their enemies. Doing so would make them no better than them. They treated their abusers like a disease that necessitated removal in a simple clinical manner. I am sure that their male counterparts would not be so lenient. They would seek to punish the crimes that had been imposed on their loved ones and families brutally and with pleasure. I learnt that they were more feared than their male counterparts as they would never surrender as they knew what would happen to them was far worse than being killed in action. I didn't mention to any of the female soldiers our recent experience, as it was insignificant compared to theirs. However, hearing their stories helped me come to terms with my own actions. It convinced me that killing the fighters on our escape from Aleppo had been the best outcome. They could no longer do to others what they were prepared to do to us without a second thought. My mindset changed; I had saved lives rather than taken them away; I could live with that.

We became attached to a young Yazidi soldier named Narin. She reluctantly told us that her younger brothers and sisters were butchered by ISIS, along with her mother and father. ISIS spared her because she was at the age of maturity, so she could be used for pleasure. Her experience was more brutal than most. The Yazidi people are considered devil worshippers by ISIS because they are not Muslim and worship a different god. Narin was traded and abused several times until she managed her escape and joined the YPJ. Although Narin had been through so much trauma in her young life, she still retained her love for life like many YPJ soldiers. She particularly liked to be around Amara and Amal; we often found them talking. I don't know what they were discussing, but I felt sure it was pleasant and had nothing to do with the war.

On the second night, sudden ear-piercing bangs woke me from sleep, followed by flashing lights and an air raid siren. The door to our room was flung open.

"Taharuk alan!" shouted a soldier loudly.

"Move now!" Amina shouted.

We followed the soldier out into the night; it was like daylight with the tracer mortars exploding above, illuminating the area. I felt we were totally exposed and being watched from above. Running as fast as we could, holding onto each other, we were shoved through a door and scrambled down some steps.

"Salama," shouted the soldier and held out a flat hand, ordering us to stay. We were inside an underground bunker with facilities enabling us to be comfortable for some time. We could hear the muffled sounds of explosions, and the ground shook slightly.

"'Salama' means safe," Amina said. "We should get as comfortable as possible."

We made ourselves comfortable on bunk beds. I drifted to sleep as Amina told the children an old Syrian folk story. We were roused the following morning by a soldier who took us to the canteen. On the way, it was evident that buildings had suffered at the hands of the attackers. We could smell burning and explosives, and there were whiffs of smoke still hanging in the air.

The canteen was full of the female soldiers breakfasting as though nothing had happened. I thought to myself that if they were men, a lot of bragging and back-slapping would be happening. The kids spotted Narin and made their way to where she was sitting; she invited us to join her.

"What happened last night?" I asked Narin.

"The usual," she replied. "ISIS are stupid. They attack us at night, thinking we cannot see them, but as soon as they fire a mortar, we can trace it immediately to the source of where it came. They then move to a different position and fire again, but we trace their new position. We then contact the Americans who send up night drones to the locations and strike out the mortar firing position within minutes. It's so easy."

"You have that technology?" I asked.

"Mortar tracing is old technology, not new," Narin replied.

"Live and learn. I didn't know that."

"The new technology is the drones. The Americans have them, but we can watch the action as they relay the pictures. Now that's fun; we can see them before they strike."

"Modern warfare, I suppose. Soon we will have robot wars," I said as a joke.

"We then send out a team that cleans up the area, ensuring everything that could assist ISIS in the future is destroyed, including men. A robot can't do that yet."

Narin was relating her account with no pride in her voice or manner, as were the other female soldiers. It was just good housekeeping, getting rid of dirt and trash, and making the place clean again.

I recalled what Ali had said regarding the YPJ, that they would be our safest bet for finding a route out of Syria and how right he was. The more we mixed with the YPJ, the more respect we had for them. They were doing so much to rid Syria of ISIS, yet the Turkish regime despised them. This made no sense to me as their goals were the same. The Turks were open regarding their hostility to the Kurds and had, over decades, tried to remove them from the face of the earth. We needed to rely on the Turks to help with our safe passage out of Syria. I expected that we would find them as accommodating to us as the Kurds.

Commander Sewsen told us that American intelligence collected information after every attack. Narin hadn't told us the cleaning-up procedures but said they were very thorough. From the dead fighters, they retrieved equipment, munitions, maps and any information that could be useful.

I met the intelligence officer, Captain Gene Werner, later that day. He was short, stockily built, smartly dressed, and spoke with a typical southern American drawl, as though he was half asleep. His drawl was accentuated by the large unlit cigar in his mouth.

"Well, I guess we better get you guys out of jail pronto," he said.

Having worked with similar Americans, I realised little thought had gone into his offer. No doubt he would have little involvement in the task ahead but would hand us to someone that would.

The following day, Sewsen informed us that a small convoy was passing through to the Turkish border, and we had clearance to join them. There was a risk of an attack, but it would be much safer than making the journey on our own.

Chapter 26

Turkey, Here We Come

On the evening of the third day, we said goodbye to the female soldiers in the canteen. We couldn't thank them enough for the way we had been accepted amongst them. The children were openly upset to leave Narin. We all hugged and kissed cheeks, knowing that we would never meet again. Amara and Amal, for the first time in their short lives, showed genuine compassion for another person. I realised they were growing up.

"Could we take Narin with us, please?" they begged.

"No, we can't," I stressed. It was impossible.

"Why? It's not fair," Amara said, sulking.

"I'm sorry; it's just impossible," I repeated, "and, yes, it's not fair."

The children were sad to leave a friend behind, not knowing what her fate would be. I hoped the traumatic event of leaving the only home they knew and witnessing the exodus would not affect them badly. Amal, younger than Amara, didn't have the same sense of danger and was excited more than scared.

Sewsen introduced us to Sargeant Wayne Brantley the following morning. Unlike Gene Werner, he was young, handsome, tall, well-built, and wore full camouflage.

He made a very imposing figure, exuding confidence. He seemed to be a proper soldier, I thought, experienced, efficient and confident. Wayne explained the situation in precise staccato sentences, which were easy to remember, like orders, I suppose.

"Keep close, keep your position," Wayne ordered. "When we move, you move. When we stop, you stop. Watch everything we do; you do the same, okay? It's only a short run, so we should have you across the border in forty-five minutes. Any questions?"

"Which border crossing are we using?" I asked.

"Zeytin Dali Kapisi, which in English translates to 'Olive Branch Gate'. I'm glad somebody had a sense of humour. Once through the gate, you are not absolutely safe, but we will escort you to a place called Kirikhan, and from there, it's a piece of cake."

Wayne couldn't resist ruffling Amal's hair, who was looking up at him in complete awe as though he was a comic book hero. I noticed Amara blushed when Wayne looked in her direction, and I smiled, realising she was growing up.

"Sync your watches; we're pulling out in twenty minutes," Wayne instructed.

I drove our car to join the convoy, and Wayne pointed out my position in the centre, flanked on either side by two M1117 sand-coloured armoured vehicles. Real boys' toys, I thought, bristling with equipment, machine guns and other tools of war.

"Maybe the kids would be safer in one of the armoured vehicles," Wayne suggested.

Contemplating Wayne's offer, Amals's face lit up. It occurred to me that adults love to see children's excitement when doing daring things. I suppose we never grow up; we are still kids in some ways.

"Can I, Baba, can I please?"

"You sure?" I asked Wayne.

"Come on, buddy," Wayne confirmed.

Amara looked excited but embarrassed. She shook her head to decline the offer, deciding to stay close to her mama. Maybe being so close to young men was a new experience for her, or perhaps she was shy.

The armoured vehicles had the Stars and Stripe's pendants flying from them. I pondered whether this was a good idea as it clearly displayed who we were. The engines started up with a tremendous roar so that I couldn't even hear my SUV. I felt insecure wedged between two large, powerful, noisy vehicles.

We drove for about thirty minutes and couldn't hear or see much due to the engine noise and the dust created by the armoured vehicle tyres. Both the armoured vehicles were slightly in front of us; we were level with the rear of the armoured cars and straddled the whole road. From a distance, the Toyota wouldn't have been visible; we couldn't see anything ahead or behind. In the Toyota, we communicated to each other using our hands and mouthed words, like, *can you see anything?*

Suddenly, the vehicle on the right side jumped in the air, followed by a flash and loud bang. The other armoured vehicle stopped, and, remembering our orders, I stopped too. Then came the ear-shattering noise of machine guns and the whistling of bullets ricocheting off the M1117s on either side of us. My first thoughts were that Amal was in the vehicle that jumped off the ground. Concern for his safety was all I could think about; 1

couldn't see what was happening but could hear the crew of four in the left-hand vehicle shouting and giving orders. Amina and Amara were lying on the floor behind the front seats, not making a sound. The noise intensified when the M1117 on our right started firing. I could hear the sounds of muffled explosions some distance away. After a few minutes, silence fell and I could feel my heart pounding. My family was in real danger again, and there was nothing I could do but put my trust in others. Thankfully, I could hear American voices outside the vehicles, moving away from the convoy. About ten minutes later, our Toyota's front doors were opened by a couple of American soldiers.

"Keep calm; everything is in hand. Get out of your car now," one of the soldiers whispered.

"Is Amal okay," I asked.

"Amal was in the vehicle with me when an IED – that's an improvised explosive device – hit us," he replied.

We watched as soldiers lifted Amal out of the vehicle. He lay motionless on the ground between the two armoured cars. Amina and Amara were crying.

"Is he injured? Is he okay?" I stammered.

We all knelt around him. Subconsciously, my first aid training kicked in, although my hands were trembling. He was breathing very fast.

"Do you want to move over, buddy?" Wayne asked.

"No, I'm fine, thanks," I replied.

"You sure?" Wayne asked again.

"Yes," I responded curtly.

I checked for the critical signs. Amal's heart rate was rapid and his breathing was erratic. He was in shock, so I checked his limbs and body for damage. His shirt was blood-stained on the right shoulder. I carefully removed his shirt and could see that his right clavicle had broken through his skin; the white bone was clearly visible.

"Wayne, do you have a first aid kit?" I asked.

He had already removed one from one of the M1117s and passed me some gloves and disinfection swabs. I cleaned the wound, covered it with a dressing and loosely bandaged the shoulder; Wayne gave me an arm sling which I managed to secure.

"Please tell me he will be all right," Amina said with tears rolling down her cheeks. She knelt down beside him and kissed his cheek.

"We have to get Amal to hospital now. He could have internal bleeding," Wayne said. Wayne ordered two soldiers to wrap him in a blanket as carefully as possible and place him on the Toyota's back seat with Amina and Amara.

"The closest hospital is the Special Sciences Hospital in Kirikhan. That's across the Turkish border. I'll guide you from your passenger seat."

Wayne ordered the crew of the undamaged M1117 to follow us as fast as they could. Once we started moving, Wayne barked his orders at me as though he was ordering one of his own soldiers. "Drive as quickly as possible, avoid any potholes, and don't wait for the M1117 behind, okay?"

Chapter 27

Kirikhan, 2012

The road surface to the border was good, with few potholes, enabling us to make good time. We were only a few minutes from the border crossing. From my rear-view mirror, I could see the M1117 had disappeared into the distance. When we arrived at the Olive Branch Border gate, the guards seemed to be waiting for us and waved to indicate there was no need to slow down.

"That was easy, wasn't it?" Wayne said. "I'm glad I told the crew of the damaged M117 to radio ahead, so the guards knew we were in a hurry."

A few minutes later, we arrived at the hospital in Kirikhan. The porters and nurses were ready with a trolley. We followed the nursing team into the emergency room, and they told us to sit in the waiting area, except for Wayne, who went with them into triage.

After about an hour, Wayne emerged from the triage room and told us what the nursing team had diagnosed so far. "He's in shock, with a snapped clavicle and still unconscious," Wayne reported in a matter-of-fact military manner.

"He's going to be okay, isn't he?" Amina asked, choking with tears.

"He's had a full MRI scan, and there were no issues found, just broken bones," Wayne added in the same neutral tone. "The clavicle will be pinned as soon as he is stable."

"What did they say about the shock?" Amina asked.

"That's pretty normal; we see it all the time. I'm sure it won't be an issue. Also, don't worry about the bill because Uncle Sam will be picking it up. We have a tit-for-tat arrangement with the Turks; we look after their casualties, they look after ours."

"How come only Amal got hurt?" I asked.

"Everyone was strapped in as normal, including Amal, but unfortunately, the seat and straps were a little large for his small frame. The force of the blast forced him through the straps. His helmet stayed on because we altered it for his head size. His earmuffs weren't in place, though, when we recovered him. As their name suggests, IEDs can be like a volcanic eruption, depending on the number of explosives available and how well they're constructed. Someone knew what they were doing with this one," Wayne explained, as though reading from a training manual.

"Was it a big one, then?" I asked.

"Well, the design of the M1117 defeats most IEDs due to the extra armoured plate underneath. The one we encountered today was large enough to lift the vehicle off the ground." Wayne hesitated. "The force was enough to knock the wind out of us; we were disorientated for a few seconds."

"What would have happened if I had run over it?"

"Well, if a flimsy Toyota had run over it, there would have been nothing left. The IED wouldn't have lifted your car but blown it into smithereens; the remains would have been scattered across the desert with no survivors."

Knowing how close we were to being killed made me feel physically sick. I realised why Wayne had formed the convoy in the way he did and why he had encouraged the children to join them under the protection of the M1117.

After a couple of hours, an elderly doctor came to talk to us. He spoke good English and seemed very caring. "Amal is stable and comfortable. Inshallah. I will operate tomorrow morning. Go find somewhere to rest and come back in the morning."

He gave us the name and directions for a hotel he recommended and suggested we return at about 10am in the morning.

We stood outside the hospital for a few moments, thanking Wayne. I suddenly realised that we were in Turkey without any visas. We had rushed through the border to get Amal to hospital. "Wayne, we have no visas!"

"No problem. Book into the hotel tonight, and your passports will be collected and stamped tomorrow. Don't worry; leave it to me. It will be fine."

Wayne was the sort of person who you felt confident would do something if they said they would. We waved as he roared away with his crew in the M1117, confident the visas wouldn't be an issue. We booked into the local hotel recommended by the doctor, tired and dusty. We showered and ordered a meal in the room.

The following morning, we walked the short distance to the hospital. A porter directed us to the operating theatre waiting rooms. The elderly doctor we met the day before joined us and told us that Amal was prepped for the operation. We needed to sign consent forms so the procedure to fix his clavicle could go ahead. He told us it was a simple operation, and the outcome should be good.

As we were signing the forms, the doctor continued with his diagnosis. "Your son has other issues; the blast from the explosion has affected his hearing."

"How bad is it? Will he get better?" Amina asked,

"I don't know. It's not my domain. He will see an audiologist tomorrow. Don't worry; it's all arranged." He beckoned Amina into the theatre prep area, saying, "Come, please."

On her return, she had tears flowing down her cheeks. She nodded that she was happy and embraced Amara and me.

After a couple of hours, the doctor reappeared to give us a report on the surgery. He said to us, "All has gone well." Then he indicated to Amina and said, "Please come."

A few minutes later, Amina came out of recovery, smiling.

"How is he, Mama?" Amara asked.

"Sleeping like a baby."

Impatiently, Amara asked, "Did he see you? Did he wake up?"

"No, he looked so peaceful; they were about to wake him up and asked me to leave."

The following day we met a young female doctor who introduced herself to us as the audiology consultant. Again, she explained the reason for Amal's hearing loss in perfect English. "The damage is within his cochlea affecting the basilar membrane."

"How serious is it? Is it repairable?" I asked.

"There's a lot of research into blast damage as it's prevalent in war zones. It is curable; the treatment is antioxidant drugs, and the success rate is reasonable. However, some of his hearing registers may not return. It's mainly his high hearing register that is affected, but the prognosis is promising. It should be okay, but it takes time to heal."

"How long will the treatment last?" I asked.

"It depends because your son is young. He will adapt and maybe not notice the damage as the very high register is rarely used. If you want to speak to me at any time, just ask reception for Nehir Avci, and I will try my best to respond."

We felt more optimistic about Amal when we left the hospital than when we arrived. We found a little locanta close by, where we had lunch and discussed the next steps in our journey. Time wasn't a pressing issue, so we decided that as long as it took, we must make the best of it, no matter what.

We returned to the hospital and checked at the admissions desk the whereabouts of Amal. The clerk told us that he was out of theatre recovery and on Ward 4, and we could visit him. Amal was sitting up in bed, looking confused. He seemed to have recovered well from the operation. His right arm was in a sling bound very tight so as not to allow movement. The three of us waved at him and called his name as we approached his bed, Amal look puzzled. The ward sister joined us and again spoke perfect English. "The operation was a success; he will be a little sore for a while and is receiving medication for his hearing loss but is still confused."

"Was it due to the explosion?"

"You could say that it's a mechanism the brain uses to block the memory of trauma sometimes. He will probably never remember what happened. Inshallah."

Amal cupped his free hand behind his ear when we spoke to him, indicating he couldn't hear. We tried mouthing words and waving hands to convey to him what had happened and what was happening to him now. Amara pulled a notebook and pencil out of her bag. She drew a picture of an armoured vehicle blown up in the air, and the border crossing, to illustrate where we were now. Amal drew on the pad with his left hand a barely distinguishable sketch of an ear and a question mark. In reply, Amara sketched a glass of water, a pill, followed by an okay. Amal put up his thumb to show he understood. I thought using a pencil and paper to converse might make it difficult for them to bicker. I smiled, and Amina did too.

"You must go now. Amal will need plenty of rest. You can come back again at 10am and again at 4pm tomorrow," the ward sister instructed.

We all kissed Amal goodbye and waved as we went.

"How long will he be in here?" I asked the sister on our way out.

"Only a couple of days, as far as the surgery goes, but they might want to do further tests on his hearing, which would be as an outpatient."

When we got back to the hotel, we were handed a package by a male receptionist. Inside were our stamped passports, a letter from Wayne wishing us good luck and a small parcel for Amal. We were still keeping in touch with Ali and Margaret and Yoran and Souzan. We didn't mention the incident with the IED; we told them that everything was fine. I wondered if they were shielding us from bad news, but kept my thoughts to myself. That evening we went out to a local restaurant called Iskenderun Citir Doner, a typical Turkish doner kebab diner. I asked Amina before entering the restaurant if it was all right.

"'Iskender' translates to Alexander. He governed most of the Middle East thousands of years ago. I think around 300 BC."

"We really needed to know that?" I asked.

"I hope the food is still fresh!" Amara quipped.

"The food probably is, but it might be the same old menu," Amina replied.

It was a small restaurant with eight tables, mainly offering kebabs, pide, rice, chips and salad. After we had finished our meal, the waiter gave us a complimentary drink of raki and water. As the glasses appeared on the table, other diners joined us without being asked. Within minutes they pushed their tables and chairs to make one large table. The Turks turned out to be friendly and tended to ask questions that I would find rude of a stranger, but they meant no harm. Curiosity seemed to be a part of their culture. Some could understand English, and they translated the conversation for those who couldn't. After the translation, they appeared happy, taking sips of raki and tapping our glasses with theirs. I thoroughly enjoyed the evening and found their curiosity amusing and not rude. On leaving, we all warmly shook hands and shouted 'gorusuruz', which I later learnt meant 'see you again'.

"That was a lovely night, wasn't it? It reminded me of Aleppo," I said to Amina when we were back at the hotel.

"Me too, but I wouldn't call it lovely," she responded.

"Whatever do you mean?"

"It was just the same as Aleppo: all men, no women. Where are the women?"

"I suppose you're right; where are the women?"

It made me think of Aleppo, and she was right. It's always the men socialising. I thought it must be an Arab thing, then I remembered Greece, and it was the same there: cafés full of men. I recalled Amina talking about the lack of freedom for women in Syria. Thinking about this concept, I recalled the Coventry working men's clubs; they were also men only! I kept these thoughts to myself; discussing them with Amina and Amara would not go well. They assumed the UK was a fair society; I knew it was more equitable, which was not the same thing.

We visited Amal the following morning. He was now on the children's ward and sitting up in bed, waiting for our arrival, his arm strapped to his shoulder. We handed him the fresh fruit we had purchased on the way in, which he delved into immediately. While he was chewing on an apple, we gave him the package from Wayne.

"Can you open it," he asked Amina.

His only free hand was engaged in its most crucial task, filling his mouth with food. His face lit up when he spotted the contents; a T-shirt and baseball cap, both with the badge of the 30th Armoured Division. There was an official letter with the heading of the 30th Armoured Division, awarding Amal a special award for bravery in action. The apple was discarded immediately, while Amal inspected the gifts from Wayne. His face showed how pleased he was with a beaming smile, and he kept repeating, "Wow, wow." Holding them up to show us, he demanded we help him put them on. The other children in the ward watched the boy soldier wearing a baseball cap and T-shirt with envy.

* * * * *

Kirikhan was not a pleasant place to be; it was a typically unloved Middle Eastern town. Every building appeared to be a run-down shop or business. The unmaintained pavements were a hazard; each step needed to be taken gingerly to avoid potholes and wares stored outside the buildings. The roads were littered with piles of firewood, building material and household trash waiting for collection.

"It's definitely not a tourist attraction," I told Amara and Amina. They both laughed.

"Let's hope we're not here very long," Amina said. "I feel everyone is watching me because I am not wearing a hijab."

"It's strange that all the men are wearing Western clothes, isn't it?"

"Different for men and women, as usual."

"I hate being stared at; it makes me want to take off my head covering, just to show them I don't care what they think."

"Me too," Amina said and smiled at Amara.

"Grin and bear it; it's not for much longer."

* * * * *

We were hoping that the Nehir Avci would give Amal a clean bill of health and permit us to continue our journey soon. The ward sister had already told us that his shoulder injury would not prevent him from travelling. As long it was strapped up until fully healed, which would be in a couple of weeks. We arranged to meet with Nehir to discuss Amal's prognosis so at least we could look forward to moving on.

"Amal is still partly deaf," Nehir explained.

"For how long?" Amina interrupted.

"The healing process will take time, and there is no benefit to him staying in hospital longer than required. I am happy for him to leave now."

"Do you mean now, this minute?" I asked.

"Let me continue; please, be patient. I will make sure Amal has enough medication to last two weeks: tablets, ear drops and earplugs that must be worn at all times. So if you come back tomorrow morning, he can leave afterwards."

"Sorry for being impatient," I said.

"That's all right. I understand. It's normal. I'm used to it. I will prepare a letter explaining the current treatment for his next doctor."

We thanked Nehir for all she had done in the usual way and kissed her on both cheeks.

"Just doing my job," she said. "I'm glad I could help."

"The people are so nice here, aren't they?" Amara said as we left the hospital.

"People are the same everywhere, well, mostly," I replied.

Chapter 28

Adana, Alanya, Antalya

We collected Amal from the children's ward the
following morning, and he said goodbye to his
new friends. Amal was wearing the oversized T-shirt and
baseball cap Wayne had given him. His new friends
looked a bit jealous of what he was wearing, or maybe
the nurses had told them of his adventurous journey and
what was about to come. The sister gave us Nehir's letter,
the medication and a copy of the x-ray of his shoulder.
We were amazed to get such good treatment in such a
run-down town. We thanked everybody involved and
made our way out of the hospital to continue our journey.

The original plan was to drive to Gaziantep and then
onto Antalya and Kas as the roads were better. We decided,
after studying the map, that the coastal highway to Antalya
was far more scenic and exciting. Though slower, there was
a better chance of finding accommodation as we were
travelling through holiday locations. I had calculated that
the driving time was about sixteen hours in total, which
would take a couple of days. So we continued our
adventure with no definite plan and decided to go with the
flow and stop where it took our fancy, giving us a feeling
of freedom. We had a target destination of Adana for our

first stop; an easy route on the D400 highway. We were driving with mountains on our right and the coast on the left. The scenery was breathtakingly beautiful, so the time disappeared quickly. It wasn't long before the car's motion induced the kids into sleep. Amina was nodding off every now and then. She probably hadn't slept much over the last couple of days from worrying over Amal.

We arrived in Adana in the early afternoon. We booked into the first hotel that took our fancy, an Ibis hotel, which surprised me. I had stayed in Ibis hotels before in the UK and found them very basic, but this was completely different. The rooms were plush, with comfy beds and luxury bathrooms, and the staff were pleasant and attentive. The town of Adana was cared for and looked inviting, so after booking in and making ourselves comfortable, we decided to walk outside, sightseeing like typical tourists. We had an early evening meal as we had an early start the following morning. The kids had never been inside a large holiday hotel before and were very curious, looking everywhere and asking questions. The waiter guided us to our table, handed us all a menu, and asked if there was anything he could get us while we waited.

"Could we have the cocktail menu, please?" Amina asked, giving me a cheeky grin.

"Memories," I said.

Amina nodded coyly.

"Yuck," Amara said. Then she asked her mother, "What are cocktails, for heaven's sake?"

"Wait and see," Amina teased.

"Would that be one with alcohol and three without?"

"No, two of each, of course," she said and then added, "to begin with."

We had a typical tourist Turkish meal of rice, chips, and kabab, followed by baklava. Amina and I finished the meal with brandy and Turkish coffee. Amina couldn't resist telling Amara how the word cocktail was derived.

Amara started to talk seriously about what she knew of Syria's problems, and I realised that we had never openly discussed the situation in Aleppo with the kids. As the conversation continued, I realised that Amara knew more than I thought and was not talking like a child but like an adult. She understood and had her own opinions of the crisis and conveyed them with thoughtful intelligence. I glanced across to Amina and could see the pride she was showing for her daughter.

"I've just witnessed the moment a child becomes an adult," I commented.

"It doesn't happen overnight, you know," Amina said, smiling at Amara.

That night, after we had prepared for bed, I indicated to Amal to take out his earplugs so that his mother could administer the eardrops. I stood behind him and shouted his name to see if he could hear me. He turned towards me.

"Did you say something?"

I nodded to indicate yes. "What did you hear," I shouted.

"My name, of course, and there's no need to shout so loud."

Amina grabbed him and gave him a big hug. "Inshallah," she said with tears in her eyes.

After a typical Turkish breakfast, we left Adana for Alanya. We all admired the scenery, which was forever changing and utterly different to Syria.

The driving from Adana to Alanya was reasonably straightforward. We all agreed that the mixture of travel and rest the previous day was just about the correct blend. We found the constantly changing arable scenery was entirely different from Syria and far more interesting, with so much more to see.

As we approached Alanya, the road skirted the coast, where the best hotels had access to the beach and ocean views. I pulled into the first one that caught our attention, the Kahya Hotel. The kids were excited as not only was there a beautiful beach but also a magnificent swimming pool. They couldn't wait to get booked in and get to the swimming pool. They could both swim as it was part of the curriculum at school. I had to tell Amal that he was only allowed in the paddling pool.

After we booked into our rooms, we went down to the hotel foyer to buy factor 50 sun cream for me and swimming costumes for all of us. Amina and Amara were looking for modest one-piece swimming costumes. They were few and far between; most of the costumes were bikinis with tiny thongs, which puzzled them. Amina had seen similar bikinis in the UK but would never wear one. Amara couldn't believe anyone could wear them in public and why anyone would want to. Eventually, they found a couple of suitable costumes. We changed in our room. I covered my milky white torso with factor 50 sun cream and we all wore the complimentary bathrobes and slippers to the pool. We strolled out onto the swimming pool patio, looking for somewhere to sit together. Simultaneously we all froze in disbelief.

Everyone was topless; men, women, young, old, fat, thin, beautiful and ugly. All were showing as much hideous, oil-covered flesh as possible, basting in the sun for the perfect tan. Some looked like overweight blubbery seals, others like overcooked chickens; it was not a pretty sight.

To me, it looked like a reasonably typical poolside scene at any Mediterranean hotel. People from countries with limited sunshine make the most of the opportunity to soak it up. A stark contrast to the grey waxen corpses I witnessed outside Aleppo. I knew which one I preferred.

Amina shook her head and glared at me angrily, as though it was my fault. "No way! We are not staying here. Come, we are going to the beach now!"

She waddled off like a mother goose and we followed behind like obedient goslings. She did a quick left turn out of the pool area, and we all dutifully followed behind her. It was a similar scene on the way to the beach, with naked flesh everywhere. Amina turned left or right quickly, avoiding looking at the overcooked torsos sprawling on beach towels in her hunt for a quiet spot.

"Don't look for somewhere too quiet as you might be even more shocked."

"What do you mean?"

"I noticed Germans when booking in, and they like to display all of their magnificent bodies, and I do mean all."

Amina stopped in her tracks and glared at me with irritation. "You don't mean bloody naked, do you?"

"Yes, but they do hide behind rocks, but the male of the species has a habit of jumping out when approached, displaying their magnificent dangly bits."

Amina pulled a face indicating disbelief whilst scrutinising the area. "That's disgusting," she uttered.

"This is far enough," she decided and plopped herself down on the sand in one graceful movement, claiming the spot.

"What is it with them? Why don't they display modesty? I don't want to see their revolting naked bodies."

"Turkey is a Muslim country, isn't it? Why does the government allow such immoral behaviour?" Amara asked thoughtfully.

Amina nodded in agreement. "Two days ago, I was stared at for not wearing a hijab," she said.

"It doesn't make sense; it's the same country, so why are the rules so different here?" Amara replied.

"Money rules," I replied.

"What has money got to do with it? It's just common decency," Amina retorted.

"The holidaymakers come here because they can do as they please," I explained.

"You are implying that the government cares more about money than decency?" Amara asked.

"In a nutshell, yes."

Amina was getting very cross. "You haven't explained why they have to be indecent."

"They don't think they are being indecent. Apparently, wearing no clothes is a liberating experience."

"I can see that," Amara said thoughtfully, "but not in public; they are forcing their nakedness on us."

"Okay, I agree, but if the government forced them to conform to your standards, there would be fewer tourists. This part of Turkey relies on tourism, so they allow them to behave differently. But what is weird is that the tourists don't behave this way in their own country; it's a holiday thing."

"Two wrongs don't make it right," Amina said, concluding the conversation.

That evening we had a lovely meal in the restaurant in a quiet corner by ourselves. Amina was still cutting up Amal's food in what I would call the American style. Knife and fork crisscrossing the meal into small pieces, so he could only eat his food one-handed with a fork or spoon.

"Don't the diners look different with clothes on?" Amara said cheekily. "I can hardly recognise anyone. Some now look almost normal."

"Imagine it! Yuck; it would put you off your food," Amina said.

I looked around the table at my family. I realised that this journey would be an education for all of us, especially the kids. I had already noticed a change in them as we seemed to form a tighter bond. The kids were becoming more assertive and provoked conversations by making sense of their new experiences. Leaving Syria and all the Muslim restraints, which they hadn't realised they had, would be an education in itself and provoke many questions.

We agreed to set off after breakfast and not stop at similar hotels but drive straight to Kas, avoiding as many tourists as possible, and possibly stop for a break at a taverna or restaurant. Our journey to Kas took longer than we thought. The road was winding, and the agricultural traffic moved very slowly along it. So, we decided to stop in Antalya, the largest town we had visited in Turkey.

Antalya was a mixture of old and new. The older part was mainly where the locals lived, and the new part mainly for tourism. The contrast between the two was massive; the older areas were like Kirikhan and appeared to be run-down and uncared for. The people were dressed similarly, too. The new areas were glitzy, with magnificent hotels and restaurants dominating the town's coastal side. Tourists walked around partly dressed; women were almost topless, scantily dressed in beach clothes. Most of the young men wore shorts only; it was the first time the kids had seen body tattoos, mainly on the men.

"Why do they write on their bodies? Does it wash off?" Amal asked.

"I don't know why, and it is permanent ink," I replied.

"Do you know what the largest organ of the body is?" Amina asked.

"The lungs," I replied confidently.

Amina laughed at my stupidity. "Wrong again; it's your skin."

"Can you poison yourself by injecting ink into an organ?" Amara asked.

"Yes," I answered, "but there are strict rules to ensure that doesn't happen. However, there are a few cowboys out there."

"Can we stop for a break but not in the tourist area or the run-down bit either," Amina suggested. "There must be a nice place between the two where normal people like us are walking around, modestly dressed."

I decided to drive away from the coast and found a local souq in an area that looked all right. It was similar to what we had become accustomed to in Syria. The souq reminded us of Aleppo, as it had a fish market with stalls on the perimeter selling fresh fish. When purchased, a stallholder delivered your selection of fish to the restaurant of your choice to cook. The restaurants were in a circle inside the perimeter of the stalls. They were all vying for business and promising good prices. We all selected a fish, sat in the chosen restaurant and decided on our side orders. It was the best meal we had eaten since leaving our home in Aleppo and so cheap.

The restaurant was quiet and not used to foreigners frequenting it, so it wasn't long before the curious Turkish waiters joined us at our table. Once again, they asked questions we might consider rude at home, but which were considered good manners. They wanted to know where we had come from and where we were going. Why Amal had his arm in a sling. Why was he wearing earplugs? Where did he get his cap and T-shirt from? Where were we from? Where were we going? They seemed genuinely interested in our answers.

When we questioned where they came from, one of them said, "Turkey," but added, "not Turkish." He proudly hit his hand on his chest. "Kurdish!"

Moving his arms in a circular motion, another said, "All Kurds here."

Proudly, the others nodded.

"On our travels, we have met many Kurdish people; they were always kind and considerate."

They shrugged in agreement. "Of course, Kurds, good people!" one of them said.

"Is there a small hotel close by where we could stay the night?" I asked.

The Turkish Kurds proved to be as helpful as the Kurds we had already met.

"Come," said one of the waiters.

We followed him through narrow side streets to a small traditional pension a short distance away from the souq and our parked car. A Turkish lady dressed in traditional Kurdish clothes greeted us with 'iyi aksamla'. She escorted us to a clean, bare room. I said, 'Iyi', accepting the room was good, and left to collect our overnight bags from the car while the others rested.

While I was away, Amina phoned Margaret to let her know where we were and how things were going and check that she and Ali were okay. When I returned, Amina told me everything was fine with them and not to worry. When we talked with them on the phone, they always said everything was fine, no problem. But we both knew they were probably telling us what we wanted to hear. The most important thing was that we stayed in contact.

As the journey should now be without worry, I had less on my mind to keep it occupied. I found this to be problematic. I felt guilty for not having had enough courage to remain in Aleppo. I knew in my heart that having a family was a convenient excuse for not staying. Even without responsibilities, I would have fled the war, and I knew it. I knew this would always trouble me. As I grew older, it would become more challenging to justify my choices.

"You would have stayed and helped alongside Uncle Ali if it wasn't for us, wouldn't you, Baba," Amara often asked.

"Yes, of course," I always replied, knowing this lie would haunt me later.

Since leaving Syria, getting my family to safety has occupied my mind. But I knew that Ali, Margaret and Amina's family would start to trouble me once we were safe in the UK. The guilt that I did not dare to stay and fled instead would be an issue hard for me to resolve.

In the morning, at breakfast, the landlady greeted us with a beaming smile. "Gunaydin," she said, "Turkish breakfast, okay?"

"That would be lovely," I said.

A young man was running from the kitchen to our table. I presumed it was the son of the landlady. He loaded the table with butter, cheese, yoghurt, honey, jam, jambon, figs, dates, fruit and different types of bread until the table was covered; they beat us into submission with food. He then placed a frying pan filled with freshly fried eggs before us, and we raised a white flag in surrender.

"No more, please," I said, pointing at my stomach and placing my hands in the air.

The lady and the young man stood in front of us with beaming smiles, as victors do.

"Kurdish breakfast cok guzel?" she said with pride.

"Evet, cok guzel," I said.

We left Antalya, following the winding coastal road towards Kas, driving past beautiful empty beaches and bays on our left, fields and typical Ottoman homes on the right. We discussed the experience so far and the different cultures in Turkey and Syria as we went. It was interesting to hear the kids' interpretations as the experiences were new to them. In Syria, they had learnt that the Turkish people were terrible and Kurds even worse, but they found them very friendly and pleasant and liked them.

I asked the kids whether they had changed their minds about anything. "For instance, the Kurds are hated by most people throughout the Arab world. What do you think of them?"

"I think the kindest, nicest person I have ever met was Narin. I know she is not Kurdish. She had been through so much herself but always put others first. I want to be like her one day," Amara said, sighing.

"I hope you don't have to endure anything like she has," I said.

Amina changed the subject and started telling the kids what Pembrokeshire was like, as though she had always lived there, and I didn't attempt to correct her. She talked about what she had experienced through her eyes.

Though not wholly accurate, I found her interpretation amusing and couldn't resist saying, "Amara, on our journey back to Syria from our holiday in the UK, your mama said she had thought she was happy in Aleppo. But then realised she wasn't, after visiting the UK."

"Yes, I did say that because it opened my eyes to a better life. A female is treated as an equal there and not a possession."

"It's going to be better for me from what Mama experienced. I will have more freedom, won't I?" Amara asked.

"Yes, you will have more freedom, and it will be better as you are so intelligent; the education system is equal for boys and girls."

"Your baba thought all the people in Aleppo, regardless of faith, caste or wealth, respected each other."

"Well, that's how it appeared to me."

"But it couldn't be further from the truth as they live in fear of each other. Your baba may have been shown respect, but that is not the same thing at all. Generation after generation bred hatred mainly through superstition.

They don't mix or intermarry but keep their distance and tolerate each other out of necessity."

"Everyone I met was polite; that's all I could go on," I replied,

"It was in their interest to be polite; they do not treat each other the same, couldn't you see that?" Amina answered, a little irritated.

"No, not really, because they were all friendly with me." I paused, hoping to end the discussion. "They were a lot happier then than they are now, and they probably wish things were as they were."

"The Arab Spring lifted the lid off a boiling cauldron of fear and hatred. They no longer had to tolerate each other but instead reverted to what they had learnt from the past generations, and that was hate," Amina argued.

"I honestly believed they were as happy as anyone else I met."

"The hatred is mainly a man thing. The women of Aleppo or any other Syrian town are kept entirely separate from the men, except within their families, of course. In the souqs, how many women did you encounter working there?"

"Honestly, I never thought about it, but I suppose none."

"That's correct! None! Women are treated as possessions, not equals. They have no say or opinions. If they do, they keep them to themselves. For all the years you spent in Syria, getting to know people, finding them pleasant, and enjoying mixing with them, they hid the hatred between themselves pretty well, didn't they?"

"Yes, they did, and I still count these people as true friends, and I couldn't take sides with any of them because they all treated me the same."

"The problem with your baba," Amina said, addressing the children, "is that he sees things through rose-tinted spectacles, not as they really are."

"Kids, please remember this conversation when you realise that things in the UK are not exactly equal either, or as your mama sees them."

Chapter 29

Kas, Meis

We drove around Kas searching for somewhere to stay and found Bougainvillea Boutique Hotel at the top of the town on a hill overlooking Kas. The hotel façade was covered with bougainvillaea, interlacing the ornate, white Creole-style wrought ironwork which covered the reception door.

"It looks lovely; this will do," Amina confirmed.

"It looks worth a try, doesn't it? Shall I book us in?" I asked them.

"Yes, please, this will do," Amara's half-asleep voice pleaded from the back of the car.

"Amara, are your eyes open or shut?" I queried, tired too. It had been a long day.

"Whatever," came from the back seat.

Unfortunately, the rest of the hotel's name bore no resemblance to its description. 'Boutique' translated into tiny, quirky and uncomfortable. We were only staying for one night, though, so we decided it would do because we were tired and grumpy. The bedrooms were tiny, the furniture was sparse, the beds uncomfortable, and the shower was minute, but we made the most of it. Amal and I showered first while the girls had refreshments at the rooftop bar, which overlooked the pretty town of Kas and the enclosed harbour. While the girls showered and made themselves ready, Amal removed his earplugs to test his hearing, as he often did.

"It's better," he said, "a bit fuzzy, and I can hear ringing all the time, but it's worse with the plugs in, as the ringing is constant."

"It sounds like tinnitus to me. Remove the plugs; other noises should compensate for the ringing, and you shouldn't notice it as much."

"Will Mama tell me off? You know what she's like for following rules."

"She probably won't notice and if she does, blame me."

Eventually, the girls arrived, so we both mimicked that we had fallen asleep by closing our eyes and snoring. "Is it morning already? Amal said.

"You should say how nice we look rather than make sarky remarks," Amina retorted.

"I'm hungry, and you know it makes me grumpy," Amal replied.

"You're always hungry; what is it with boys?" Amina said while looking at me, indicating she meant me as well.

"Come on, the two most beautiful women in my life, I'm starving, and that also makes me bad-tempered," I said, smiling at both of them.

We had a quick meal at one of the harbour bars. Amal and I left the girls at the bar while we went to the Meis Express booking office to check the ferry schedule. Captain Osman Muslu greeted us, and we enquired about a one-way trip across to Meis and the Rhodes ferry timetable. Osman was amiable and spoke perfect English. When he realised that the journey was only one way, the typical Turkish curiosity kicked in, so we had to relate to him the story of our adventure so far. Osman genuinely appeared concerned about the Syrian war.

"We are all Muslim: refugees are fleeing Syria like yourselves, attempting the same route, but, without money, passports or paperwork, they have little chance."

"Yes, I know. We saw thousands on the road, some walking, carrying everything they could."

"I feel sorry for them, but there was nothing I could do but turn them away."

"It really was a pitiful sight," I recalled our journey to him, though only a brief account.

"Just outside of Kas, there are camps of refugees living in tents, women and children mainly, and a few men. Their situation is desperate, and each day it gets worse as more arrive."

I planned to leave the Toyota in the harbour car park with the keys and paperwork inside with a note reading 'finders, keepers'. Still, after Osman told me about the refugees' plight, I thought it would be a kind gesture if the vehicle could help those in most need. It could help in a small way if I gave the car to them, as we couldn't take it with us. We could also leave anything we couldn't take with us in the car. The vehicle and contents might help someone, making me feel less guilty that I hadn't been able to help before.

"Would it be possible to leave my car and some superfluous possessions to the refugees?" I asked Osman.

"Legally, it's difficult, as all vehicles sold have to go through a 'Noter' in Turkey. The seller and buyer must sign a transfer, and a Noter must witness the transaction."

"All the paperwork is in the car, in my name, and notarised in Syria. The green insurance paperwork is there too. I can leave a letter for the 'Noter' and a copy of my passport. Would that do?"

"Not really," Osman replied, "but let me think for a few minutes. Meet me in the Zuhutu Meze Cocktail Bar at about 9pm. I will make a few phone calls, and we will see what can be done."

We met the girls back at the restaurant and went over the discussion with Osman.

"The bad news is that we have to meet him at the Zuhutu Meze Cocktail Bar shortly."

"That is terrible news," said Amina sarcastically, "and what are cocktails?"

"Mama, not again," Amara said.

"The timing is good for us as it will give us plenty of time to get rid of unwanted baggage we no longer require. That means one suitcase each, only, please. Be ruthless. Remember, most of your clothes will look out of place in the UK. We can replace things bit by bit as we go along, okay?"

"Okay," Amina and Amara replied at the same time with tired voices.

We met Osman at the bar as arranged. He was with another man who introduced himself as Sener. "Sener will be able to help, maybe, as he is a Noter."

"If you get all the paperwork to me at 9am in the morning, I will draw up a power of attorney, naming Osman as the new owner. Documenting that the sale proceeds will be transferred to the Syrian refugee charity."

"That sounds good, so the money will be shared amongst the refugees."

I bought another round of drinks so we could toast the deal. We had an enjoyable evening talking to Osman and Sener; the cocktails helped loosen all our tongues. We told them about our friends, Ali and Margaret, still in Syria, saving lives. Osman raised his glass to the National Defence Team as he proudly toasted them. I noticed tears in Osman's eyes; he was a caring, honest man.

"Gurusus," we called to them in Turkish as we left.

"Iyi akshamla, gule gule," they replied.

We replied, "Goodnight, goodbye."

We all were up early in the morning after a poor night's sleep on very uncomfortable beds. We breakfasted on the hotel's roof terrace, from where we could see the Meis Express pulling out of the harbour on its first trip of the day. The previous evening, we had learnt from Osman that there was a duty-free shop on Meis. Some passengers were not nipping across just for a visa but also to purchase tax-free goodies, mainly booze.

I met Sener in the morning as arranged at the Noter office. Osman had already signed the power of attorney papers. Sener took photocopies of my passport and all the other documentation as proof of ownership of the car. I wrote and signed a letter regarding the proposed donation. Thanking Sener for his help induced a feeling that this was another step towards our new life. Strangely, getting rid of possessions can bring an emotion of freedom, like removing shackles. It was one more step, one less worry removed, and I started to feel we were so close now to our new life.

Approaching our hotel bedroom door, I could hear raised voices.

"You don't need that," Amina was shouting.

"You don't need that, either, Mama," Amara was yelling back.

I opened the door to see a pile of clothes littering the beds and half-full suitcases. Amal was sitting in a chair in the corner of the room, his small bag packed beside him. Amal's mouth was half-open. He had a look of amazement on his face, which I had never seen before.

"What's going on?" I asked.

Amal threw his arms upwards, shrugging his shoulders. "You tell me, they are supposed to be the clever ones!"

"We haven't got a lot of time. Have you both lost the plot?" I addressed my words to both of them.

"It's hard knowing what to pack," Amara said.

I found it hard not to laugh. "You pair are not very bright, are you? Think about it! Take the minimum that you need, and you can buy new later, which means shopping – your favourite occupation!"

They both froze in their tracks as though I had pressed a switch in their brains to pause mode. They looked at each other.

"Well, in that case," Amina said, turning her suitcase upside down, "I will need a smaller bag."

"Me too," Amara said, and they started laughing.

"What the hell were you thinking?" I asked, feeling the need to have the last word.

I packed the unwanted stuff in the suitcases and placed them in the car boot. We drove to the harbour car park, where we would leave the SUV.

"It feels strange, saying goodbye to a lump of metal and having feelings similar to leaving a friend behind, doesn't it?" Amina said.

"Really, Mama, do you think she will miss us? It's just an object with no feelings." She smiled as her mama would after making a clever remark.

"Amara, why did you call it 'she'? It's not a person but a lump of metal," Amal remarked.

"We haven't the time for a detailed explanation on the gender of objects," I interrupted before they could debate further.

"But..."

"Sorry, we haven't got time. Maybe later, Amina," I said, engaged mentally on our itinerary.

We boarded the Meis Express carrying a small bag each. Osman checked our passports and I slipped him the Toyota keys, thanking him with a handshake. Once the crew cast off the boat, I turned to the three of them.

"In 45 minutes, we will be on the island of Meis."

"No, we will be on the island of Kastellorizio," Amara said confidently.

"It means red castle, but the proper Greek name is Megisti," Amina added.

"I thought it was called Mice Island because of all the mice on the island," Amal said. We all laughed. "I can't help my hearing, and you shouldn't laugh at the afflicted; that's not nice, is it," Amal sulked.

"Sorry, Amal; we shouldn't laugh, but your hearing is good. Meis is pronounced mice, so I can understand why you misunderstood."

Looking at the children, I could clearly see a difference in their demeanour in such a short time. They were openly more confident, which had developed through their recent experiences. The worry that was part of their young lives was slowly lifting, and it was clear that they were happier.

The crew docked the boat in a small horseshoe-shaped harbour with duty-free shops and tavernas dotted around the shore. Meis was a tiny island with almost as many names as it had occupants. We were surprised by the number of cars parked close to the dock.

"Look at all those she's parked up," Amal said.

"You know why they're called 'she'," Amina asked.

"Please, not now, as we have things to do first! Later, please," I said quickly. "Let's get sorted first."

We said goodbye to the staff and quickly made our way to an inviting taverna. We didn't have long to wait as the Rhodes ferry docked at 1.40pm and departed at 2pm, and it was already noon.

We ordered lunch as soon as we sat at a table. The waitress took our selected orders of moussaka as it was conveniently pre-prepared and ready to serve. Amina phoned her parents while we were waiting and told them that we had arrived safely, as usual. Telling white lies previously in the circumstances was the best solution. They were not aware of what we had been through and never would. I thought her parents were probably doing the same thing. She told them we were in the European Union on a small Greek island, off the Turkey coast and not to worry, as we are safe and well and would soon be in the UK. They were delighted and wanted to speak to Amara and Amal and told them they were looking forward to seeing them sometime soon. As Amina said goodbye to her parents, we all shouted, "Hope to see you soon; love you."

Amina sent a text to Ali and Margaret, which read,

In the EU, safe and well, ashkurak, inshallah (thanks to you; keep in touch) xxxx

The moussaka was delicious, and the Greek waitress was amicable and helpful. Sitting outside, shaded from the sun, looking at the sparkling, crystal-clear water, listening to the enchanting music from *Zorba the Greek* was delightful. It played softly through the restaurant speakers, creating an ambience of warmth and relaxation.

"We are just a couple of miles from a Muslim country, yet it's so different, pleasant, and calming; don't you agree?" Amina remarked.

"It's lovely, Mama. The music is infectious; what is it?" Amara asked.

"It's from a film about war, set on a small Greek island similar to this one. And, yes, the music is infectious: traditional bouzouki. Men and women dance together in Greece, and it sounds even better when you are dancing."

"I hope it's going to be like this everywhere," Amara replied.

"You will find most people will be friendly as they think we are on holiday."

Amina removed her head covering and shook her head, so her black wavy hair fell loosely onto her shoulders. Amara did the same as her mama. It was such a simple thing, but the effect was profound. I looked across to Amal, and I could see it affected him the same. We both watched them transform before our eyes by simply removing a piece of cloth from their heads. They looked so different, and their manner changed.

"You are both so gorgeous," I said, smiling at them.

"Money, please," Amina asked, holding out her hand.

"Money, please," Amara said, copying her mama.

"What for?" I asked.

"Head coverings, of course; remember you said we could buy new," Amina replied.

"But you have plenty of money yourself, don't you?"

"Yes, but when you said we could buy new, I took it to mean you would be buying." She and Amara made the 'gotcha' sign with their fingers.

I looked across at Amal, who was still wearing the cap that Wayne had given him. He didn't seem to ever take it off and he wasn't a bit interested in the conversation.

I handed the girls twenty euros each, realising that they had gained a minor victory over me. "Buy me one as well, something soft that can be packed easily and large-size. Amal doesn't need one."

"Obviously," Amara said, smiling at the inattentive Amal.

I watched the two of them walk jauntily away towards the shops; they seemed very pleased with themselves. It started to dawn on me that maybe the 'packing' incident earlier that morning might have been contrived. They had laid a trap that I had jumped into enthusiastically with both feet. *Who's stupid now*, I thought and laughed out loud.

"Take a look at that." Amal pointed to his returning mama and sister.

Amina wore a large sun hat with floral ribbons down to her shoulders. It seemed very Audrey Hepburn-ish, but I kept that to myself. Amara wore a very colourful baseball cap, back to front. Her hair was tied in a ponytail and hung behind the cap peak resting on the back of her neck and shoulders. The transformation in their body language was enormous; they were proudly walking with an exaggerated swagger, like models on a catwalk.

"Wow, Baba, it looks like a fashion show; that's my mama and sister."

When they realised that we were not the only ones gawping at their performance, they stopped their exhibition immediately, looking embarrassed. They waved to us, hoping the people watching realised they were just having a bit of fun. They now looked confident, modern and sophisticated. It amazed me that such a simple change in their head coverings made so much difference to them.

On the way to board the ferry, I put on my sun hat, and it made no difference to how I felt at all. For them, removing their head coverings and replacing them with sun hats was an expression of liberation. Whatever they wore was now their own choice and they exuded an aura of liberty.

Chapter 30

Rhodes at Last

The ferry appeared on the horizon.

"Here she comes," Amal shouted.

As soon as he had said it, he looked as though he regretted using the 'she' word in front of his mama and sister

"Why is a boat a 'she'?" Amara asked as quickly as she could.

Amina was impatient to tell us why.

"Go on, clever clogs, tell us," I teased.

Amina related the reason as though she was reading from a book. "Well, sailors relate to the idea of goddesses and mother figures playing a protective role in looking after a ship and crew. So this is linked to the common practice of giving ships female figureheads and female names."

I saw an opportunity to wind the two girls up. "There are alternative reasons. Amara, which of these definitions do you agree with? A ship's running costs are high, similar to women. Or here's a definition I prefer; it takes an experienced man to handle a ship correctly. Without a man at the helm, she is entirely uncontrollable."

"Baba, that's very sexist and stupid; I agree with Mama," Amara remarked with a frown.

"Well, Baba, I couldn't have said it better myself; you've hit the nail on the head, and it takes a lot of paint to keep her good-looking, as well."

"Well spotted, Amal, I forgot about ongoing maintenance; it looks like a draw in that debate."

We departed from Megisti to Rhodes on time. We spent most of the journey watching the turquoise sea and the beautiful coastline of Turkey, in awe of its beauty. The cleanliness of the rugged, primarily uninhabited coastline, with small fishing boats bobbing in the ocean, often with only one crew, was quite magical. The scene was so different from the war zones of Syria; the only noise was the chugging of the ferry's engine and the occasional seagull. I could feel the responsibility for my family's safety lifting from me. The possibility of them being brutally taken from me often flooded my head. I was desperately trying not to remember how close we came to not making it. The details Sewsen had so vividly described would never entirely leave my mind. I was crying without realising it until I felt a tear roll down my cheeks. I turned towards Amina, and she was crying too. We hugged each other, whispering, "It's okay." The kids joined in, and we embraced in a circle. No words were needed; we all knew why we were crying.

We were almost at the start of our new life, safe and protected by our status. I thought how easy it was for us, with our privileges, compared to the refugees attempting the same journey on a wing and prayer. How many would make it, and at what cost? We docked at the ferry port and hailed a taxi.

"Could you take us to a quiet hotel that suits a family for a few nights?"

The driver did a quick search on his mobile phone and then made a quick call. It was evident from the conversation that a friend was on the receiving end, as his voice changed to a soft, friendly tone. "Okay," he addressed us in his business voice, "we are going to the Koukis Rhodian Guesthouse, and I hope you like my choice."

"No problem," I replied.

His choice was good and precisely what we required. We settled into a large family room. I collected some 'must-see' brochures from the hotel lobby to look at while we dined in the hotel restaurant. Rhodes was one of the largest Greek islands with so much history. Entrepreneurs have developed many historic buildings and created must-see tourist attractions over many years.

I tried to book our flights from Rhodes to London Gatwick that night while Amina and the kids were fast asleep. The internet was incredibly slow; it always annoyed me when the laptop screen froze, but my impatience was on a different level now. I swore to myself, my hands shook, and I hit the keyboard excessively hard; nothing happened. It seemed to take ages.

I felt Amina gently place her hand on my shoulder. She whispered, "It's okay, love. I will take over; tell me what you are trying to do."

Angrily, I snapped, "I'm fine. Go back to sleep."

Amina whispered, "Allan, your continual shouting is going to wake the kids up."

"I'm not continually shouting, for Christ's sake."

"Yes, you are. Let me take over. You haven't slept for days; you look exhausted."

Her hand was still on my shoulder; I could feel it attempting to stop my uncontrollably trembling. I didn't understand why I was repeatedly uttering, "What have I done, what have I done."

"Come on, darling, come to bed, try to sleep; you will feel better in the morning."

Amina put her arms around me; I could feel her hands patting my back like you do when trying to get a baby to sleep. "It's okay, love, it's okay," she repeated.

I did sleep deeply for the first time in a long while. I awoke and felt ashamed and couldn't understand my performance last night. How could I be shouting out loud and not realise it? What was wrong with me? When Amina stirred, I asked, "Are you awake?"

She replied, "Yes, love, are you okay?"

"Sorry about last night; I don't know what came over me."

"Sorry for what? You have nothing to be sorry for."

"We have all been through the same thing. Why can't I come to terms with it, like you?"

"Allan, you have been the strong one; you got us where we are now. We have all been leaning on you, expecting you to pull us through, and you have."

"Why do I feel this way?"

"Allan, I am not a psychologist, but I think your mind has been on one thing – to get your family to safety – and you haven't had a chance to think of anything else. Now we are almost there, and you are not under so much pressure. You have other things popping into your head that you don't want to remember. Don't get upset if I say maybe you have PTSD."

"Amina, that's a disease soldiers get, isn't it? I haven't been through anything like they have."

"Bloody hell, Allan, don't be stupid. Of course, you have. We all have."

"What does PTSD stand for, clever clogs?" I knew she wouldn't have said it without knowing.

"Post-traumatic stress disorder. It's not just soldiers who get it. Different types of stress cause it. Just think of all the stress you have been through."

"And you. Does it go away?"

"I believe the treatment is anti-depressants and therapy, and it does get better."

"If you think I am acting weird again, can you let me know?"

Jokingly, Amina replied, "That's going to be complicated. Do you mean weirder than usual?" Then she did the gotcha sign with her finger.

"Thanks, love, maybe just tap your nose. After breakfast, shall we book the flights together? Perhaps we can go to a travel shop; no rush."

We had breakfast at a restaurant. I felt less stressed; the kids helped me as they had brought the 'must-see' brochures and were excited, flicking through them. They were a joy to watch and made me feel proud.

The only flight left was in three days, so there was nothing to do but enjoy the few days we had in Rhodes. We spent the next three days mixing sightseeing and relaxing. The following days weren't planned, and I realised that this was the first time they could freely pick and choose things to see. We didn't talk about what we had been through to each other. I realised from the previous night that the kids had been through the same emotional roller-coaster. I was unsure of how they were dealing with it. I was still struggling to keep myself together, hoping it didn't show. Without my family around me, I probably would have failed. For me, it was the best thing at this time; I had been obsessed with getting my family home to Wales.

Most things were new to them all, and they bombarded me with questions: Did I know this? Did I know that?

"We will only have time to visit one choice each," I said as we browsed the brochures.

They all started quickly reading as much as they could. My children were just like their mother, researching ardently. I would only look at the photos and choose on impulse. Surprisingly, they all selected different sights to see.

"For me, it's got to be the Palace of the Grand Master of the Knights," Amal said.

"I was thinking of that too," said Amara, "but I've chosen the Castle of the Old Town."

That left Amina, who was still reading the brochures. After a long pause, she said, "I think that I would most like to see the Mosque of Suleiman."

"Come on, Baba, what would you like?" Amal asked.

"An uncrowded, quiet beach and a bar serving ice-cold beers."

"And maybe a cocktail or two, for me, don't you think?" Amina added.

The short welcome break was over, and we were all getting excited that we would be on the last leg of our journey. We had booked four seats together on the plane. Amal, of course, wanted a window seat, and so did Amara. Amal came up with the winning excuse that it was more comfortable for his strapped-up shoulder. To be fair to him, he had never complained about his shoulder, so we gave him the window seat. His ears were still a concern, so I insisted he used earplugs during the flight. I thought it might help with the change in air pressure during take-off and landing. Amina sat next to him with Amara on her other side and me in the aisle seat, buffered by trolleys and passengers. It was the first flight for my very excited kids. After a short period, they all fell asleep, except me. I had a long drive to West Wales ahead of me when we landed; they still weren't quite home.

Chapter 31

Safe in the UK, 2012

I collected a hire car and started our drive to West Wales. Helen had rented a holiday cottage by the coast, close to Freshwater East, for as long as we liked.

"Why is it grey and cold here?" Amara asked as we drove west on the M4.

"The weather here is very unpredictable, nothing like Syria. In Syria, the seasons are very defined. In the UK, one summer day can be warm and sunny, and then, for absolutely no reason at all, the following day can be grey and cool."

"So it could be nice tomorrow?" Amara replied.

"Inshallah," I replied.

"Why are the roads so busy? Where is everyone going? Why are we going so fast, but keep stopping?"

"Notice when we stop, the drivers aren't beeping their horns like in Aleppo," I pointed out.

"Perhaps they're not in a hurry," Amal said sarcastically.

"Too many vehicles, traffic jams and the bad weather: you must get used to it!"

"When we were in Alanya, everyone was practically naked. You said they don't do that here; I can see why now."

We arrived safely at the cottage after a long and tedious drive. Helen and Paul were there to greet us. It was two years since I had seen them. We had been in regular contact over the internet, using Skype, to begin with. They also sent short videos and photos by email; in the later years, we FaceTimed each other at regular intervals. That didn't prepare me for seeing them in the flesh. I did feel guilty as an absent father; it's not what I wanted. They recently told me they realised it was not what I wanted. Meeting my grown-up children face to face didn't go as expected. It really was face to face as they had grown so much. I thought we would hug each other and say how much we missed each other. I didn't expect that my children would be so openly emotional.

When I was young, it wasn't the done thing to show emotion; it was classed as a weakness, so I avoided it as much as possible. I had been like that all through my life until Amina showed me it was a good thing. The kids today are taught differently. They don't have any inhibitions; if they love you, they tell you so. They were the words my children whispered in my ear; I whispered back, "I love you too." It flashed through my mind with regret that I never said that to my own parents. Their response would probably have been an embarrassed, 'away with yer'.

I said to them with glassy eyes, "You only have to turn your back for a short time and look what happens. You both look amazing. Just look at you two. You're both amazing." Before I knew it, Helen and Paul were hugging me. I saw Paul waving at Amina, Amara, and Amal to join us. We all embraced together in a circle.

Helen said, "Thank God you are all safe; we were so worried about you."

Paul said. "It must have been awful; Syria has been on the news all the time."

I replied, "We are some of the lucky ones, inshallah."

"Dad, you haven't changed much, except you've shrunk a bit. Did someone put you in a hot wash?" Paul teased. "You're lucky as you don't need a good thatch on an empty cottage," he joked about my thinning hair.

"Haha, very funny; it comes to us all eventually," I said, looking at his unkempt hair. I quipped, "You don't need a roof on a busy thoroughfare, either."

Helen went straight to Amina and gave her a big hug. "It's more like having a big sister back than a step mum," she said, smiling.

"That's nice. I've never had a sister; I will hold you to that."

Helen greeted me with another big hug, as though I was a second thought, and whispered in my ear, "Lucky Man."

"I know," I said, "you don't have to keep reminding me."

"Hi, buddy," Paul said, greeting Amal, "how are things doing? Looks like you have been in the wars; are you okay? I like your cap and T-shirt; where did you get them?"

"Just a flesh wound," Amal said, grinning proudly. "A Yankee soldier gave me the hat and shirt."

They both high-fived, and Helen went over to hug Amara. "You are your mum's double; later, you must tell me all about your adventures," she said. Then she turned to Amal and hugged him, saying, "Now for the best-looking man in the room!"

Amal blushed and didn't say a word; he was not used to being hugged by a female, so he looked at me for help. I shrugged back at him and smiled, thinking he must get used to it.

"You're going to break the girls' hearts around here, with that curly blonde hair, golden tan and your mother's eyes. It's a shame about your dad's bits, though; that might put a few off."

"Haha, very funny. Well, I think you all take after me," I chipped in.

"Hope not," was muttered in turn from all of them.

Helen made tea in the Welsh way. Amara and Amal liked tea, or chai, as they knew it, but were confused about chai in large mugs, not small clear glasses. They watched as Helen added milk turning the clear golden brew into a brown muddy solution. They both looked at me for help; they had been taught it was bad manners to refuse hospitality.

"Is there something wrong?" Helen asked, noticing their discomfort.

"No, not wrong, just different, that's all. It's going to be a learning curve; they are used to chai, Arabic-style."

"Oh, I didn't think, sorry. I made the tea without thinking."

"It's not your fault. They're going to have to adjust or go thirsty."

"What would you like to drink?" Helen asked.

"Many things are different; sometimes they will feel weird. If Helen and Paul ventured into the Middle East, they would expect to behave according to that culture, wouldn't they?"

"Sorry if we offended you," Amara said, "we shouldn't have turned up our noses before trying it."

"Don't worry," I said, "here it's different, as nobody will be offended if you say 'I don't like that', or 'I want it this way. Just ask politely. One thing more, you don't know whether you like something until you try it."

Amina picked up a mug of tea and took a sip. "Just about right for me," she said. "It's lovely. Try it, both of you," she said, addressing Amal and Amara.

"Oh my God, I've ordered takeaway fish, chips and mushy peas for supper, and it comes wrapped in paper," Helen suddenly blurted out.

"That sounds great, doesn't it, Amal?" Amara said.

"Sounds lovely," Amal replied, trying hard not to show displeasure but not quite managing it.

We all laughed. Surprisingly, the kids enjoyed the meal but were unsure about the vinegar.

"Yuck, it smells like sour wine. I'll give that a miss," he said, pulling a face.

Helen studied at Bath University and had grown into a confident and intelligent young woman. She was a good host and took complete charge of the situation, making us feel comfortable. Somehow, she managed to control everyone by ordering us about in a friendly natural way. So we all adhered to her plan without realising it. We were all bystanders as she took control and made sure everyone was happy. As I expected, we all talked away well into the night. All the family got on well, and Amal joined in the conversation. However, I was unsure how much he heard clearly or understood. I noticed Paul had matured and talked in whole sentences rather than grunts. At last, he seemed interested in other things outside his own small world.

I asked Paul, "What do you think is the best car for us? The hire car goes back next week."

After a short pause, he said, "SUV, probably a seven-seater, would be your best option as we could all fit in. It also gives you flexibility as the seats fold out of the way, so there are handy for moving things."

"What make? There are so many to choose from."

"Yeah, there are loads of makes and styles. Do you want me to ask one of my mates; he works as a car salesman?"

"That would be great, yes, please."

"I'll give him a ring. I will tell him what you are after. Do you want old or new?"

"Not bothered as long as it's in good nick."

"Well said; what's the point of throwing money around just to get a new registration plate? Bonkers, if you ask me."

My dad's logic jumped to mind, realising it had moved on to another generation. I said, "You sound like Grandad."

Paul replied, "Hope so; thanks for the compliment."

Paul rang me a couple of days later to tell me, "Move fast; my mate's got the ideal car."

I picked Paul up right away. His mate, John, showed us the car, saying excitedly, "It's that just come in; it hasn't been through the standard inspection. You will get a better deal buying it 'as seen' right now."

"Isn't that a bit risky?" I asked John.

Paul butted in and said, "Dad, you will save thousands. If you want, I'll wash it?"

John said, "It's low mileage and fully serviced by us; it's a snip. If you don't snap it up now, it will go through the garage into the showroom; you will regret it."

As it was Paul's mate telling me this, I held out my hand and shook John's to confirm the deal.

I was now the proud owner of a seven-seater Peugeot 5008. Driving home with Paul, I realised the advantages of living in a small town, rather than a big city where you know everyone.

So I said to Paul, "Are you glad we moved out of the city into the sticks?"

"Too bloody right, I'm glad. I hate cities."

The following day, Helen insisted that we all go to the beach for a swim as the weather was sunny, for once. Obviously, this was part of her pre-planned 'I am in charge' programme.

"Okay, I'm up for it, but can we walk to the beach nearest here? It's not the prettiest beach, but it would be the easiest for Amal to negotiate."

"We're having a picnic as well," Helen pointed out.

"Fine by me," I replied.

"I'm afraid there's not much in the pantry. How do cheese sandwiches, fruit and flasks of coffee sound?"

"That sounds great," Paul replied.

"Fine by me," Amal shouted, and the rest of us echoed our agreement.

"It's nice and sunny, but it feels pretty cold to me," Amal pointed out on the walk down to the beach.

"Don't worry! The closer you get to the sea, the colder the wind gets, and you'll be glad to get into the warm water," Paul joked.

"It doesn't look warm. Look at the waves crashing and the noise," Amal fretted.

"Amal, can you hear the waves," I asked?

"Yes, and the ringing in my ears has gone."

"Great! Don't forget to put your earplugs in before you go into the sea, will you?"

"Okay," Amal sighed, pulling a face.

"Amal will love it, won't he, Amina," Helen said.

"It's an experience," Amina laughed, "that I will never forget, and I can't wait to do it again!"

We found a spot on the beach and settled down.

"There are only a few people on the beach and not many dressed for swimming," Amara said.

"They're wimps, not from around here. You'll love it. Wait and see," Paul butted in.

We stripped into our swimming costumes, trying not to shiver.

"It's amazing how the wind chill invigorates your bare skin," Paul shouted. "Last one in is a wimp."

He ran towards the sea, and I couldn't help but notice how his physique had changed; it was obvious he had worked out and had the body of an athletic young man.

Helen quickly followed behind, shouting, "Come on, you lot!"

"You go first; I'll get the towels ready, then I'll follow," Amina said. As the kids ran towards the sea, she turned to me, grinning, and said, "I can't wait to hear their screams."

Paul and Helen were already in the sea, riding the rolling waves, waving at the rest of us to join them. Amara reached the water and stopped in her tracks, ankle-deep.

"What's up, wimp?" Paul shouted

"Nothing's up; it's lovely. Just waiting for Amal," Amara replied, smirking.

Amal found it difficult running with one arm strapped up and reached the sea a few seconds after Amara. He ploughed into the water as fast as he could, knees raised high, splashing the water up Amara's back.

"That's not bloody funny," she hollered at him angrily.

Amal stopped and screamed as loud as he could, "It's bloody freezing."

"Wimps! Come on, get in!" Paul shouted back.

Amara splashed with both hands, showering Amal with water in revenge for his splashing her. Gingerly, Amara and Amal ventured up to their waists in the sea, splashing each other in a contest. Amal was hindered, using only one arm, but was giving as good as he got.

Amina was enjoying the show with tears of laughter. "I think I will give it a miss," she said, wrapping a towel around her shoulders and sitting down. All the kids were now fully in the sea, waving at us to join them. Amina shook her head vigorously, indicating, 'no way. She then shrugged at them as though she didn't understand, cupping a hand close to her ear.

The kids continued to call us. "Come on, wimps!"

I couldn't resist the temptation. I scooped Amina up and carried her to the water's edge. "You dare! Just you dare!" she screamed at me. The wriggling of her arms and legs trying to escape was like a red flag to a bull. I waded further into the sea and rolled her out of my arms into the freezing water. She yelled in anticipation before she hit the sea. Her piercing scream enticed the kids to splash us both with water.

"I will get you for this," Amina threatened, but joined in the fun just the same. She put on a brave face. "See, I told you it's lovely once you get used to it," she grimaced. "Actually, it's bloody freezing!"

An exhilarating splashing war followed, all inhibitions gone. We took it in turns to drown each other in the foaming sea. The water fight seemed to distract us from the freezing water, and we became accustomed to the cold.

"I told you it would be good fun," Paul said.

"I can't wait to do it again," Amina said, pulling a face that indicated the opposite.

Afterwards, we sat in a circle wrapped in towels, holding our hot coffee mugs for warmth while our teeth chattered.

Amal took out his earplugs. "The whistling goes when I take them out; all I can hear is the sound of the sea."

"Amal, it sounds like tinnitus to me. Any noise will mask the whistling. It should continue to get better." Amina confirmed what I'd already suspected.

"I really did enjoy that, and I did get used to the cold," Amara said. "Does anyone want to join me for another paddle?" She pulled a face as Amina had done, so we knew she wasn't serious.

"I'm up for it," Paul called her bluff.

"Only joking," Amara said, smiling at him.

The rest of us ignored the suggestion.

* * * * *

Helen and Paul had to return to their studies the following day. Helen to Bath University, and Paul to Bristol

Technical College. After they had left, it seemed a little strange, just with the four of us again. But it gave us time to ourselves and reflect on our next steps. We needed to find a place to live, and the kids had to be enrolled at school. The school catchment area was an essential factor to consider. We spent the next couple of weeks on the internet, all four of us looking at properties we could afford. It was no surprise that the kids were very enthusiastic and had different ideas of 'ideal'. Even Amina and I had opposing ideas. Somehow we had to find a compromise.

Once we had a shortlist of properties, we drove to view them outside before asking for an internal viewing. Distance to a school was important. We eliminated anything brand new from the shortlist, as they tended to be tiny houses on small plots. Eventually, we settled on finding an older property, preferably with a private garden on the outskirts of Pembroke. After many visits to estate agents and trawling through hundreds of brochures, we eventually settled on an old detached double fronted stone bay house built in the forties, with two large reception rooms and a large kitchen. It needed extensive updating, rewiring, central heating, kitchen and bathrooms. It was new on the market and fitted all the criteria, so we moved quickly and snapped it up. So we extended the rental on the holiday cottage whilst the purchase went through and gave us time to renovate our new home before moving in. I already knew the best builders in the area by reputation, so I picked one that would project-manage and bring in various trades at his convenience. The house was finished to a high standard, and we were pleased that it only took a couple of months to complete.

We enrolled the kids at Pembroke High School shortly after the term started. Both kids were excited, and I didn't anticipate any issues regarding their mixed race. In the beginning, everything was fine, with no problems. The school uniforms were similar to those in Syria, blazers and grey trousers for the boys and grey skirts for the girls. Amara hadn't worn a head covering since Meis, and that was not the only difference. She had to come to terms with the short, tight skirts worn by all the girls. Amara enjoyed the mixture of learning and making new friends, and she excelled at both. I noticed the odd bruise on Amal from time to time; when I questioned him, he told me everything was fine and not to worry.

At the half-term parents' meeting, the form teachers had nothing but praise for Amara. They told us she was polite and intelligent and everything seemed easy for her, and her classmates liked her. It was the opposite for Amal. We were told he was always getting into fights and didn't make any friends. His form teacher asked us to find out why he was not mixing with the other boys. That evening, we talked to the kids one at a time to pass on to them what their form teachers had told us. Amara was delighted that her teachers had given such a good report. Amal was stubborn, and we had to prise out of him what the issue was. Eventually, he told us other kids called him the 'Arab boy'.

"You should be proud of that; you are an Arab," I told him.

"No, it's an insult, the way they sneer it right in my face and spit at me."

"No, that's not right! Sorry, son. Why didn't you tell us?"

"Because, Baba, you have always drummed into me to look out for myself."

"This is a different, son. If you are being bullied, you have to let me know, straight away, always, all right? How are they bullying you?"

"They take my school bag off me, pretending to search for bombs and throw my stuff everywhere, shouting 'boom boom' as they do it."

I was unsure what we could do without making matters worse. "It's just because you are different. The novelty will soon wear off. Stick in there, son. There will be other boys watching what's going on who won't like it. Try to make friends with them."

Later that night, when the kids were in bed, we talked as parents do when concerned. "It's strange that they single out Amal. Amara's features are more obviously Eastern; his blonde, curly hair, dark olive skin, and dark brown eyes are unusual. Does that make him a target for abuse, maybe?"

"Maybe it's his striking looks and athletic build. Maybe he's seen as a threat to the other boys?"

"Girls are different to boys, aren't they? More sociable naturally?"

"You could be right," Amina replied thoughtfully.

"Amara is petite, gentle, attentive and pretty like you and doesn't bring attention to herself. Don't you think?"

"Well, Amal is just the opposite: clumsy, untidy, has the concentration span of a gnat and gives back as good as he gets. He won't be pushed around, just like his father. That could be his problem. As you know what it's like being at school here, will you talk to him? Ask him to try a bit harder not to stand out."

"Yes, and I will visit the school. I'll ask his form teacher to keep an eye out for bullying, but not to make an issue out of it. I will have a word with Amal too, but you know what he's like."

"Yes, just like you, unfortunately. Now, put the light out. Goodnight, darling."

* * * * *

I was interviewed at a local refinery and found a position as a tutor in the apprentice training academy. Amina found a job at a local college teaching English. We settled into our new home, and on the surface, things were going well. Beneath the surface, though, the concerns regarding our closest friends and family in Syria were always on our minds. The media reports didn't make it easy for us; we continually saw horror stories on the television regarding the war. The situation seemed to worsen every time a news item contradicted what we were hearing from Yoran, Souzan, Ali, and Margaret. They insisted it was fine on our weekly phone calls. Still, we both knew that life was a lot harder than they were making out; their assurances didn't alleviate our worry, but at least it didn't compound it. I remembered a phrase an Arab friend had told me: 'I tell you what you want to hear rather than the truth, as it is more welcome'.

We all eventually settled into everyday life, and we were comfortable in our skins, as they say. The house was perfect for us. The garden was a work in progress and something else to occupy us. We started to make new friends through neighbours and work colleagues. Our social life was different from the one we had experienced in Aleppo. Amina mixed well with some of my old friends, including Derek and his wife, Liz, and we made new friends through our work. We invited friends around to dine and play cards or board games in the evenings. This provoked memories of the times we had spent with Ali and Margaret but never replaced those times; we still missed them. However hard we tried, they were always in our thoughts. Although we were in contact regularly, and they insisted they were fine, it was their presence we missed most. We joined the local pub quiz team, where Amina excelled. "How does she know so much?" our teammates and competitors would ask. She was always the first choice to join a team. I was handy for getting the drinks in.

Amal's issues at school eventually settled down. The turning point came for him the first winter when the rugby season started. Amal knew nothing about what he thought of as a silly game with an odd-shaped ball, hard to kick and pass. Although I sometimes watched it on television, he would sooner play and watch football. In the evening, after his first rugby practice game, Amal told me that he was placed on the wing and had no idea what to do. Eventually, he received the ball and ran the entire pitch length because he didn't know the rules or how to pass the ball properly. His classmates discovered he was a fast runner. Somebody nicknamed him 'Gump', which I had to explain to him. He thought it was an insult until I told him it was funny as Gump could run forever. I suggested he stay on in the evenings for rugby practice. Amal then told me that one of the boys had asked him to join the local rugby club as there was no after-school practice. So Amal's interest in rugby began.

It wasn't long afterwards that we noticed a difference in him, and the school reports improved vastly. He was soon picked to play for the school team. I went to see his first game without him knowing. No other parents were there, so I watched from a distance to avoid his embarrassment. I knew that there was fierce competition between rival schools, and games were often violent, brutal events. The schoolboys played for their school badge just as rugby internationals played for their country's flag, with the same pride and no-holds-barred mentality. The bigger boys were usually selected as forwards to gain territory by winning or retaining the ball using brute strength. The backs relied on speed and guile, receiving the ball once the forwards had won the hard yards. Amal's team's pack of forwards drove the opposing pack off the ball, and suddenly there was space for the backs to run into.

I heard our school's supporters shouting from the sideline, "Give it to Amal!" Eventually, the ball was passed to him. He was off like a greyhound out of a trap, sidestepping forwards, outpacing centres, rounding the backs and placing the ball under the posts for a try. I expected to see a beaming smile on his face; instead, he showed no emotion, as though he had done nothing special. I wanted to clap and shout, 'well done, Amal!' but I managed to control my pride with difficulty.

After the game, as the losers clapped the winners off the field, Amal was patted on the back by his opposing number, who said, "Good game." I then watched as his team walked off excitedly as mates together, with their arms around each other's shoulders, congratulating themselves after their win. Amal was no longer different to them but a valued team member.

Chapter 32

Pembrokeshire

We had hoped the war in Syria would fizzle out rapidly, but that was not to be. The media reports from Syria always grew worse. We were unsure how accurate the information was, as many different countries were involved, all with different agendas. It was difficult to see a solution unless one side completely obliterated the other. That could never happen as America and Russia were the leading players on opposing sides. Many countries and organisations with different agendas, like Iran, Turkey, Israel, NATO, ISIS, the EU and the Kurds, were involved.

We lost contact with Ali and Margaret without warning: the phone calls and texts stopped abruptly for no reason. Yoran and Souzan were still in touch, and from what they told us, which was confirmed by the BBC news, life was almost back to normal where they lived. It was occupied in the main by people loyal to the government and defended well.

We tried without success every way we knew to contact Ali and Margaret through mutual friends. We left messages without any response. We always kept our Syrian mobile phones on charge at all times and checked them often, in hope. Waiting for news from them was difficult to bear as another year passed by. Without knowing why we could not contact them, we became highly concerned for their safety. We couldn't accept that anything terrible had happened to them, though. Ali, in our eyes, was indestructible, so we adopted the phrase 'no news is good news.

Amara and Amal were doing well at school. Amara was taking her A level exams, hoping to go to university. Amal had changed so much and now had friends at school and the rugby club. Being bullied at school and being called an Arab was well behind him. He didn't excel academically like Amara; he was an average student but good at sports. He went through the typical teenage growth spurt. We thought he would never stop growing or eating, but still, he was always hungry. Then, thankfully, the growth spurt slowed, the teenage spots disappeared, and he became a very good-looking, popular boy. Because he looked different and stood out in a crowd, Amal was never short of friends, boys or girls. He always had things to do that were more important than learning, and he was always busy. He was the complete opposite of Amara. Learning was her top priority; her goals were utterly different. She took after her mother and was like a sponge. The more information she gathered, the more she sought.

Amina and I were watching the BBC 10 o'clock news in August 2015. We were shocked when the newsreader announced that Khaled al-Asaad, the famous Syrian archaeologist, had been executed by ISIS. His brutal beheading by so-called religious zealots was done on the pretence that retaining history was against their faith. We had only met him a couple of times, but his brutal death came as a shock to us. The atrocity inflicted on someone we had met and admired increased our feeling of the futility of this stupid war. Watching the broadcast on British television, showing the destruction of Palmyra and photos of Khaled while he was still alive, brought back memories of our time there. We could not understand why a life devoted to saving history for preservation was taken away by so-called religious fanatics. Khaled was 81years of age; Palmyra had been his whole life. He was a truly gentle, kind man and no threat to anyone. His beheaded body was tied to a lamp post in Palmyra town square. His severed head was placed between his knees as an example to others because he hadn't submitted to ISIS's demands and surrendered artefacts hidden from them. He had done this to stop them from being destroyed with the rest of the beautiful city of Palmyra. So sad what one human can do to another; even more painful is the belief it's done in the name of religion.

Chapter 33

September 2015

On a Saturday evening in September, we were both dozing, half-watching something on television, when our Syrian mobile phone started ringing. Amina jumped up nervously to answer. "It's not the usual time for my parents to ring," she said nervously, obviously expecting bad news.

I could see she was concerned, so I stood next to her to offer support if the news was terrible. I watched her face closely, ready to comfort her, as her puzzled look changed to one of joy.

"It's Margaret," she cried.

"Margaret! Oh my God," I cried out, "is she okay?"

"Shush, Allan." Amina was listening carefully.

"How are you, Margaret? Where have you been? Is Ali with you?" Amina enquired with tears rolling down her cheeks and not allowing Margaret time to answer any questions. I was crying too. Amina pulled me close and turned the volume up so we could both hear the conversation. We had so many questions to ask.

"Slow down, please," Margaret said. "I will tell you later why we haven't been in contact, but there's too much to tell over the phone. This call is to let you know we will be in the UK next week."

"Can I talk to Ali?"

"It's difficult at the moment, but soon," Margaret replied. "We are flying into Heathrow next week, and I will text you the flight details later."

"You can stay with us," I said excitedly.

"That would be great, but we have to go somewhere else first," Margaret replied.

"We will meet you at the airport, regardless," I said.

"I'd prefer if you didn't," Margaret said.

"We will meet you at the airport. It's not a problem; we can't wait to see you both."

"I will text you the details later. Love you both, bye for now."

The phone went dead.

We looked at each other, tears rolling down our cheeks. We hugged and exclaimed 'bloody hell' in unison. I poured two brandies, and we sat down in shock, staring at each other.

"I never expected that! I wonder where they've been. Why now? Thank God they're safe."

"That was entirely out of the blue; I wasn't expecting that," I said while topping up the brandies.

Amina lent towards me with her glass. "To Ali and Margaret," she sang as she clinked my glass.

"We must phone the kids and tell them that Uncle Ali and Auntie Margaret are safe and well."

"Texting them would be better; it's Saturday night; they could be anywhere," I replied.

Amal and Amara were delighted, and both texted back very quickly that they wanted to be there when we met them. Amina texted them back to explain that it wouldn't be possible as Margaret had asked us not to come. We would tell them everything when we got back.

The following Wednesday, we enthusiastically drove to Heathrow to meet them at Terminal 2. We stood outside the arrival gate, excited, waiting for them to appear. When I first saw Margaret, I was confused, expecting the beautiful, vibrant, confident lady we had said goodbye to in Aleppo. It was a shock to me when I saw her; I felt Amina's hand in mine, and I realised it was a shock to her as well. She looked thinner; gone was her jet black hair, gone was the beautiful, flawless complexion, and gone was her jaunty walk. I expected to see Ali walking beside her, but it was just Margaret pushing a baggage trolley on her own. I was scanning the area for Ali, as was Amina. We both spotted a porter at the same time pushing a wheelchair occupied by a grey-haired old man. It wasn't until Margaret turned to him and smiled that I wondered why I realised who he was. Then it came to both of us simultaneously, and we turned to each other and said, "Ali."

"Hold it together, don't look shocked," I whispered to Amina as I squeezed her hand firmly, and we walked towards them. I was trying not to show the anxiety I felt. Amina ran to Margaret with arms wide to hug and kiss her. Ali slowly lifted himself out of his wheelchair so he could greet me. The last time I hugged Ali was when we had escaped from Aleppo. Ali had been taller then. I held the power of his embrace for as long as I could. I was now hugging a shorter, frailer version of Ali: where there was once muscle and power, there was now only skin and bone. I was afraid of hurting him; his strength had gone, as had his beaming smile. He was trembling with the effort he had just made to stand. We didn't say anything for a moment. Still, I couldn't help myself say what I thought, although I immediately regretted it.

"What have they done?"

"Can we sit and have a coffee so I can tell you what our plans are," Margaret said.

Amina was hugging and kissing Ali. "It's okay now. We will look after you," she assured him.

Over coffee, I caught Margaret's eyes to query what had happened. "Later, not now," she whispered.

Ali gave us no eye contact; he looked away as though he was uncertain of his surroundings.

"I'm taking Ali to Frimley Military Hospital for treatment. It's all arranged by James Le Messurier of the White Helmets. Do you know him?"

"Why Frimley?" I asked. "And yes, I do remember the White Helmets."

"It's been arranged for Ali to have specialised treatment there." Margaret indicated it was not a good time for questions by putting her index finger to her lips.

"We will take you there. That's not a problem for us, is it, Amina?" I pleaded.

"Of course not! We will do anything, anything at all. Please, Margaret, let us do this little thing?"

"Thanks for your offer, but it's arranged. We're being collected from here soon. The ambulance is here at the airport, just waiting for them to pick us up."

Ali was still avoiding eye contact and didn't utter a word. He was just staring away into the distance. When I tried to make eye contact, he half-smiled and looked away.

The ambulance crew arrived and whisked them away; we watched until they were out of view. Later, we sat in the airport car park, looking out of the car windows at nothing, without speaking.

"I didn't expect that," Amina said, openly crying. Black lines were streaming from her eyes; she wiped her cheeks with the back of her hands.

"Nor did I. What a shock. Anything it takes, anything. We will be there for them, won't we?"

"Of course, anything. He looks like an animal that's been beaten almost to death, frightened to make eye contact with us," Amina sobbed in anger.

We drove all the way home, not stopping or talking, except for the occasional query to each other that we were okay and patting each other on the knee for reassurance.

After about a week, Margaret rang. "Could I come and stay with you for a bit?" she asked.

"Of course, you can. We would love it if you could stay with us."

"Ali is not coming, though. It will be just me, I'm afraid."

"Is Ali all right?" Amina asked.

"He's okay but is still having treatment."

As we drove to Frimley Hospital to collect Margaret and bring her home, Amina shared something she had learnt. "I have spent a lot of time on the internet recently."

"Nothing unusual," I said.

"Please don't interrupt. I need to explain what could have happened to Ali in Raqqa. I have been reading accounts from ex-prisoners and how they broke them."

"Shouldn't you wait until you're told?"

"Maybe you're right, but you know me."

"I have also read a bit but probably not as much as you. I know they use mental as well as physical torture."

"Yes, you're right. One mental torture is the white cell; everything is painted white. There are no windows, no natural daylight, and no means to distinguish night and day. The lights are very bright and switched on and off at irregular intervals. Food and water arrive intermittently as well to confuse even further. The light could be left on for days or switched off after minutes until the prisoner loses all track of time."

"How long does it take to break a prisoner?" I asked.

"Months, weeks; it depends on the person."

"One prisoner recalled an interview room where the interrogators forced him to sit opposite them, strapped in a chair, as they completely ignored him. The guards ate and drank from a table covered in food and acted like he wasn't there. He was starving and craving food and water; he could smell and virtually taste the food. The mental torture went on for days, and he was never fed. These are just some of the psychological techniques they used; there were others."

"I can't imagine that would break Ali; he would be aware of what they were doing. He is so strong-minded, don't you think?"

"I'm not so sure; caged in a room alone, month after month, with no natural daylight, little food and water. A smelly toilet bucket keeping you company, and nothing to occupy your mind, other than the light being switched on or off, would drive anyone mad, don't you think?"

"I suppose that if mental torture failed, there was always physical torture to fall back on," I added. "The bastards!"

"It's actually far easier to recover from physical torture than mental torture because the body can heal, but the mind is more complex."

"Physical scars are easy to see. Mental scars; they're a different matter, aren't they!"

"Yes, they are. We don't know what they did to him, but it must have been something awful." Amina hesitated. "Sorry I started this conversation. I think we should concentrate on Margaret as she looked like she'd been through hell."

"I was shocked. I would have walked straight past her if we weren't deliberately looking out for her."

We were hoping to see Ali at the hospital, but we were told it wasn't possible as it would interfere with his treatment. Margaret and one of his female counsellors met us in a day room. She was middle-aged, pleasant and informative. She told us the team treating Ali had decided it was in his interest to recover physically and mentally before mixing with people he remembered. They also emphasised that physical recovery would be relatively easy compared to mental healing, which would take more time and care.

"Ali is such a proud man in every aspect; his physical condition and appearance have always been important to him. Will getting that back help him mentally?" I asked.

"Who knows how much of the old Ali we will get back, or what he has been through," the counsellor answered curtly. "Only he knows that!"

"Inshallah," I said.

"God has nothing to do with it," she replied.

"Sorry," I said. "It's just a remark Ali would have made, and he's not a believer either."

Chapter 34

October 2015

On the journey back home, I was unsure what to say to Margaret, so we drove in silence for quite a while. Margaret was looking out of the window and appeared to be deep in thought. When she did speak, her voice was trembling as though answering an unasked question. "It was more challenging than either of us imagined."

"If you want to tell us, that's fine, but only if you want or need to," Amina said.

Still staring out of the window, hiding her face from us, Margaret began her story, shaking and sobbing and wiping away the tears as she spoke. "I need to talk; maybe then I can make sense of what happened. Ali worked with the White Helmets all over Aleppo; wherever there was an airstrike, he would be there. Russian fighter jets, helicopters, drones, and the army were striking areas assumed occupied by opposition fighters. The opposition didn't act as a united force, and some were even fighting each other. Some were changing sides and fighting the people who were once allies; it was a mess. These areas were occupied mainly by ordinary people, who may have had allegiances with the militants, but were not soldiers; they were primarily the old, women and children.

The White Helmets sent their people into attacked locations, regardless of the occupants. I was told later that Ali entered an area infiltrated by ISIS fighters. We are not sure how ISIS knew that Ali was once in the Syrian Army, but they did. ISIS disapproved of the White Helmets anyway; they didn't want non-supporters of their so-called holy war rescued. ISIS wanted the world to see Asaad's army butchering the innocent Syrian population because it was good propaganda."

"I saw a documentary claiming that ISIS had infiltrated the White Helmets," I interrupted.

"That makes a lot of sense," Margaret replied.

"So many good men were killed along with the innocent while the world looked on," Amina said.

"ISIS captured Ali and tried to break him down over a long period and convert him to one of them. They also thought he might have vital information, which he probably had. According to the Geneva Convention, prisoners of war only have to give name, rank and number. Ali was no longer in the military, so his name was all he needed to give. They imprisoned Ali in an interrogation centre in Raqqa, where he spent the last year. They used all sorts of techniques to break him, psychological and physical; they are experts at this with much practice."

"Why didn't you let us know that Ali was missing?" I asked.

"I didn't know. One day he didn't come home. That was not unusual, but the days turned into weeks. I was unable to discover where he was. What I saw from day to day was horror. What one human can inflict on another, and then display as a warning to others, is sub-human, sub-animal."

"You sure you're all right to continue?" Amina asked gently.

"Yes, I need to. After a while, my life turned into a fantasy, walking past heads on spikes, body parts littering the pavements, witnessing innocent victims thrown from tall buildings. The bastards would round up bystanders and force them to watch them commit their atrocities with glee as a warning to comply. I must have become normalised to these acts; I became numb to any emotion. I wore clothes that wouldn't draw attention, with my hair and skin covered at all times. I kept to myself and spoke to no one. My work at the hospital was mainly cleaning to make way for the new arrivals. Cleaning was removing the dead to the mortuary and preparing a place for new arrivals. The deaths were noisy and traumatic. Some fought for days to hang onto life, with no morphine or drugs to help with the pain. The doctors and nurses never gave up, each success urging them on, but there were few of those."

"Awful; bloody awful." I wiped my eyes to see where I was driving.

"Talking to someone in the real world would have taken me over the edge, so I never told anyone. I wasn't in your world, and you were never in my thoughts. The only thing allowing me to keep myself alive was waiting for Ali to appear on his white charger and gallop me away out of the nightmare. He never came; the hell continued. All my days consisted of was helping victims and sleeping; I had to be exhausted to sleep."

While Margaret was talking, Amina held her hand and didn't say anything. My mind was racing. I wanted to know everything. How long ago was Ali released from prison, and how had it come about?

"When did you find out Ali was safe?" I asked.

"Two months ago, I received a text message from James Le Messurier. It simply read 'Ali is safe'."

"You don't have to say another word," Amina said, still holding on to Margaret's hand.

"He wanted to know where I was and wrote that someone would collect me as soon as possible."

"Please, only talk if you want to," Amina stressed.

I realised it was getting hard for Amina to hear Margaret's story.

"I was in shock, confused, unsure if it was true, and I wanted to know where he was. I remember texting back with my hands trembling. I couldn't see the keyboard for my tears. I managed to text back my location. I packed a few things and sat at the entrance of our apartment and waited."

"Did you wait very long?" Amina enquired.

"I'm not sure how long; I wasn't sure if I was being tricked. A car eventually stopped. In Arabic, a man shouted out through the window, 'get in'. I shook my head; I was scared. He shouted, 'me friend, get in!' I got in the car, and he said, 'wife of Ali Mansour, yes?' I said yes. He said, 'me friend of Ali Mansour'. I asked him where Ali was, and he said he didn't know, but he had been instructed to take me to Jindires as soon as possible."

"When we arrived at Jindires, I was met by Commander Sewsen Birhat. She told me that an American helicopter had transferred Ali to Antalya Hospital in Turkey as he needed urgent treatment. She was involved in the recovery of Ali. They had successfully attacked the prison in Raqqa with the help of the American Army. They removed all the prisoners, and the sickest were transferred to Antalya for urgent medical treatment; Ali was in the first wave. Sewsen told me I could go on the next available wave. She didn't know how bad Ali was but told me he was in good hands."

"What I find so strange is the YPJ are arch enemies of the Turks, but some of the prisoners rescued by the YPJ would have been Turkish soldiers. It makes no sense to me."

"Absolutely no sense at all. The Turkish doctors and nurses were fantastic; nothing was too much trouble. They even found me an overnight room at the hospital. I was allowed to see Ali the following day. He was in the intensive care unit; it was a shock when I first saw him. I thought it was a mistake, that it wasn't my Ali they had taken me to see. The nurse took me to a frail person covered in sores; his skin was dark, sort of bluish, bruised, I suppose. The frail body on the bed had tubes and wires attached and looked nothing like Ali. I shook my head at the nurse, and I said, 'this is the wrong man'. The nurse asked me who I was looking for. 'Ali Mansour,' I replied. She told me to put my ear close to his mouth and listen. I did, and I could hear him faintly say 'Ali Mansour, Ali Mansour'. Then I looked closer. In my mind, I could only see my Ali, which wasn't the face I could see, but I realised it was him.

"The shock was too much; I must have fainted. When I woke up, I was in a bed next to him. The beds had been pushed together, so I could reach his hands. I placed my hand in his and gripped it tightly. There was no response. I held a frail, bony hand that was nothing like the powerful warm assuring grip I was accustomed to. I turned on my side to look at him. His profile was gaunter than before, but there was no mistaking the nose and brow; it was Ali. I tried talking to him and got no response; I could see his chest rise and fall slowly. I called a nurse over to ask her whether he would be all right. She told me he was in good hands but delirious; they needed to get his body fluids up and slowly introduce vitamins and proteins. He had been starved of nutrients, and his brain needed time to repair itself. The nurses thought he was hanging on to one piece of reality, his name, which he kept repeating. They told me that if Assad's men had captured him instead of ISIS, he would have been in Saydnaya Prison. Where ninety per cent of prisoners disappear and the torture is worse; over a million have been imprisoned there."

"Why are the Syrian government destroying their own citizens? For what purpose?" I asked.

"I don't know if there's a reason," she answered.

"It's bloody madness," I said. "Sorry, Margaret, please carry on."

"Over the following days, which rolled into weeks, Ali improved slowly. The colour of his skin returned almost to normal, and he gradually regained a little weight, thanks to the team looking after him. Everyone concentrated on his physical well-being, getting him to stand and walk. Ali would raise his head and look down at his body and mouth, *sorry*. I told him he had nothing to be sorry for, just be himself. Many physical issues had to be worked on. The bastards had done so much damage. There wasn't a part of his body that they had not tortured in some way. One psychological torture he endured was being strapped to a chair with headphones fixed to his ears. He was forced to listen to deafeningly loud recordings of prisoners screaming for mercy as they were being tortured to death. Ali's hearing had been damaged, which is one of the issues we hope will be fixed at Frimley. Another is dental work; beatings to his face and malnutrition mean most teeth are missing. That's one of the easiest treatments as it's purely cosmetic. However, the psychologist told me that, although straightforward, it's a big part of his rehabilitation. Getting him back to looking close to what he did before will help with his self-esteem."

"One of my first memories of Ali is how he flashed his white teeth," I said.

"Me too," Margaret said, "but that was a long time ago. After about a month in the hospital, Ali started to talk about life before his imprisonment; slowly, his memory returned. Every day he was getting better. He's so much better now than when I first saw him."

"How long will his treatments take?" I asked.

"Possibly months, maybe years, but I don't think he will fully recover."

"He won't be in the hospital all the time, will he?" Amina asked.

"No, not all the time. Ali will be allowed out for short breaks when a little better. But he will require medical, physio, dental, audio and psychotherapy treatments, which they have already started. He will continue these for a long time."

"As long as it takes, you can stay with us; you need some rest and pampering and looking after too."

We were both concerned about Margaret's state of health and often discussed how ill she looked. We decided to treat her as though nothing had happened, but at the same time, to be there if she needed a shoulder to lean on. For the next few months, we took Margaret to visit Ali most weekends. We stayed at a Travelodge close by, as Margaret was the only visitor allowed. Eventually, we were allowed to see Ali, although only for an hour.

Before meeting Ali, his rehab team explained that he looked better visually but still remained fragile emotionally. The primary instruction was not to ask him any questions about his capture, which we both thought was obvious.

"How should we behave?" Amina asked.

"Don't go over the top. Hide your emotions. Act normal, and it will be fine."

We met Ali in a day room; he was sitting in a bay window overlooking the garden. The sun's rays were streaming through the windows, creating a haze. As we walked toward Ali, he stood up out of his chair to greet us. Immediately, the instructions we had received were ignored. Amina couldn't restrain herself. She ran to Ali to embrace him, and I joined them in the embrace; the three of us were all sobbing onto each other's shoulders.

"Okay, that's enough of that. Please, let's sit," Ali said.

It was a different Ali; he was greyer, thinner, with bonier cheeks, and his new teeth were evident when he smiled; they seemed a little too large. He had a round button attached to the side of his head above his right ear. I was curious but didn't ask. I presumed it was something to do with his hearing, as he could hear us clearly now.

"When can you visit us?" Amina asked.

"The sea air would be good for you, if only for a short break," I encouraged.

"That would be nice. Just to get out of here for a bit. I will ask my care team if it would be possible."

It was a subdued Ali we were talking to, but it was Ali. His uniqueness was still there, the way he shrugged his shoulders and crossed his arms if he disagreed but then carried on as though it didn't matter. The smile and confidence, or arrogance, as some people thought, had disappeared, but at least he was talking. It encouraged us; he was on the mend. We were relieved that he would be back to his old self one day. The visit was short and must have been timed, as a nurse asked us to leave at a convenient moment. I wondered if perhaps she had been observing us.

Later we discussed with the care team what we needed to do for Ali to be able to stay with us. They gave us a list of must-do things. First, his bedroom light must not be bright; we were to use only low wattage bulbs and leave them on at all times. His bedroom must be decorated in a warm neutral colour: pastel colours would be good. The bedroom door must be held open, and soft music would be helpful. We were to remove all door handles and make sure nothing attached to a wall could support his body weight.

"Why?" I asked. "Is Ali suicidal?"

"Who knows what's going through his head, but at the moment, there are no signs. The better he gets, the more the bad memories will return. He suffers nightmares now and is on a knife edge; Margaret will be in charge of his medication. Anything could trigger bad memories. His subconscious could be woken by anything. Things like lights going on and off, doors banging, shouting, complete silence or sudden noise could all be a trigger."

"What happens if he flips?" I asked. "What do we do?"

"Margaret has been trained. She has all the contact details. She knows what to do, so she must be close to him at all times. Before Ali can stay with you, I will arrange occupational therapy to inspect your property to make any changes required. Is that okay?"

"Yes, of course," I replied. "I will start with the other jobs you have given me straight away."

Chapter 35

December 2015

We collected Ali from the hospital at the beginning of December. We wanted him to stay for as long as he could cope with being away from the hospital. Armed with all his medications, instructions and contact numbers, we started the journey to Pembrokeshire.

Ali sat in the front with me; he insisted he wanted to ride 'shotgun'. It had been a long time since he had been to England, and it would be his first trip to Wales. He spent most of the time looking out of the window like he was recharging his memory bank as we drove.

"What is the first thing you would like to do?" I asked Ali to break the ice.

"Drink a pint of real ale and eat a pie in a pub, or maybe a pickled egg," he said, licking his lips.

"Only the one pint," I replied, smiling.

"Probably followed by a few single malts."

I then said something I wished I had not. "Still not a good Muslim then."

"I have witnessed what good Muslims do," Ali uttered in anger.

"Sorry, Ali," I said quickly.

He put his hand on my knee. "No problem, my friend. Be yourself… Sorry if I'm a bit tetchy."

Margaret's health had improved while staying with us, but she was still nothing like before. Amina was responsible for the improvement, helping her with her hair and make-up. Amina had now reversed the roles as she took Margaret shopping and looked after her. Her hair was no longer naturally black but dyed and styled by a hairdresser. Her make-up hid the worry lines on her face brought about by the trauma and stress she had been through. She was now taking more care of herself, seemed happier, and gained weight. However, she was not the witty, devilish Margaret we remembered. We would often find her crying, although she tried to hide it from us.

We did have a pie and pint from time to time, but mainly we played cards and had a glass of wine at home. We talked about the old times and recalled how our friendship had developed. We never spoke about the war, which was still ongoing. There were often news bulletins regarding how bad it was, but we never talked about Aleppo or Syria.

Amal was due home from Bristol Technical College at Christmas. His apprenticeship included a three-month residential term away at college every year and the rest at the refinery training school. He wasn't allowed to work at the refinery until he was eighteen. We worked at different refineries, so the father teaching the son wasn't an issue but an advantage. He was reluctant to ask for help, preferring to work things out for himself; that way, he remembered better, or so he said.

Amal couldn't wait to see Ali and Margaret and vice-versa. Amara was returning from Bath University for her

Christmas break, so we would have a full house. We had told both of them to be as normal as possible, not to play loud music, no practical jokes, not to shout or argue and to be careful what they said.

There had been a few nights when Ali had nightmares; Margaret would find him curled up in the corner of their bedroom and we could hear her gently coax him back into bed. However, Ali and Margaret began to smile and laugh and take short walks together, holding hands. They seemed content in each other's company. I often saw them sitting on a rock with their arms around each, looking out towards the sea. Watching waves rolling in and crashing onto rocks was very therapeutic to me. It made me think the world would continue regardless, despite our efforts to destroy it. I wondered what they were thinking; perhaps they were thinking of different things. One evening over a glass of wine, I asked them.

"What are you thinking when watching the tide ebb and flow?"

"The magnificent power of the ocean crashing into the rocks is mesmerising," Ali said. "No two waves are the same: the noise, the pure white spume, and it has been that way since time began. Then the following day, there is hardly a ripple."

"I agree with Ali," Margaret said. "It's mesmerising, but I see the beauty created by nature, nothing to do with man. But man will do his best to destroy it, and one day he will succeed."

"Can I join in?" Amina asked. "And I agree with all of you, but what astounds me is what causes the tide, which is the sun and moon creating a gravitational pull on the ocean. Man hasn't found a way to destroy them yet!"

I raised my glass. "I would like to toast to getting back to old times!"

When Ali met Amal, he was amazed at his size. He was no longer the little boy in Aleppo. He was as tall as Ali and similar to the old Ali in build. They hugged and greeted in the Arabic way. They asked each other questions and answered with nods and high fives. Amal was always a little in awe of Ali; I was proud of how he handled seeing him now, as though nothing had happened.

The following day, Amara arrived from university. Margaret was the first to greet her when she walked into the room. "She is the image of you, Amina. Unbelievable, a carbon copy. What a beautiful young lady you are. You're gorgeous. What do you think, Ali?"

"Oh, to be young and free again. You are your mother incarnate."

"I was never that beautiful," Amina retorted quickly.

"Yes, you were," Ali said. "I remember you were the second most beautiful woman in the world once."

"But you told me just a little too late. I was already married," Amina replied jokingly.

"As I remember," Margaret butted in, "he preferred Souzan." She then made a 'gotcha' sign in the air with her finger.

"Well, Amina picked me, so she can't be very clever," I joined in.

"You're just a very fortunate man, punching well above your weight," Margaret reminded me.

Everybody laughed. It was like old times, and after the banter, we all talked through the night.

On Christmas day, Helen and Paul popped over for Christmas dinner. They knew what Ali and Margaret had been through. We told them to just be themselves, as Ali and Margaret would spot right away if they were holding back or being false in any way.

After dinner, the ladies retired to the lounge and sat around the fire, drinking glasses of wine.

We men tidied up the kitchen. Ali was sitting at the table watching as Paul started to tease Amal.

"Men against boys," challenged Paul.

"Wait until tomorrow. We'll see," Amal responded.

I didn't get the gist of what was going on but realised it was all good-hearted fun as they were laughing.

"We will stuff you," Paul said, grinning.

"In your dreams," Amal replied,

"Your worst nightmare, you mean. I will run all over you," Paul said.

"You won't even see me," Amal replied.

"I haven't a clue what's going on," I said to Ali.

"Are you two playing some kind of game tomorrow?" Ali asked.

"Not really. It's called hammering. It's too one-sided to be a game, as that's between two equal sides."

"In that case, you may want to concede now," Amal said.

"I gather that they're playing rugby against each other tomorrow," I explained to Ali.

"Who do you play for?" Ali asked Paul.

"The Quins."

"Amal, who do you play for?"

"The Quins."

"I am confused," said Ali. "Are you both playing for the same team tomorrow?"

"No, we could do, but Paul isn't good enough to get in mine," Amal said, laughing.

"Explain!" I demanded, flummoxed now.

"No need," said Ali. "I think I know what's going on. Is it exiles against the first team?"

"Something like that. It's the exiles against the youth team. It shouldn't be allowed, really, men against boys, lambs to the slaughter," Paul answered.

"How did you that work that out," I asked Ali.

"I did go to Oxford, you know," he replied.

"So you've seen rugby before?" Paul said.

"Better than that; I played a few games for my college."

"In what position?" Amal asked.

"Guess!" challenged Ali.

All three of us looked at Ali, who was trying to look as big as possible by puffing out his chest.

"In the olden days, the forwards were relatively small, so I presume you must have been one."

"I saw what Uncle Ali looked like before," said Amal and then stopped, realising what he said. He turned to Ali and said, "Sorry."

"No need to apologise. It's the truth; what position, Amal?"

"Flanker; you were built like a flanker," Amal replied.

"I can tell that both of you are backs, correct?" Ali said. They both nodded in agreement. Ali said, "I used to hang around with rugby players myself; now can you guess my position?" They both shook their heads, indicating no. "Well, I made it pretty evident that I was a back like you, not a proper rugby player. The forwards called us the girls and not proper players." They both laughed.

"I bet you were a centre, correct?" Paul said.

"Yes, 'crash ball' was my speciality; mind you, the ball was not that important."

"A bit like me then," Paul replied.

"You might see me coming, blink, and I will be gone. You will be crashing into my shadow tomorrow," Amal teased.

The rugby match was typical of a boxing day game between two teams from the same club: more talk than action, probably due to the Christmas celebrations. Apparently, little duals were going on between the players trying to win bragging rights in the club afterwards. Side bets of pints of beer were placed between each other in their individual contests. It was good-hearted and entertaining, but in no way could it be considered a classic contest. Both Amal and Paul claimed they won their side bets, so they bought each other a drink. Paul did tackle Amal a few times, and Amal scored a try, so their personal match was considered a draw. Ali watched the game showing little emotion, as though his mind was somewhere else. After the game, we had a few drinks in the bar. Margaret pulled me to one side and asked if they could leave as soon as possible because the raucous noise of the players and supporters was too much for Ali.

On New Year's Day, Paul and Amal persuaded us that the annual sea swims at Saundersfoot would be a great idea. Somehow, they managed to convince all of us it would be fantastic. Apparently, the colder the weather, the wilder the wind, the rougher the sea, the better the conditions for swimming. Margaret and Ali agreed they would like to watch us enjoy ourselves from a distance.

There were hundreds of similar lunatics on the day. Most swimmers did the dip for charities or drunken promises made over the festive season. Some did it every year; some wussies wore wetsuits, some wore silly costumes, and others wore ordinary bathing costumes. When the hooter sounded, the crowds raced towards the sea. We were at the back. Being new to it, we didn't want to upset the locals by being first in; that was our agreed excuse. We held hands, Paul and Amal on the outside, Helen and Amara next to them, and Amina and me in the middle. We ran into the sea, dragged along by Paul and Amal, holding our hands in a tight grip. We had discussed no screaming; we would show them we were brave, not wimps. Running as fast as possible was the agreed tactic. We hit the water, and none of us yelled, although at first as the cold took our breath away. Then like everyone else, we were screaming and trying to appear as though we were enjoying the experience. We were also determined not to be the first to turn and run back out of the sea.

Ali and Margaret watched from the road; they were in charge of towels and hot toddies. We ran back up the beach to them, feeling colder out of the water than in; the wind chill encouraged us to run faster, no longer an organised group. It was every man for himself as we ran to Ali and Margaret to be first to grab a towel; I was last to arrive as usual. We wrapped ourselves in towels and stood huddled, shivering, drinking hot toddies, congratulating each other. We were saying things like 'Amazing', 'It wasn't as cold as I expected, 'It was bloody freezing', 'I can't feel my fingers or toes,' and 'Why do teeth chatter when you're freezing cold?'

Ali had been quiet for a while, and then spoke to me quietly. "I promise you, next year, I will join you."

"No problem, you can take my place," Amara said merrily.

"Margaret, you can take mine. Honestly, I won't be offended," Amina added.

I put my arms around Ali's shoulders. "Inshallah, that would be great, my friend," I whispered.

"No way, it's towels duty for me," Margaret joined in.

"To next year," we all said as we toasted with our hot toddies.

* * * * *

Ali and Margaret continued to visit Frimley Hospital throughout the following year, and they saw us often. Ali's recovery was slow; he had improved slightly physically, but mentally he was still suffering. Margaret was told it would take time and patience and not to worry. We were all optimistic that Ali was past the worst of it and was at last on the mend.

We had a message from Margaret in November that Ali had become ill. She told us tests confirmed he was suffering from an immunodeficiency virus and also had tuberculosis. We were both in shock as we drove to be with Margaret. We comforted each other, saying things like, 'He is in the best place', and similar words to convince ourselves it was not happening. When we next saw Ali, he was in the intensive care unit, hooked up to all sorts of equipment. It had only been a short time ago that we thought he was winning his battle to recover. Now he was being kept alive by machinery, his chest rising and falling, aided by medical devices. I remembered what Margaret said when she saw Ali in the Antalya hospital. She didn't recognise him, and I knew what she meant. Then I remembered the 'alien' that forced me to the ground with such power and speed; that was the Ali, I remembered. This was not him on the bed before me, but a husk of him. There was no way that I could have recognised him from memory. I had the same thoughts as Margaret. This was not Ali. Holding his hand was no longer a challenge for me, but now he would never know.

We were told it was only a matter of time before he would pass away. So we waited for our friend to die, unable to help in any way, watching, useless and heartbroken, as devices keeping him alive were turned off. Audible beeps from the machinery monitoring his bodily functions confirmed he was still alive. I sat there, coming to terms with the knowledge that they would stop soon. I was numb with disbelief. The person I thought was indestructible was about to leave us. The beeps stopped; the nurses didn't rush to his bedside. We sat around his bed, not speaking, crying or looking at each other. It was difficult for me to handle my own grief; I wasn't strong enough to accept the suffering of others.

The nurses then came to us. "Sorry for your loss," they whispered and pulled the bedsheet over Ali's face.

This action induced tears to fill my eyes. I moved to where Margaret sat to comfort her. Amina was already there, tears rolling down her cheeks, hugging Margaret, who was shaking but not making a sound.

When the shock wore off, I grieved alone and realised that grief was personal and shared. I cried afterwards on my own. I am sure the others also cried when private memories of Ali flooded back. I regretted never telling Ali I missed him, but now it was too late to say it. I wished I had.

Ali was dead. There was no religious ceremony; the inclinations he held towards religion had been lost to him well before the actions of religious zealots.

The following New Year's Day, we made sure that Ali made good on his last promise to me. Amina, Amara, Amal and I joined hands and walked into the sea at Saundersfoot. Margaret watched from the road as Ali joined us in the water. We set him free, and he did join us in the ocean as he promised he would.

We are still in touch with Margaret but rarely see her. She now works for UNICEF, doing her best to help where she can. When we meet or talk, she is not the same Margaret we first met; gone are all the clever innuendos, the make-up, the jet black hair, the unblemished face. If I hadn't seen her over the years and was asked to recognise her, I would fail, the same way she was unable to recognise Ali after he had been rescued.

Epilogue

Ali's eyes are always the memory trigger for me and would always appear first in times of reflection. The first time we made eye contact, his eyes were bright, alert and curious. They immediately subdued me and made me very careful to answer his questions honestly.

Later they immediately became open and friendly and encouraged me to be the same. When I saw Ali at Heathrow Airport, he made it difficult to make eye contact with him. It is only now that I realise that perhaps Ali couldn't cope with the message my eyes were giving him. He possibly read that message as pity; it hurts me more now, realising that my eyes didn't show him the empathy he deserved.

I also remember what Margaret said about Amina's eyes when she told me to 'look into them and see what happens.' The first time I looked into Amina's eyes, she looked away. I realised later her actions were because she thought a relationship between us was impossible. Amina's eyes filled with tears of joy when she saw her parents after having been kidnapped by the Bedouins and with happiness when I proposed marriage to her.

Margaret's eyes are a puzzle; they could trick me into believing she was serious. It took time to realise that she was being wickedly clever and fooling me for fun, as she would say, 'because she could'. Her eyes no longer have this ability; they have lost the sparkle and now show little emotion of any kind.

It's always the eyes we look at to gauge the feelings of another. I don't understand how they involuntarily send a signal to our brain without our knowledge or how our brain interprets the message to reflect a sign back to another pair of eyes. How are tears of joy and grief translated through our eyes to confirm?

When confronted with a picture of a tortured animal or child, their eyes always confirm the suffering that emotionally affects us. Those who torment others use the eyes of the wretches as a guide to how successful they are at inflicting pain.

When the eyes of the child who was sent to trap us opened, my brain immediately knew something was wrong. The involuntary eye signal my subconscious interpreted didn't match the situation, triggering my alarm.

I wonder whether a reason Doug was so irritating was that life had placed curtains over his eyes, curtains that never opened. After talking to him and explaining things carefully, he absorbed nothing: his eyes never showed emotion.

This story would not have been written if the recruitment agency had done its job correctly. I would have never met Doug. My life would have followed a completely different path. I wouldn't have met Amina, so my children would not exist. I probably would not have become friends with Ali or met Margaret. I now have beautiful memories because Doug instigated a series of events. So I ask myself: if I were to meet Doug now and explain his effect on my life, would it register? Would I see recognition in his eyes?

About the Author

Like the main character in this story, I was born into a working-class family in the industrial midlands of England and moved to Pembrokeshire to set up a new life with my family. I also worked in Syria and Saudi Arabia for several years. After my wife and I retired, we moved to Turkey, where we lived for six enjoyable, exciting and challenging years.

I have always been fascinated by the cultural differences of people I come into contact with and their varied beliefs and customs. The people I mixed with were usually working-class like myself. Most had the same preconceived impressions of foreigners as I held. Things changed once they were offered the respect I was expecting to be shown by them. Friendships developed, and the differences I expected to be an issue weren't there. I have tried incorporating some of my observations into my story, and I hope you enjoyed reading it.

The author with his Saudi crew, 1984